ACCLAIM FOR BRYAN CASSIDAY

"A fast-paced detective novel, enhanced by exceptional characters and a striking ending."—*Kirkus Reviews*

"A potent shot of contemporary LA noir that will have readers hooked from page one."—*BestThrillers.com*

"A deftly crafted roller coaster of a ride for the reader, Bryan Cassiday's novel, *Bolt*, is a truly riveting read from cover to cover."—*Midwest Book Review*

"Fans of Dennis Lehane and James Ellroy will love *Force of Impact*."—*BestThrillers.com*

"This series is great. It keeps you expecting and delivers a lot of unexpected turns. I recommend this if you love post-apocalypse reading material."*****—Amazon reviewer

"*Sanctuary in Steel* made me feel like I did the first time I watched Romero. Fresh, exciting and engaging like any outbreak story should be."—Iain McKinnon, *Domain of the Dead*

"*Sanctuary in Steel* is way up there with the best of the zombie stories in terms of plotting and pacing, propelled by great characters and unique twists."—*Readers' Favorite*

"Cassiday blends thoughtful suspense and pulse-pounding terror to deliver a novel with both bite and creeping dread."—David Dunwoody, *Empire*

BOOKS BY BRYAN CASSIDAY

Horde (Zombie Apocalypse: The Chad Halverson Series Book 6)
- *Crime Blotter USA*
- *Murder LLC (Scott Brody Thriller 2)*
- *Bolt (Scott Brody Thriller 1)*
- *Riptide of Fear*
- *The Payout*
- *Force of Impact (Ethan Carr Thriller 4)*
- *Wipeout (Ethan Carr Thriller 3)*
- *Dying to Breathe (Ethan Carr Thriller 2)*
- *Countdown to Death (Ethan Carr Thriller 1)*
- *The Bus Stops Here—and Other Zombie Tales*
- *Two Moons Rising*
- *Alien Assault*
- *Comes a Chopper*
- *Zombie Apocalypse: The Chad Halverson Series Books 1–5*
- *Helter Skelter*
- *The Anaconda Complex*
- *The Kill Option*
- *Blood Moon: Thrillers and Tales of Terror*
- *Fete of Death*

ICE IN THE BLOOD

BRYAN CASSIDAY

Bryan Cassiday
Los Angeles
ISBN 9781732976399
Printed in the United States of America
First Edition: August 17, 2021

Table of Contents

Razor

He wanted to make her brief life feel as uncomfortable as possible.

That was half the fun.

But it was also necessary for his plan to work.

They had met at Twelve Step. They both had a drinking problem. He could tell she wasn't attracted to him. He knew she wouldn't be. That wasn't the point. The point was to get her to open up to him so he could make this work. He needed to find out what was driving her to drink. He could take it from there. Whatever the cause, it was bothering her, and he needed to work on it so she would need him.

It was difficult to get to know anybody in Los Angeles. The county sprawled over almost five thousand square miles. It turned out that Twelve Step was a good place to meet people, because everybody had problems—and some resorted to alcoholism.

He had followed her one night to her Twelve Step meeting without her knowledge. It was part of the plan.

The bit he didn't like about Twelve Step was the big speech everybody was required to make about how they had messed up their lives and resorted to drinking. What a bunch of self-indulgent nonsense. Who wanted to listen to these guys wallow in self-pity? He didn't. But that was part of the program. He could wallow as well as the next guy. He was good at making up stories. He was a born storyteller. If he didn't have another job, maybe he would have become a writer.

For his Twelve Step speech he concocted a story about what a rotten life he had and how it had driven him to booze.

They were sitting on uncomfortable white plastic chairs that formed a circle when they gave their mea-culpa, what-a-fuckup-I-am speeches. The steel frame of his chair was cutting off the circulation in his legs.

When it was his turn, he rose to his feet and made up a story about his mother being an alcoholic who had committed suicide when he was a teen. He told them he couldn't handle it. He didn't know what to do with his life. He had no one to turn to for guidance, since she was a single mother and he was an only child. He ended up following her example. Not the suicide bit. The drinking bit.

None of it was true, of course, but he wanted everyone in the room to feel sorry for him. If your life story sounded wretched enough and your voice broke as you related it, the members would tear up and clap when you were done. Which apparently was what you were supposed to do, he decided. It was like going to confession. Like he knew anything about confession. How could he? He never went to church.

He took his seat.

He earned her sympathy after his sob story.

She must have got the impression she knew him after his "confession."

She had dark wavy hair and hazel eyes. He couldn't recall ever seeing her smile. For that matter, he hardly ever saw anyone smile at Twelve Step. If they did smile, their eyes were swimming with tears.

She stood up awkwardly, as though she was torn between wanting to stand or remain seated. He got the impression she was reluctant to make her speech. Not everyone enjoyed baring their souls in front of a group of strangers. She lingered in a semi-upright position for fifteen seconds, trying to make up her mind how to proceed, her hand aimed at her chair as if she wanted to grab it and seat herself, or as if she might fall any minute and wanted to make sure the chair would be there to break her fall.

"It's all right, Belinda," said Chairman Bob, a middle-aged guy wearing jeans and a grey T, the leader of the group.

He looked like he spent a lot of time in the gym. He had told them he was a substitute NFL referee and had reffed several games for Tom Brady when Brady was the quarterback for the Patriots.

"We're here to help," Chairman Bob went on. "You'll feel better after you tell us a little about yourself."

Belinda managed to stand up without leaning to her side and feeling for her chair with her hand, reaching for it like it was a life preserver and she was drowning.

She took a deep breath and launched into a long rambling speech about being alone in LA and not knowing how to connect with anyone. At first she was reluctant to talk about herself, but the longer she talked the more comfortable she felt speaking to the group.

As she told it, unable to form bonds with people, she resorted to drinking and pills as substitutes for a social life. Her doctor was glad to prescribe her any pill she requested. Soma, Valium, Halcion, whatever she wanted. Taking them wasn't enough to make her feel better. She felt empty and drank.

She was in her early thirties. She had come from New Orleans to LA to seek a job in Hollywood as a makeup artist five years ago. Things didn't go as planned. She was working now as a hair stylist at a Supercuts. She couldn't get her foot in the door in Hollywood, even though she had been trying like crazy the whole time she had lived in LA.

Now she was coming to the conclusion she would never make it in Hollywood, that she would end up at a Supercuts or another salon chain for the rest of her life.

She felt like a failure. She felt doomed. She couldn't come to grips with her botched life. Yet she couldn't bring herself to return to New Orleans. To return would be tantamount to conceding defeat. There was still a part of her that could not accept defeat.

Her mother and father were both alcoholics, and they had made her life miserable back in New Orleans. For them life was one long Mardi Gras to be savored in a drunken stupor. They had told her in no uncertain terms that it was her job to support them now that she was old enough to support herself. She couldn't wait to get away from them.

Things didn't pan out in Los Angeles. As she saw it, she was stuck here with her life swirling down the drain.

She didn't know what she had done wrong. She had honed her cosmetic skills to the best of her ability. And now she was stuck in a dead-end job. She could have gotten a job at a Supercuts in New Orleans. She didn't have to come all the way out here to Hollywood. What had happened to her dream job in Hollywood?

She saw no way out of her predicament. So she drank.

She started fidgeting as she stood, at a loss for words, wishing she was elsewhere.

"Do you feel better now that you've talked to us?" said Chairman Bob, noting her chagrin.

"I—I—guess so," she said.

"There's nothing to be embarrassed about here. We're all in the same boat. Our lives haven't turned out the way we wanted. There's no shame in that."

He didn't like Chairman Bob. There was something condescending about him. Like he was some kind of uppity schoolteacher who thought he knew everything. He wanted to break Chairman Bob's jaw.

He even found the guy's droning, supposedly sympathetic, voice annoying. He could see through Chairman Bob. The guy was on a power trip. It was why the guy worked as a referee—so he could order the multimillionaire, pampered celebrity football players around and penalize them if they didn't play according to the rules. Listening to a bunch of besotted losers made Chairman Bob feel like a champ. But he wasn't a champ. He was a chump. He wasn't a celebrity football player. He was just a referee. And his paycheck proved it. So he came here to lord it over the alky flops in life who couldn't stay sober.

No doubt Chairman Bob had been a lush at one time. Otherwise, why would he be here? Maybe he still was.

He hated Chairman Bob. A total fraud who thought he had all the answers, but didn't have even one.

"Do you want to tell us anything else, Belinda?" said Chairman Bob.

"No. I guess not," she said, looking uncomfortably at the floor.

Prompted by Chairman Bob who clapped with a fulsome expression on his face, the others began clapping for Belinda with teary eyes.

She grabbed her chair like she thought it would escape before she had a chance to sit on it. She exhaled with relief as she sat down.

Of course, she was messed up, he decided. It was why she had joined these down-and-out juiceheads. Little did she know, he was going to mess her life up even more. He was going to make her wish she had never been born.

Fear was the key. What he needed to do was work on her fears. And she must have had them, or she wouldn't be abusing alcohol. They didn't call it *Dutch courage* for nothing.

It wasn't like she was going to be his first victim. He had done the same thing to his other victims. Played on their fears, then preyed on *them.* As in murdered them. To make his plans work, he had to incite fear in his victims—without their knowing he was the one behind it.

He was sitting two seats away from her. He looked at her and applauded along with the others in the group, a smile of approval on his face. The smile was feigned.

In actuality, he hated these losers. Just sitting among them made him feel like a loser. They made his skin crawl. He wondered if they could tell he wasn't one of them. Would they turn on him like jackals and tear him limb from limb if they found out he wasn't one of them?

When was this stupid, interminable meeting going to end? he wondered.

He supposed he could walk out any time, but he wanted to stay and eavesdrop on what Belinda had to say. He needed to know what scared her. Not that he could ask her point-blank about it. But he wanted to sound her out, being subtle about it, to uncover her fears, without addressing her directly and drawing attention to himself. He would eavesdrop on her as she spoke to fellow members. Maybe he would start a conversation with someone else, and Belinda would chime in and reveal herself and her hidden fears. Deep down, everybody was afraid. You just had to dig a little to find the source of their fear.

He thought he had her figured already—just from her little speech. She was afraid to date men in Los Angeles. And who could blame her with all the wackos here? You could be hooking up with the likes of the Hillside Strangler or the Night Stalker. Even Ted Bundy had spent time in these parts.

The meeting started breaking up. Finally.

Chairman Bob had a hot date lined up, he announced, and he didn't want to be late for it. Chairs scuffed the hardwood floor as group members stood up to leave.

He didn't care about Chairman Bob's hot date. The guy had said the same thing at their last meeting. Bragging. Why did he think anyone cared?

Chairman Bob's eyes lingered on Belinda for an instant then cut away.

Interesting, he decided. Maybe he could work on something there. It might be nothing, but then again . . .

He had had enough of Chairman Bob. He wanted to get out of here. He didn't like feeling he was being bossed around, especially by some smarmy guy pretending to be your good buddy who was deeply concerned about your drinking yourself into an early grave.

He couldn't stand the place anymore. He left before he had a chance to eavesdrop on Belinda.

# # #

Belinda walked down the hallway to her apartment, fumbling in her purse for her keys. Her cell phone chimed in her purse. Pausing her search for her keys, she came to a halt in the corridor and took the call.

"Hello," she said.

Nobody answered.

She thought she could hear someone breathing on the other end of the line.

"Hello," she repeated.

Nobody spoke.

Not that creep again, she decided.

She terminated the call, continued walking, and resumed her search for her keys.

"You don't look too happy," said Zelda, opening her apartment door just as Belinda passed it.

Belinda's heart stopped. She let out a little gasp. "Oh, Zelda. Hi."

"What happened?"

"Nothing."

"Things aren't so hot, huh?"

"I'm just looking for my keys," said Belinda, continuing to rummage around in her congested purse.

"Want to come in for a cup of coffee?"

"What? Oh, I don't want to bother you."

"No bother. It'll give you a chance to find your keys before you reach your door," said Zelda with a smile.

In her early thirties, she was wearing pale greyish pink lipstick, which made her lips look bloodless and harmonized with her limpid grey eyes. She had a full head of brunette hair that tumbled down the back of her powder blue shift in bouncy coils.

Belinda hesitated. "Well—"

"Did you ever think about joining a cult?"

"What?" said Belinda, unsure she had heard Zelda correctly.

"A cult. It would improve your self-confidence."

"What's wrong with my self-confidence?"

"Not to put too fine a point on it, you look, shall we say, downtrodden or browbeaten. Take your pick."

"I don't like either one." Belinda's face registered confusion. "What's joining a cult got to do with it?"

"Come in for a drink, and I'll tell you."

Raising her eyebrows, Belinda entered Zelda's apartment.

"Have a seat," said Zelda, and retreated into the kitchen to fetch their drinks.

She returned with two glasses of ginger ale and handed Belinda one.

"I don't have any coffee ready," said Zelda. "Is ginger ale OK?"

"Fine," said Belinda, sitting on the sofa in Zelda's well-appointed apartment.

"I've only been living in this town for six months. The first thing I learned is it's hard to meet people here. I don't feel like hanging out at the local Erewhon browsing through the raw kelp noodles to form relationships."

"There's always Twelve Step," muttered Belinda.

"What?"

"Nothing."

"I think you have the same problem."

Belinda didn't feel like talking about it. "What's this about a cult?"

Zelda sat beside her. "I joined one, and I'm convinced it has improved my self-confidence. It would do wonders for yours, too."

"It was just someone harassing me on the phone. You know how that is. You answer the phone, and they hang up on you."

Belinda took a pull on her ginger ale.

"That's why you should think about joining a cult," said Zelda. "A cult will help you deal with your enemies by building your self-confidence."

"What's a cult got to do with self-confidence? Cults are slave camps that program you to follow their orders."

Zelda laughed. "That's what the media wants you to think. It's propaganda. I thought the same thing before I joined one. They're not at all like the fake news says. At least the one I belong to isn't."

"I suppose it depends on the cult."

Belinda didn't want to mess with cults. She had never heard of anything good come of joining a cult.

She got up to leave. This conversation was making her uncomfortable.

"Gotta run," she said.

"So soon?"

"What I need to do is find my keys," said Belinda, flustered. "They're not in my purse, so they must be in my car."

She headed to the door.

"If you change your mind about the cult, look me up. I can get you in. It's not easy to get in. You need to be recommended by another cult member, which is me in your case," said Zelda, smiling brightly as she stood up and followed Belinda to the door. "It will do wonders for you."

Do I look that miserable? wondered Belinda with disquiet. Compared to Zelda, she probably did. Was that why Zelda was so happy? Because she had joined a cult?

Belinda's cell phone chimed.

She answered it.

Silence.

"Hello?" she said. "Who is this?"

The caller hung up.

"Was that the creep?" said Zelda.

Belinda nodded yes.

"Do you have any idea who it is?" said Zelda.

"No."

"Did you turn somebody down for a date lately?"

"What's that got to do with anything?"

"He could be the one harassing you."

"You think it's a man?"

"I'm telling you, you should join this cult I'm in. They'll empower you. You won't be scared of these stupid phone calls from pervs."

"This caller could be a homicidal maniac for all I know. Maybe he goes to bed with a chain saw at his side with trophies of body parts under his bed."

Zelda chuckled. "Your imagination is working overtime."

"There are a lot of crazies out there," said Belinda, opening the door and walking into the hallway.

"I can take you to one of the cult's meetings any time you want. Just let me know when," said Zelda, standing in the doorway. "They'll empower you so you won't be so frightened of everyone."

"I'm not frightened of *everyone*. Just the creep that keeps hanging up on me."

"Not everybody is a psycho."

"Now you're making fun of me."

"Not at all. I want to help you."

This cult Zelda was talking about must have done a good job of brainwashing her, decided Belinda. And yet . . . Zelda *did* look happy and carefree, with eyes that glowed. Belinda doubted she could ever look like that. She didn't think it was in her genes.

There was something unnerving about Zelda, though. Like she was a Stepford wife. Even though she wasn't married. What had that cult done to her? On the other hand, what was so sinister about being happy?

Why was she so distrustful of happy people? wondered Belinda. Maybe she was jealous. Maybe Zelda was onto something with this cult she was yammering about.

Maybe Belinda should take Zelda up on her offer of introducing her to this cult. Why did they call themselves a cult? The word *cult* had ominous connotations. What had prompted Zelda to join them? Something to think about.

In the meantime Belinda had to find the keys to her apartment. Maybe her disconcerting speech at Twelve Step had had something to do with her misplacing her keys.

She exited the apartment house's lobby, descended the cement stairs, and walked onto the sidewalk toward the gated underground parking garage.

Her cell phone chimed.

She halted on the sidewalk, rooted through her purse, and fished out her mobile.

"Hello?"

Nobody answered.

Not again.

It was getting so she couldn't answer her phone anymore.

She was getting the message loud and clear. This guy wasn't going to leave her alone. Was he going to break into her apartment?

Edgy and unsettled, she thrust her cell into her purse and resumed walking. She noticed a security guard's patrol car parked near the sidewalk.

Maybe that was what she needed, she decided. To hire a security guard to keep watch over her and her apartment. She noted the name of the security agency printed on his car and committed it to memory. Direct Action Security. Maybe she would give them a call. You could never be too careful in this crazy town.

Out of the corner of her eye she picked up on a stocky middle-aged man with a hirsute face on the other side of the street staring at her with black eyes. He was wearing a grey linen flat cap pulled down low on his forehead and smoking a cigar.

She cringed.

Was he the creep that was harassing her? she wondered.

She was going to go batshit if she kept freaking out every time a man stared at her. She told herself to relax.

She used her remote to open the garage's metal gate, descended the driveway's cement incline, sidestepped a discarded sky blue plastic baggie of dog turd, and reached her parked Mini.

Her apartment keys must have fallen out of her purse. She pressed her car fob to unlock the car door. As she swung the door open, the dome light went on, and she could see her keys lying on the leather passenger seat on the spot where she had set her purse while she had been driving.

Sighing with relief, she retrieved her keys, locked her car door with the fob, and returned to her apartment, where she let herself in.

While she was thinking about it, she decided to call the security agency to find out their rates and what services they provided.

"Direct Action Security," said the receptionist.

"Hi. Could you give me a rundown of your services?"

The receptionist went over their different types of services and their prices.

"What is the best service to keep someone from harassing me?" said Belinda.

"I could send a guard to your apartment to help you with that. With each service you can customize your account and add on certain features that suit your needs, and he would go over the details of the pricing for you."

Belinda thanked her and hung up.

Less than thirty seconds later her cell phone was chiming.

Thinking it was the security agency she answered it.

Silence on the other end of the line. Then a click as the caller terminated the call.

This had to stop, she decided. She wasn't going to spend the rest of her life dreading whether to answer her phone. It would turn her into a nervous wreck.

She wasn't keen on the idea of shelling out money to a security agency to protect her, but she felt threatened. What if the harasser decided to break into her place and attack her? The cops wouldn't get here fast enough to help her if she called 911. A security agency would react quicker, if they were in her employ.

Keyed up, she started when she heard a knock on her door.

She eyed the door and noticed she hadn't locked the dead bolt. Her heartbeat kicking up a frantic racket, she stole toward the door, dreading the stranger might try to enter. She reached the door, turned the dead bolt, and breathed a sigh of relief.

She peeked through the door's peephole and saw Zelda standing in the hall facing her door. Belinda unlocked the door and let Zelda in.

"Did you hear the news?" said Zelda.

"What?"

"What's with you? You're shaking like Shelley Duvall in *The Shining*."

"I thought you were the guy that's stalking me."

"I'm telling you, you need to chill. Did you hear the news?"

"No."

"I thought that's maybe why you're strung out."

"What news?"

"The trade paper *Variety* received a letter from a serial killer saying he was going to kill again in LA."

"You tell me to chill in one breath and then you start talking about a serial killer in the next."

"I thought maybe that's why you're so anxious."

"Ignorance is bliss, I guess. I didn't know anything about any serial killer's letter."

"You *do* know a serial killer is at large and has been at work in LA for the last year?"

"The guy that uses a cutthroat razor on his victims? I *do* know about that. And thanks for reminding me," Belinda said dryly. "I got enough stuff going on without thinking of that."

Zelda stroked her chin in thought. "Do you think the guy stalking you is the serial killer?"

"Why did you have to go and say that, Zelda?"

"I'm not trying to upset you. You look like you're just this side of a nervous breakdown as it is."

"I've had better days."

"Anyway," said Zelda, angling to the couch, "the letter's in the headlines because talking heads are casting doubt on its authenticity. They say the letter's nothing more than a skeevy publicity stunt by a movie producer desperate to open with a boffo box office for his new slasher flick."

"Fake news?"

"That's one way to put it."

"What do the cops say?"

"They're withholding comment until their forensics crew has a chance to inspect the letter. These Hollywood people will do anything to generate buzz for their flicks. I wouldn't put it past them to fake a serial killer's letter."

"I can't believe they're that hard up for publicity."

"It's hard to tell these days between fake news and real news. It feels like we're always being manipulated by the media."

"It's almost like they want us to live in constant fear for our lives."

"You can't go around being scared of everything, Belle. It would do you a world of good to join our cult. The cult preaches empowerment. That's just what the doctor ordered for you."

Join a cult to escape a stalker and a serial killer. Yeah, that made sense, decided Belinda. As much sense as anything else, she supposed. Now that she thought about it, were the stalker and the serial killer one and the same? No wonder she was coming apart at the seams.

She crossed the carpet to the cellarette and withdrew a bottle of Smirnoff vodka. She poured herself a drink and took a pull on it.

"Do you want a drink?" she asked Zelda, holding up her shot glass of vodka.

"No, thanks. I don't need booze to feel good."

"I'm trying to cut back, but life doesn't let me."

"We use certain drugs in the cult to open the doors of perception. They would work wonders for you."

"The cult? All you ever talk about is 'the cult.' Doesn't it have a name? Like the Peoples Temple or the Manson Family?"

Zelda laughed. "You make it sound so diabolical. Why is a cult that makes you feel good considered evil?"

"It makes you feel good till you start swilling the Kool-Aid."

"You're so funny sometimes. I assure you, it's quite harmless. We don't go around offering human sacrifices to Satan while conducting a black sabbath in the middle of the night dressed in black robes chanting and burning incense."

"Then what do you do?"

"We empower each other. It's a lark. Come and find out. You don't want to sit home alone all the time and waste your life watching TV, do you?"

Belinda ignored the dig. "So what's the name of this outfit?"

"The Cult. That's its name. Simply, the Cult."

"Like it's the one and only, huh?"

Zelda shrugged. "Don't knock it till you've tried it."

Belinda was used to taking care of herself. She wasn't on the lookout for a group to take care of her, especially one that called itself a cult. She was already a member of Twelve Step. How many damn groups was she supposed to join?

"I don't think I ever asked you. What's your line of work, anyway?" said Zelda.

"I'm a cosmetician."

"How interesting. For the movies?"

"I'm trying to get into Hollywood, but haven't got there yet."

Zelda gave an enigmatic smile. "You'd be perfect for our group. As a Hollywood artist you must get a truckload of rejections—like an actor. This is where the cult comes in. It empowers you, enabling you to endure rejections and soldier on, stronger than ever."

"If the cult is so wonderful, why haven't I heard about it sooner?"

"They avoid publicity. They know the media will launch a smear campaign against them to take them down, so they fly under the radar. So far, it's worked. The media hasn't gotten wind of them. I'll let you in on a little secret."

"What?"

"Cults are all the rage in Hollywood circles. We have scores of actors in our group, some of them quite famous."

"If the cult is such a secret, how do they get new members?"

"Other members, like me, recruit them."

"Why recruit me? I'm not a famous actor."

"Not all of our members are actors. We have people from all walks of life."

"So why me?"

"Because you need empowerment. You're always moping around when I see you." Zelda paused and changed the subject. "The cops say this serial killer has killed at least twelve women so far."

"I can't keep up with that stuff. It bums me out."

"They believe the victims invite him into their rooms. Can you imagine?"

"Maybe he's a charmer. Or maybe he's a she."

"Hello?"

"How do they know the killer isn't a woman? Women would be more apt to admit another woman into their homes than admit a man."

"How many women serial killers do you know?" scoffed Zelda.

"None. I hope."

"That's my point. Most serial killers are men."

"I think we should change the subject," said Belinda, uneasily.

"Of course. But admit you like talking about serial killers. Everybody does. It's a guilty pleasure."

"Maybe at another time."

"The killer sending a letter to one of the trades is hard to believe. I mean, why send it to them? Why not to the *Times*, which has more readers?"

"I dunno. Maybe it's for real. Didn't the Zodiac Killer send letters to a San Francisco paper?"

"That's right," said Zelda, snapping her fingers. "They were in code. And they never caught him. They recently decoded the letters, which prove conclusively he was stark raving mad."

"Why are all the psycho killers from California?"

"I guess they like the weather here, like everybody else." Zelda thought about it. "But not all of them are located here. Son of Sam was in New York. And then there's the Milwaukee Cannibal. And the 'Killer Clown' John Wayne Gacy was from Illinois. And . . . ," Zelda trailed off. "You know what the papers are starting to call our killer?"

"I thought we agreed to change the subject. Not everybody is a serial killer."

"The Gouger. That's what they call him. Imagine that. It gives me goose bumps just thinking about it," said Zelda, screwing up her face, crossing her arms and rubbing them. "What does he do to his victims to earn such a grisly moniker?"

Belinda didn't know which was creepier—the Gouger or the Cult. Then again, maybe she should check the cult out. Maybe it was on the up and up. Brimming with energy Zelda *did* appear to be in a lot better shape than her. Belinda could do with a little pep in her step.

"When are you going to the cult?" she said.

"We could go right now."

"I didn't say 'we.' I said 'you.'"

"Let's go. It'll do you a world of good."

Zelda strode to the door, opened it, and waited for Belinda with her hand on the knob.

"What's that perfume you're wearing?" said Belinda, sniffing.

"Nice, isn't it? Good Girl Eau de Parfum by Caroline Herrera. It comes in a dark violet glass bottle shaped like a stiletto shoe."

"Sometimes you seem like another woman bustling around with all this energy you never used to have."

"Joie de vie, my dear. That's what it is," said Zelda, unleashing a toothy smile. "Now come with me. I command you," she added in a deep voice, smiling, beckoning to Belinda.

Belinda decided to go. She hoped she wouldn't regret it. She was curious about this cult and how it had enlivened Zelda. If she didn't like it, she could always walk out. There was no law that said she had to stay for one of their meetings or black masses or whatever they called their get-togethers. If Zelda didn't want to leave with her, Belinda could call an Uber to take her home.

"My curiosity is piqued," said Belinda, and headed out the door with Zelda.

They piled into Zelda's spick-and-span navy blue BMW Z4 convertible in the underground garage.

Sitting in the driver's seat, Zelda reached over Belinda's lap to the glove compartment and retrieved a Trader Joe's canvas tote bag.

"You have to put this over your head, I'm afraid," she said.

"What?"

"If you're not a member, the cult doesn't want you to know where they're located. I can't take you there unless you're blindfolded."

Belinda was beginning to regret her decision to accompany Zelda. What was she getting herself into? Belinda wondered with a measure of apprehension. On the other hand, it sounded exciting. She placed the empty tote over her head.

"That wasn't so hard, was it?" said Zelda, and fired the BMW's engine.

Whether it was due to the darkness of the hood over her face or to something else, Belinda felt herself nodding off minutes after they left the apartment house. She lost track of time, listening to the throb of the BMW's engine lull her to sleep.

# # #

She found herself bound to an X-shaped wooden cross with plastic zip ties secured around her wrists and ankles. The cross was erected in an empty warehouse with a cement floor and a cathedral ceiling. The only items she could see in the warehouse were wooden pallets stacked in a pile next to the door.

She shivered with cold. She looked down at her body as she hung from the cross and realized the reason. She was buck naked.

Her wrists were killing her. The tight zip ties were digging into her flesh as she hung from them.

A shirtless, brawny, tattooed, fortyish guy wearing a black leather mask and matching trousers strode across the floor toward her, a bullwhip in his hand. Coming to a halt twenty-odd feet away from her, he started snapping the bullwhip over his head in her direction. The whip wasn't long enough to reach her, but she flinched nonetheless.

Zelda cut across the cement floor toward her.

"It's all about empowerment," she told Belinda, as she stood near Leather Mask and watched her hanging from the cross.

"What the hell are you talking about, Zelda?" said Belinda, wincing in pain, feeling like her arms were going to tear out of their sockets any minute as she hung spread-eagled. "What's empowerment got to do with hanging naked from a cross?"

"This is how you learn to face and endure the brutality of the world. You suffer and learn how much pain you can endure."

Leather Mask cracked the whip above his head again.

"You got the wrong girl, Zelda, if you think I'm a nutso masochist."

"This isn't about masochism. It's about empowerment. Imagine how good you'll feel after we untie you and let you down."

"This is the cult you were talking about? A reject from a wrestling match wearing leather tights cracking a bullwhip?"

"Suffer and be grateful. Be happy you're alive."

For the first time Belinda picked up on small puddles of blood coagulating on the cement floor beneath her. Had Leather Mask cut her while she was unconscious? she wondered with alarm. She didn't feel like she had cuts on her body. The pain she felt was emanating from her wrists and shoulders.

"Another prospective member was reluctant at first, like you," said Zelda, noticing the direction of Belinda's gaze.

Belinda felt a frisson of fear go down her spine.

"You're gonna start shanking me if I don't join your cult?" she said.

She wanted to sound indignant, but deep down she was terrified to her very marrow.

"The initiate before you needed persuasion. She didn't understand what a good deal she was getting by joining us. This is an exclusive club. You can't join unless you're invited, and very few people *are* invited."

"You're brainwashed, Zelda. Can't you see? Did they hook you on drugs?"

"You should feel honored we invited you, instead of bent out of shape and rebellious."

"This sick joke has gone far enough. Let me down this minute. Or I'll scream," said Belinda, in fear for her life now.

"Go ahead. Nobody will hear you. We're in the boondocks."

"What do you want from me?"

"I want you to feel empowered," said Zelda, raising her arms and spreading them at her sides, a feeling of ecstasy washing over her. "The world is yours for the taking. All you need to do is join us."

They had really done a number on Zelda, decided Belinda in despair. How was she going to get off this cross and out of here? She saw no way.

She cut loose an ear-piercing scream. She couldn't help herself.

###

A loud crash from the green garbage truck beneath her bedroom window collecting trash awoke her as she lay in bed the next morning. She saw sunlight percolate through her window into her room trapping dust motes swirling inside its cone of light. Her head ached.

She rubbed her eyes, wondering how she had got here.

The last thing she remembered was a nightmare in which she was bound to a cross in a deserted, clammy warehouse, screaming. Was it a nightmare or had Zelda really driven her to the warehouse hooded with a Trader Joe's tote bag? At this point Belinda wasn't sure. If she really had been at the warehouse, how did she get back here in her bed? She had no memory of returning to her apartment.

What a horrible nightmare.

And yet her wrists felt sore.

She inspected her right wrist. What could have been a red ligature mark marred its flesh. If it was a dream, how did that mark get there? Had Zelda really tortured her?

Muddled and terrified, Belinda sat up in bed, trying to get her bearings.

The garbage truck continued generating a racket then left, grinding its gears. With the truck gone she could hear someone knocking on her door. What time was it? She glanced at the electric clock on her nightstand and saw it was ten past eleven in the morning according to the lime numerals. She never slept this late, even on weekends. Zelda or the cult must have drugged her. The ginger ale?

Belinda scrambled out of bed, flung on some clothes, ducked into the bathroom, and considered herself in the mirror. Not so hot. But she had just woken up, with a headache to boot. What could you expect? She fluffed her hair and strode across the living room carpet to the front door, where the knocking continued.

"One minute," she called out.

She peeked through the peephole in the door and saw a guy in his late thirties in a security guard's grey uniform standing in the corridor. He was clean-cut, with a nondescript face.

And yet he looked familiar somehow.

She opened the door.

"Good morning, Ms. Townsend," he said. "My supervisor at Direct Action Security told me you want to discuss the different services we provide for clients."

"Oh, yes. Come on in."

"Did I come at a bad time?" he said, searching her face.

I just woke up, is all, and I have a pounding headache.

"Not at all," she said, forcing a smile. "Do come in."

The guard entered her apartment.

"Have we met?" she said, her face creased with a frown.

"Not that I know of. Maybe you saw me outside one day. This is my route and I have several clients in this area. You could have seen me sitting outside in my patrol car."

"That must be it," she said. "Have a seat."

"Which is strange, because most people don't notice me. I'm good at blending into my surroundings."

She shrugged. "I guess I'm more perceptive than most."

"How much service are you in the market for?" he said. "By the way, my name is Zack."

"Pleased to meet you. You can call me Belinda. In regard to your question, I'm not sure. I'm hoping you can help me with that."

"That's my job."

"I'm being stalked by someone. He's been harassing me for weeks, and I'm worried he might try to kill me."

"Sad to say, that's not surprising. More and more women are living alone these days and are concerned for their safety."

"And then there's that serial killer that's terrorizing the city."

Zack nodded yes. "Our company is getting twice as many calls as usual from prospective clients."

"You never know who your neighbor might be nowadays."

"Before we get down to the nitty-gritty, could I use your bathroom?"

"Of course. It's over there," she said, pointing toward it. "Would you like something to drink?"

"A glass of water would be fine."

Zack retreated to the bathroom, Belinda to the kitchen.

In the kitchen she flicked on the radio on the gold-flecked white Formica countertop. Maybe some music would cheer her up. The pop music station KIIS-FM was playing “Let ’Em In” by Paul McCartney.

Despite his bland unmemorable face, it dawned on her where she had seen the security guard. She hadn’t seen him in his patrol car. She had seen him at Twelve Step. He had a drinking problem, like her. It was a small world, she decided.

Before he reached the bathroom, the man calling himself Zack slewed around and stole after Belinda. He whipped out a straight razor from his trouser pocket, opened it, and guided the gleaming stainless steel blade toward the carotid artery pulsing in her graceful white throat.

“Did you read my letter in *Variety*?”

“No, but I did, douchebag,” said Zelda, appearing in the doorway, and shot him in the back of the head with a Beretta nine mil. “I’ve had my eyes on this dweeb in his dinky rent-a-cop car. I thought *I* was the one he was stalking.” She paused and smiled at Belinda. “You didn’t think I’d let him take you away from me, did you, my dear? Now how about a nice glass of ginger ale?”

Quagmire

When Kidd answered the door, he beheld a large middle-aged man in a brown blazer with a bull skull bolo tie standing on the porch in tan hand-tooled cowboy boots looking at him.

"Is this the Darren Kidd residence?" said the man.

"Who wants to know?" said Kidd, in khaki chinos and a sky blue polo, looking young for his thirty-five years.

"Victor McClory. I'm a special agent with the US Marshals Service," said McClory, withdrawing his badge from his blazer's inside breast pocket and displaying it.

Kidd felt his heartbeat put on speed. "What can I do for you?"

Maybe this is about something else, he thought. *How much you wanna bet?*

"Could I enter?" said McClory.

"Why, of course," said Kidd's trim wife Rose, pushing thirty, clad in jeans and an apricot viscose blouse, over his shoulder. "We're always ready to help the police."

"I'm not the police, ma'am. The US Marshals Service is a federal enforcement organization separate from your local police department. We work for the Justice Department."

"Of course. You know what I mean. You guys can arrest people like the cops."

"So we can. We have the power to enforce warrants and apprehend subjects."

Kidd felt his palms sweating. He would have to let the cop—the marshal, that is—in. He had no other options. He backed away from the doorway to allow McClory to enter.

Six feet and then some, the guy had to weigh over two hundred pounds, decided Kidd.

"Have a seat and tell us what this is about, Marshal," said Rose, gesturing to the Naugahyde-upholstered couch in the living room.

"I'm here to make an arrest, ma'am," said McClory, holding his ground.

"Arrest?" said Rose, befuddled. "Arrest who?"

"Your husband Darren Kidd."

"What for?" said Rose, taken aback. "Have you been speeding again, Darren?"

"No," said McClory. "He's wanted for the murder of his wife."

"That can't be. *I'm* his wife."

"His previous wife."

Rose gazed at Kidd.

"His ex-wife," said McClory. "We have reason to believe he strangled her to death with one of her scarves."

"You got the wrong man," said Kidd. "I didn't do it."

"You're denying you're Jane Kidd's husband?"

"I *was* her husband. Not anymore."

"Because she's dead, and you killed her."

"I didn't kill anyone."

"What's this all about?" said Rose, flicking her eyes from McClory to Kidd in consternation.

Kidd could see the telltale bulge under McClory's blazer where a handgun was snugged in a shoulder holster.

"Your boyfriend—"

"My husband, you mean."

"If you say so. He's wanted for the murder of his wife Jane."

"I know there must be some mistake," said Rose.

"If his name is Darren Kidd, there's no mistake."

"I'm not the one that killed her," said Kidd. "Somebody else did it. They tried to pin that on me five years ago, and they dropped the murder charge because they had no case, no evidence."

"Why didn't you tell me about this?" said Rose.

"It's water under the bridge," said Kidd, flustered.

"You never said anything to me about your previous wife being murdered."

"I didn't want to upset you."

"Upset me?"

Kidd squirmed. "I thought you might reject my proposal if I told you about it."

"Because somebody killed your wife?"

"That's right. I mean, look at you. You're all bent out of shape now that you know about it."

Rose stood nonplussed, digesting the unthinkable.

"I don't care about your personal problems, Kidd," said McClory. "I have a warrant for your arrest."

"Impossible," said Kidd, incredulous.

"New evidence was found implicating you in your wife's murder."

Kidd shook his head no. "There can't be any such evidence. I didn't do it."

"Tell it to the judge."

Worked up, face hectic, Kidd strode across the living room away from McClory.

Thinking Kidd was trying to escape, McClory tore after him, tripped on the carpet, toppled forward, and slammed his forehead into the edge of the walnut coffee table, wrenching his neck and breaking it.

Raising her hand to her open mouth, Rose stifled a scream of dismay.

Kidd's face turned wan as he gazed at McClory's motionless figure with its face blood-smeared and its neck twisted at an unnatural angle.

"Hell," Kidd muttered.

Rose was the first to come to her senses.

"We have to call 911," she said, darting to the landline phone on the coffee table.

Kidd dashed over to the body and, staring at it, shook his head.

"Don't," he said. "He's already dead. Look at his eyes."

McClory's eyes were indeed glazed and staring into infinity as he sprawled on his side.

"Are you sure?" said Rose.

"Look at his neck. He broke his neck in the fall."

"Still, we have to notify the authorities he's dead," she said, leaning down to lift the handset from its cradle.

"Don't," he said, bolting over to her and staying her hand.

"What are you doing?"

"Don't call 911."

"Why not? Are you worried his family will sue us? We have an umbrella insurance policy for a million dollars."

"I'm not worried about a lawsuit."

"Then what?"

"Look at him. If you call the cops, they'll say I killed him."

"We'll tell them the truth. It was an accident."

"He was here to arrest me. You think they're gonna believe he died by accident?"

"But it's the truth."

"It looks like someone bashed his head in. They'll charge me with another murder."

Rose pulled her arm out of Kidd's grasp. "Then what are we supposed to do?"

Kidd clutched his forehead. "Let me think."

"If they find out we're concealing his death here, for sure they'll blame you for murdering him. Is that what you want?"

"If we call 911, and they find him like this, they'll bust me, especially with that murder warrant out on me," said Kidd, sweat beading over his upper lip.

"We can't just leave him here."

Kidd made a beeline to the picture window. Fortunately, the white sheer linen drapes were drawn shut. He inserted his hand between the opening in the middle of them, and peeked out the window at their neighborhood. He wondered how many people had seen McClory enter his house.

Kidd didn't see anybody walking around outside or working in their yards. All was quiet. He saw no sign of activity. Cars were parked in their driveways. No kids around. The neighbors were at work. Lawns were deserted. Blades of grass bowed softly in the late afternoon breeze. Not even a dog was being walked.

It was possible nobody had seen McClory enter their house, decided Kidd.

Removing his hand between the drapes he slewed around to face Rose.

"We have to get rid of the corpse," he said.

Rose shook her head no. "We need to call 911."

"We can't let them know he died here. I'm telling you, they'll blame me for killing him."

"If I help you get rid of the body, that makes me an accessory."

"An accessory to what? We didn't kill him."

Rose thought about it. "Accessory to hiding a dead body. Isn't that a crime?"

"If we do this right, nobody will ever find out. We'll have nothing to worry about."

Rose demurred. "We really should call 911. It's the right thing to do."

"Do you want them to throw me in the joint for murder?"

"We'll tell them the truth. He tripped and fell and hit his head."

Kidd turned away from her and paced in a semicircle, his head down. "He comes here to arrest me and dies because he trips? They'll never believe it. His head's busted up. Look at it," he said, wheeling around and stabbing his finger at McClory's blood-streaked head.

"They'll have to believe it. It's the truth."

Kidd laughed cynically. "A lot you know. They'll say I resisted arrest and killed him. I know how those guys think."

"They won't do anything to us if we tell them the truth."

Kidd wasn't listening to her. "We have to hide the body." He paused in thought. "Or destroy it."

He returned to the picture window and peeked through the curtains at the street. "Which car is his? Do you know? I don't see a federal marshal's car out there. He must have used an unmarked vehicle."

She approached the window and peered out the corner of it.

"That dark blue car parked down the side of the street," she said. "I don't recognize it. Maybe that's his."

"Looks like a Charger. Luckily he's not parked in front of our house. Maybe we can leave it where it is. But that might be dangerous. When the authorities find it, they're gonna know McClory was in our neighborhood before he disappeared."

"Let's just call 911 and get this over with, without digging ourselves into a hole by messing things up."

"I suppose I could use his car keys to move the car."

Backing away from the curtain, Rose confronted him. "Why didn't you tell me you had been married and your wife was murdered?"

"I thought it might scare you away from me—even though I didn't kill her. I thought it was best to avoid the subject."

"You should have told me. It's almost like lying by withholding it from me."

"It would have made you suspicious of me."

"Better to have it out in the open than conceal it from me. Concealing it makes you look guilty."

"I was going to tell you—eventually. But not before we got married."

"Why do they think *you* killed her?"

"Because they're clueless. A neighbor told the cops we had a fight the night before the murder."

"And did you?"

"We argued. That's all. I wouldn't call it a fight."

"If you didn't kill her, who did?"

"Beats me. I'm no detective."

"You must have some idea. You were her husband."

He turned away from her and eyed McClory. "All I know is, I didn't do it. Let's talk about this some other time. We need to take care of this stiff."

"I deserve an explanation. I'm your wife."

"What's to explain?" he said, facing her. "Somebody murdered her. What more can I tell you? Let's drop it. You don't want me to go to jail, do you?"

She scrunched her face. "What else have you been hiding from me?"

"Nothing."

"I don't understand why they think you killed your own wife."

Kidd changed the subject.

"What if we made it look like McClory was in a car accident? His injuries could be consistent with a car accident. The blow to the head. The broken neck," he said, making a sweeping gesture toward McClory's head.

"If you didn't kill her, you have nothing to fear by calling 911 and reporting this accident right now."

"Easy for you to say. You're not the one they would cart away to the joint for murdering a cop."

"He's not a cop. He's a marshal. You heard him."

"That's even worse."

"I'll back you up."

"A wife can't testify for her husband."

"Are you a lawyer now?"

"Everybody knows that."

"I don't want you to get me involved in a crime."

"What crime? We're simply moving this body out of here, so the cops will find it elsewhere."

"Moving a dead body without notifying the cops? That must be a crime. Especially since this guy is a US marshal."

"We didn't commit a crime. He died by accident." Kidd strode to the window and peeked out between the curtains. "It'll be dark soon. Then we can move the body without the neighbors seeing us."

"I can't believe we're having this conversation."

"We need his car keys."

Kidd crossed the carpet to McClory's body, hunkered down, and rummaged through the body's trouser pockets.

McClory groaned and flicked his wrist.

"Jeez," cried Kidd, bolting to his feet and reeling backward.

Rose screamed.

"Shh," said Kidd, grimacing as he regained his balance. "The neighbors."

Rose clamped her hand over her mouth, eyes bulging in fear. "He's still alive. We need to call 911. If we don't and let him die, it's the same as murdering him."

Kidd scrutinized the body as he stood over it. "He's already dead. Look at his eyes. They're dead man's eyes. They're open, but they can't see a thing."

"He groaned and moved his hand. You can't deny you saw it."

Kidd shrugged it off. "Some kind of reflex of the nerves after you're dead."

"That doesn't explain his groan."

"Uh—air. Air trapped in his lung escaped and sounded like a groan. Look at him. He's not moving now."

Circumspectly, Kidd squatted back down near the body and resumed rooting through McClory's trouser pockets in search of the car keys, apprehensive of the body moving again. He located the keys and dredged them out.

"Voila. We're good to go," he said, standing up and holding up the keys in triumph.

He caught Rose staring at him.

"Why didn't you tell me you were married before?" she said.

"Are you gonna harp on that again?"

"It's something you should have told me before we got married."

"What did you think? That I was a virgin? I had a previous life before I met you. Just like you did. We don't live in vacuums our entire lives. We all have histories."

"I've never been married before. I would've told you if I had."

"And what about your previous boyfriends? Why didn't you tell me about them?"

"It's not the same thing as marriage," said Rose, withdrawing into herself, shaking her head.

"Why not? What's the difference?"

"And what about kids? Do you have any kids that you haven't told me about?"

"No. No kids. And what about you?"

"Kids? I've never been married. I don't have kids."

"So you used to be a nun?"

Rose laughed. "Actually, I used to be a stripper before I became a History teacher."

Kidd did a double take. "A stripper? You never told me anything about stripping."

"Why should I have told you? There's no law against it. There *is* a law against murdering your wife."

"How many times do I have to tell you? I didn't do it." He paused. "So you used to take your clothes off in front of a pack of drooling pervs in raincoats ogling you in a sleazebag strip joint?"

"I had to pay my college tuition along with my rent."

"And what about lap dances? Did you perform lap dances for your customers in the backrooms too?"

"No. No lap dances."

"And you kept this hidden from me?"

"I saw no reason to tell you before we got married. Like I said, it's not a crime. I'm telling you now. What's the big deal? You, on the other hand, are wanted for murdering your wife."

Rose didn't know why she was confessing about being a stripper now. Maybe it was out of spite for Darren's not telling her about having an ex-wife. Otherwise, she probably never would have brought it up.

"We don't have time for this," said Kidd. "We have to get that body out of here. Every minute it's in our house increases our risk of being found out."

Rose thought about it then gazed at Kidd. "He's a US marshal. He said he had new evidence you murdered your wife. How could that be if you didn't do it?"

"Whatever evidence he had couldn't prove I did something I didn't do. I didn't kill her."

He approached the window and checked out the neighborhood. It was still quiet as the sun set, bobbing like a lava orange globe over Vic Andrasi's salmon-colored Spanish-styled stucco house across the street. If Kidd wasn't so keyed up, he would have drunk in the picture-postcard scene.

"The sun's setting," said Kidd. "We can take the body to McClory's car pretty soon."

He spun around and saw Rose wiping her hands.

"I don't want anything to do with this," she said.

"I need your help. I can't do this alone."

"Why not?"

"I'll drive him out of here and stage the accident. Then I'll need a ride back here. You follow me in our car so I can get a ride back with you."

Rose collapsed on the sofa.

"I'm not cut out for this underhanded stuff," she said, slumping forward, holding her head in her hands.

"Do you think I am?"

"You must be. You've got it all figured out."

"No, I don't." He thought about it. "What kind of an accident is it? He needs to hit something hard enough that the impact would kill him in such a manner that would break his neck and fracture his skull."

"You sound like someone who has experience in this sort of thing," said Rose, raising her head and eying him with suspicion.

"I'm thinking on the fly. You really think I've done something like this before?"

"I'm beginning to think I don't know you very well."

"Just because I didn't tell you I was married?" he said in exasperation.

"Not just that. Your mind seems devious, the way you're plotting to make it look like McClory died in a car accident."

"What's your solution?"

"Call 911, and let them take care of it."

Kidd shook his head no. "They're trying to pin one murder on me already. If they find a dead US marshal in my house who had a warrant for my arrest, five will get you ten they'll say I killed him."

Rose got to her feet and threw up her hands in dismay. "Why?"

"We have to look at this logically. And you know what I say is true. We can't let the cops find this stiff in our house." He approached her and lowered his voice. "We're in this together."

Rapping on their front door made them both jump.

"Who can that be?" said Rose, eyes bugged out.

Kidd stole across the living room and peeked around the curtain toward the front stoop.

A thickset man with a tonsure in his late thirties wearing a cream button-down shirt with its top two buttons unbuttoned and blue jeans was standing in front of the door. Vic Andrasi, a sales rep for Honda who lived across the street.

Kidd was torn between answering it and pretending no one was home. But what if Andrasi should see him leave the house after Kidd didn't answer the door? Andrasi would become suspicious. Kidd decided he should answer it.

He strode to the door and edged it open.

"Hey, Darren," said Andrasi. "How about a game of golf this Saturday?"

"Oh, yeah, Vic," said Kidd, keeping the crack in the door narrow so Andrasi couldn't peer into the living room and make out McClory's corpse sprawled on the carpet. "Sure."

"Anything wrong?"

"Not at all. Why do you say that?"

"I dunno. You look like you're hiding behind the door or something. Did I come at a bad time?"

"Well—uh—I don't have any pants on."

"Oh," said Vic, laughing nervously. "I'd be embarrassed, too, if I had chicken legs like yours. I didn't mean to disturb you."

Kidd smiled politely, trying to look insincere enough that Andrasi would take the hint and leave. "No problem."

"I'll leave you alone. Oh, while I'm over here, do you know whose car that is parked over there?" said Andrasi, pointing at McClory's car.

Kidd's heart skipped a beat. "Can't say that I do."

"I know most of the cars in the neighborhood. I don't recognize that one."

"Somebody probably visiting a friend."

Andrasi shrugged. "I guess. See you on Saturday early. Be ready to go at seven sharp," he said, smiling. "I've spent the day trying to figure out how to spend the twenty bucks I'm gonna win from you on the links."

He turned away and retreated down the flagstone path to the street.

Kidd closed the door with an audible sigh of relief.

"Who was it?" said Rose.

"Vic. He noticed McClory's car."

"He knows a US marshal's here?" said Rose, her voice tight.

"He just asked whose car it was. He doesn't know who parked it there."

"There goes our plan."

"Why do you say that?"

"He must be watching that car."

"He can't keep watching it 24/7. And how's he gonna see it in the dark? We don't have the best-lighted street in the world. He won't see me take McClory out to his car."

"He's not gonna see you drag a dead body out of our house?" said Rose, incredulous.

"I'm not gonna drag him. I'll help him out with his arm around my neck, like he's juiced."

"And how do I know you won't do the same thing to me?"

"What are you talking about?" said Kidd, frowning with bafflement.

"How do I know I'm not gonna end up murdered like your previous wife?"

Kidd shook his head. "I'm innocent until proven guilty. They can't prove I killed her because I didn't. You worry too much."

He paced around the room for the next ten minutes, which seemed interminable, waiting for the darkness.

"Will you stop doing that?" said Rose. "It's driving me crazy."

He peeked out the window. "It's dark enough. I'm leaving."

"An innocent man wouldn't sneak a corpse out of here in the dark."

"We've been all through that. You're like a dog worrying a bone."

Rose angled to the closet in the hallway, opened the louvered wooden door, stepped inside the closet, and returned to Kidd, holding up a Ruger 9 mm pistol in her hand.

"Then why did you hide this gun in the closet?" she said.

Kidd stared at her. "It's for self-protection. You know I prepare taxes for a living. Some of my clients don't like the results they get from me. If they don't get refunds, they get pissed. And they take it out on me. Some of them get downright hostile. You know that."

"Why didn't you tell me it was in the closet? I happened to find it one day when I was cleaning."

"I confess, I don't tell you everything I do," said Kidd, nettled. "I didn't see any need for you to know it was there."

"All you had to do was tell me."

"Well, I didn't."

"We can't have so many secrets between us," she said, shaking the gun. "Were you headed for the closet to get this when McClory said he was arresting you?"

"No."

"Then where were you headed?"

He shrugged. "I was trying to make a run for it."

"Even though you're innocent?"

"That's right."

"How many more lies are there between us?"

"Everybody's a liar. That's what society does to us. It turns us all into liars. You weren't born yesterday. You should know better."

"I'm not sure what I know anymore."

"Let's concentrate on what we have to do here," he said. "We have to get rid of this body."

Rose tossed the gun on the sofa in disillusionment.

"That's better," said Kidd.

She gave him a look he couldn't decipher.

He had no time to get into it with her. He stooped, draped McClory's arm around his neck, and, grimacing, lifted the dead weight with the strength of his legs. He hauled the body to the front door.

"Get the door for me," he said, his face flushed from the heavy lifting.

Rose opened the door, stepped outside onto the stoop, and checked to see if the coast was clear.

"I don't see anyone," she said.

He hauled McClory out onto the porch.

Rose flicked on the porch light.

"No," hissed Kidd. "Kill the light."

"You'll trip on the stairs in the dark."

"Someone will see me with McClory in the light."

Rose doused the light.

"Get in the car and follow me when you see me leave," he said.

He manhandled McClory down the stoop's creaky wooden steps, straining to maintain his balance despite the stiff's weight. He felt sweat from his armpits trickling down his flanks. One misstep and he would pitch forward and crack his skull on the ground. His straining back was killing him.

He reached the flagstone path and horsed McClory down it toward the sidewalk, keeping his eyes peeled for any sign of movement in the dark neighborhood. The glowing blue light of a TV set dancing in Andrasi's living room window comforted Kidd. If Andrasi was watching TV, he wouldn't be watching a dark figure in the night hauling around a corpse, decided Kidd.

Kidd dragged McClory's feet across the flagstones and reached the cement sidewalk, gasping for breath. He paused to catch his wind. But pausing didn't lighten the two-hundred-pound-plus weight hanging around his neck. The sooner he got the stiff to the car, the better.

He resumed hauling McClory down the sidewalk.

Picking up on headlights blazing from a car approaching on the street, he froze in their beams.

The car slowed down as it neared Kidd. Sweat was pouring out of his armpits now, soaking his shirt. The car was coming to a halt. Kidd held his breath.

Braking the car to a halt, the driver powered down his window.

"Sorry, I missed the party," he cried, tipping his thumb in front of his open mouth like he was drinking, and laughed at his joke.

He accelerated and drove away.

Kidd trudged forward, schlepping the corpse down the sidewalk twenty-odd feet from McClory's parked car, which turned out to be an unmarked Dodge Charger without government license tags. McClory had wanted to surprise Kidd by coming in unannounced, decided Kidd.

Kidd figured the Charger had to be McClory's. He didn't see any other cars that didn't belong in the neighborhood parked on the street. To make sure it was McClory's he stopped on the sidewalk, keeping McClory's body propped up, fished McClory's car fob out of his trouser pocket, and pressed the fob's button. He heard the Charger's doors unlock.

He pocketed the fob and shuffled the rest of the way to the car with McClory's limp arm hanging around his neck. Reaching the Charger he approached the passenger's-side door, opened it, and manhandled McClory's limp body into the front seat. He straightened out the body, placed its legs in the footwell, and laid the back of the head against the headrest.

McClory's head kept tilting to the side and sliding off the headrest. Kidd decided it was a losing battle to keep the head against the headrest. He angled the body so the head leaned down on McClory's chest.

He circled the hood, swung open the driver's-side door, and slid onto the driver's seat. He checked the sideview mirror for any sign of Rose. He didn't see her. She should have been pulling out of their driveway by now so she would be able to hang a tail on him without losing sight of the Charger. He thought he could see her opening the front door of their house, framed in the golden light emanating from their living room.

###

Inhaling the jasmine-scented night air, Rose got in their BMW, fired the ignition, backed out of the carport, and down the driveway onto the street. As she pulled onto the road, she picked up on the Charger's lights flicking on and its engine revving. She followed the Charger as it pulled onto the road and headed out of the neighborhood, knifing through the darkness.

She hadn't told Darren the whole truth about her previous relationships with men. Did anyone ever reveal the whole truth to anyone else, especially to their spouses? Besides her stripping, she had hooked a few times to pay for her college tuition at UC Irvine.

She didn't come from a rich family. Her mother worked as a secretary at a used car dealership. Her father was a clerk at the post office. She learned early on in life she had to earn her way, one way or another. Back then when she was young, she wanted to experience everything in life, and why not turn a trick or two? She never saw anything wrong with turning a couple of tricks. On the other hand, she would never do it again.

She wondered if Darren knew where he was going to stage the accident that had supposedly killed McClory.

Darren was a guy who had too many secrets, she decided. She doubted she could ever trust him again. Everyone had secrets. That was a given. But Darren had more than his share. His secret about being suspected of murdering his wife fanned the fires of suspicion inside her. He should have come clean about it before they had gotten married. His concealing it made him look all the more suspicious in her eyes.

Through the windshield she watched the chiaroscuro of the Charger's red taillights puncturing the black velvet night, her heartbeat beating a crescendoing rataplan as she anticipated the forthcoming accident. Her mind revolved her plans of what to do after the accident. Her palms sweated inside her driving gloves as she gripped the BMW's steering wheel.

To make this work she could not make any mistakes. She had to think and rethink everything she was going to do after the impending crash. It would help if she knew what kind of accident Darren was planning. She doubted it would involve another car, which would add another person to the brew whose actions could not be predicted. Darren wouldn't want any witnesses.

The Charger turned down a winding road, which was even more ill-lit than the road they had been on. It would make sense to stage an accident here, she decided, negotiating the turns, speeding up so as not to lose sight of the Charger on the tortuous road.

There was less traffic on this road, she noticed, as fewer headlights of oncoming traffic greeted her. She wished Darren would slow down. She didn't want to lose sight of him. Her tires protested as she rounded a hairpin turn.

Why did disguising the cause of somebody's death come so easily to Darren? she wondered. She could think of only one answer, and it made her tremble with apprehension. He must have had experience. With his ex-wife? What if he had more ex-wives that he hadn't told her about? And what if they had been murdered?

She found herself pressing the gas too hard, causing her to swing wide in a sharp curve. All but losing control of the car, she straightened out after fishtailing, to avoid running off the road. She told herself to calm down.

Hearing a crash up ahead, she started in her seat. She took her foot off the gas, slowing down, squinting to see through the darkness what had happened in front of her.

She rounded another curve. And she saw it.

The Charger had crashed into an oak tree, triggering its airbags, which had deployed and filled the front seat. Wisps of smoke snaked upward from the contorted hood.

She tooled toward the driver's side of the Charger, whose front end had crumpled in its collision with the tree, ripping through grey oak bark, exposing a long, deep gash of bone white wood.

Darren, sandwiched between the airbag and his backseat, his head turned sideways, looked at her and waved for her to help him out of the vehicle. She stopped across from him and powered down the BMW's window.

"The door's jammed," he said. "I can't get out. Help me."

Rose raised Darren's pistol, which she had brought with her from their house, and drew a bead on his head. Her hand was shaking out of control, throwing off her aim. But she had to do this. She had no other alternative. To let him live would jeopardize her life, leaving her at his mercy.

"What are you doing?" he said, his face twisted with baffled fear.

She steadied her arm and fired twice, discharging two bullets point-blank into his head as he faced her.

She had to do this quickly, she decided.

She tossed the pistol through the Charger's open driver's-side window, where it struck Darren's motionless face and fell beside his seat. Not what she had planned. She had wanted to toss the gun past Darren's head so it landed near McClory, but the gap between the back of Darren's head and the back of his seat was too narrow for her to thread, and the gun had struck Darren's face with her lousy aim.

Eying his blood-streaked face she wanted to throw up.

A car approached from the opposite lane and passed them.

Checking her rearview mirror Rose saw there was no traffic behind her. She backed up the BMW and parked on the grassy verge that skirted the street. She cut her eyes to the sideview mirror and saw the car that had passed her pull to a stop.

She decided she had better report the accident before the other driver called for help. Otherwise, the cops might suspect she had something to do with it. She whipped out her mobile from her purse, punched 911, and filed a report.

"I heard an explosion, and I can see a car wrapped around a tree in front of me," she said.

"Are you near the accident?"

"I parked behind it."

"Stay away from it in case the car explodes."

Rose hadn't thought of that. Actually, it would be a good thing if the Charger did blow up, because it would confuse things even more, throwing the cause of the two occupants' deaths into dispute. Maybe she should toss a match onto the wreckage. She rechecked her sideview mirror. The other car was parked not far from her. The driver must have been calling 911 like her. Too dangerous for her to get out of the BMW now and light a fire. The other driver might see her.

Rose couldn't risk it.

"Where are you?" said the emergency dispatcher.

"I'm—I'm not sure," said Rose. "I don't know the road's name." She scanned the road up ahead for a sign. "I don't see any signs."

"OK. Don't worry. Stay on the line and the paramedics can track your cell's signal in their ambulance."

"All right," she said, her voice quavering.

"Stay calm."

She glanced at her sideview mirror. The other car wasn't budging. Waiting for the cops like her, no doubt, she decided. She went over her story in her head, preparing her answers for the cops.

She heard a siren's wail slice through the night.

If she had had more time, she could have planted the gun in McClory's hand making it look like he had shot Darren. Too late now. She dared not approach the wreckage with the other car parked across the street. Best to wait.

The cops arrived ten minutes later, blue lights flashing on their light bars.

Two uniformed patrolmen climbed out of their black-and-white and inspected the accident.

Shaking with apprehension, Rose got out of her car and stood beside the front fender, watching them.

A fortysomething bald cop approached her after investigating the crumpled Charger, a wallet in his hand, which was wearing a blue surgical latex glove.

"Did you see what happened, ma'am?" he said.

"I heard an explosion in front of me and when I drove around the curve I saw that car over there smashed into a tree."

"You heard an explosion?"

"Yes."

"What kind of explosion?"

She shrugged. "I dunno. A loud noise."

"Could it have been a gunshot?"

"I—I—uh, maybe."

"Take it easy, and try to remember. Take a couple of deep breaths."

She took a deep breath. "It could've been a gunshot."

"The reason I ask is because the driver was shot in the face."

"Oh no."

He inspected the wallet. "His name is Darren Kidd."

Rose gasped. "Ohmigod."

Her eyes filled with tears.

"What's wrong?" he said.

"He's—he's"—she sobbed—"my husband."

"Your husband?" he said, taken aback.

"My—my husband."

"I'm sorry for your loss. I had no idea. The man he was with must have shot him and died in the accident that followed."

Rose sniffled. She wiped her tearing eyes. She wasn't faking her grief. The realization that her husband was really dead was finally hitting her. Even if he was a murderer, he had been her husband.

"Sarge, I ran a check on the passenger," said the other cop, who was muscular, close cropped, and in his twenties with a bulbous nose, as he approached them, McClory's badge in his hand.

Rose wished he knew the meaning of the word *deodorant*. He smelled like raw onions and manure mixed together. If she didn't have a case of the sniffles, she probably would have wretched at the foul odor.

"And?" said the sergeant. "Out with it, Penske."

"His name's McClory. His badge says he's a US marshal."

The sergeant turned to Rose. "Why would your husband be with a US marshal?"

Pretending to be dumbfounded, Rose shook her head. "I have no idea."

Furrowing his brow Penske scratched his temple. "The funny thing is, I ran a check on him, and it turns out there's a BOLO on him."

"Who? McClory?"

"Yeah."

"For what?"

"He's wanted for impersonating a US marshal and shaking down murder suspects by lying to them there's a warrant out for their arrest because new evidence has been found against them."

If Rose wasn't ashen-faced before, she was now.

"Kidd must have refused to pony up, so McClory shot him and died in the ensuing accident," said the sergeant.

Rose's knees buckled, and she fainted.

Mug's Game

Vince Macy had a rap sheet. He had done time at San Quentin for check kiting.

He was going straight now. Straight to poverty row the way he saw it. Working as a rent-a-cop wasn't paying enough money to keep him or his wife happy. Honesty was supposed to be the best policy, but experience had taught him otherwise. In financial terms honesty was the worst policy.

He had turned thirty-five last week and felt stuck in a rut. More and more fights were erupting between him and his wife Katherine. Half the time he didn't even know what they were fighting about. He figured they were both on edge because he wasn't making enough dough.

He became concerned that Katherine was getting ideas about walking out on him. He didn't want her to leave. Which meant he needed more dough.

He was standing in his living room gazing out the window across the street at Grimes's digs in his San Bernardino neighborhood of tract houses, one-story pastel stucco bungalows with red tiled roofs.

Grimes was standing outside watering his garden of jasmine next to his stoop with a green plastic hose. Wearing wire-rimmed round bifocals and clad in a white polo and beige chinos, the middle-aged CPA had a receding hairline. Not the best-looking guy in the neighborhood, but Macy envied him.

Normally Macy didn't envy paper pushers. It wasn't Grimes's job that Macy envied. It was what Grimes had told him the better part of an hour ago.

Grimes had told him he had won the lottery. And yet the guy was out watering his garden like winning the lottery was an everyday occurrence.

If Macy had won the lottery, he'd be out celebrating at Halloran's pub, hoisting brews, tying one on. But not Grimes. Grimes celebrated by watering his flowers. It took all kinds, decided Macy.

Maybe Grimes didn't need the dough, decided Macy. Maybe it meant nothing to him. It was always the guys who didn't need the shekels that ended up winning the lottery.

Macy bought lottery tickets all the time. The only time he won, he won pin money.

He got on the horn to his buddy Porter, a guy who had also done a little time and was going straight—for the time being, anyway.

"Did you hear the news, Porter?" said Macy. "My neighbor won a million bucks in the lottery."

"He's got it made. Invest it in the stock market, sit back, and you're set for life."

"Life isn't fair, is it?"

"It's a coldhearted bitch is what it is."

"You got static on your line?"

"I hear it. Bad connection. You shoulda used your cell."

"Guess what he's doing? I'm watching him right now through my window."

"Shooting off fireworks?"

"You're not gonna believe it when I tell you. He's watering his garden."

"Oh, man. All that money going to waste. I can't stand the idea of moolah going to waste."

"Me neither. Especially when I'm behind on my mortgage," said Macy, his expression sour as he watched Grimes aiming his hose at the jasmine, their wet white petals glittering like snowflakes under the hot sun.

Porter had done time for manslaughter, Macy knew, which was the reason he was calling him. Porter had beat a bum to death with his bare hands for laughing at him. Porter had a temper. He did a five-year stretch for it in San Quentin, where Macy had met him.

"How's life treating you?" said Macy.

"Like a hooker with the clap."

"That bad?"

Porter heaved a sigh. "Employers don't like hiring ex-cons. Where's the love?"

"Good luck finding it."

"How about you?"

"The same as you, is why I called."

"Is this a scheme you wanna pull off?"

Macy nodded yes. "There you go."

"I'm interested in hearing your proposal, considering my future ain't looking rosy and bright."

"I thought you'd be interested."

"Shoot."

"What say we liberate that winning lottery ticket from Grimes?" said Macy.

"That your neighbor's name?"

"It is."

"He didn't cash it yet?"

"Not from what he told me. He said he just found out he had won when he saw me getting out of my Mustang in my driveway."

"Whoever cashes in that lottery ticket owns the dough."

"It'd be a lot easier to swipe the ticket than the dough."

"Agreed."

"I know what he's gonna do. He's gonna transfer his winnings to his bank account electronically, and nobody's ever gonna see the dough. He's a CPA. I bet he knows how to do that stuff."

"How do you know he hasn't done it already."

Macy stared at Grimes, who had his back to him hosing down the jasmine.

"He doesn't look like a guy in a hurry to cash in his ticket," said Macy. "A lot of these lottery winners consult lawyers before they cash in the ticket and ask legal advice to make sure they pay the least amount of taxes and don't violate any laws. Maybe he'll set up a trust fund or move his winnings to an offshore bank account. Once you get that much money, it's all about hiding it from the government. To do that you need a lawyer. Grimes hasn't had time to get legal counsel." Macy paused in reflection. "He's still got that ticket on him. I'd bet my bottom dollar on it."

"We could save him the trouble of hiring a lawyer. Is that why you're calling me?"

"I'm thinking that lottery ticket wants a new home. Can you get here tonight around nine?"

"Got it."

Macy cradled the handset on the coffee table.

Something was eating at him. Why was there so much static on the line? he wondered. It could have been a bad connection. Or somebody had been listening to him and Porter on a wiretap.

###

That somebody was Scott Brody, PI, who was sitting in the back of a battered old white van he had rented and parked a block away from Macy's house. Headphones on his head, he heard Macy hang up. Brody had tapped Macy's phone for his client, Macy's wife Katherine, who suspected Macy was cheating on her and had hired Brody to find out the identity of Macy's inamorata.

Hair cropped, wearing jeans and a grey sweatshirt with frayed, cut-off sleeves, Brody removed the headphones from his head. At six two, and all muscle, he cut an imposing figure.

He wondered what he should do with the intel about the impending robbery of Grimes.

Eavesdropping on phone conversations wasn't Brody's favorite activity, and he normally avoided resorting to it, but he hadn't had any luck catching Macy carrying on a clandestine affair. Either Macy was too careful at covering his tracks, or he wasn't seeing anyone on the sly.

To find out the truth, Brody had decided to tap Macy's landline. The biggest problem with tapping phones in California was its legality. You weren't legally permitted to tap a phone without the permission of the two speakers.

Brody didn't break the law if he didn't have to. Bending it was an altogether different matter. He had been known to bend it several times in his profession. Bending the law gave him that extra edge he sometimes needed to crack a case.

The info Macy had just imparted was useless in a court of law because Brody had obtained it illegally.

He fished his cell phone out of his trouser pocket and called Katherine Macy, a short redhead with fiery green eyes—green in color and green with jealousy—and an even fierier temper.

"Your husband is planning to rob a neighbor's winning lottery ticket tonight," said Brody.

"What?" said Katherine in disbelief.

"Macy found out Grimes won the lottery."

"That idiot. He's got a record, you know. If he gets caught committing armed robbery, they'll lock him up and throw away the key."

Brody nodded. "A million bucks is nothing to sneeze at."

"A *million*?"

"A nice chunk of change."

Silence on the line.

"Hello?" he said.

"I'm here."

"How do you want me to handle this?"

"What do you mean?"

"Do you want me to call the cops?"

"No. That would implicate me."

"In what way?"

"Because you're working for me, and I don't want my husband to know I hired you. The cops would get that out of you."

"I can keep my mouth shut."

He had no wish to tell the cops about Macy's planned heist. He'd have to admit he had illegally tapped Macy's line, lose his private investigator's license, and do time. The DA had almost tried him the time he had left a dead, rotting trout on a guy's doorstep as a warning to back off Brody's client. The DA had decided not to prosecute, since he couldn't prove the dead fish was a threat. Sometimes a cigar was just a cigar.

Brody wondered why Katherine didn't want him to tell the cops. Maybe she liked the idea of Macy adding a million bucks to the family nest egg.

"There's no point in telling the cops," said Katherine. She paused. "What about the other woman?"

"I haven't found one."

"Keep looking. He'll trip up one of these days. What time?"

"What?"

"What time is he planning to rob Grimes?"

"Nine o'clock tonight."

She terminated the call.

Interesting question, decided Brody. Why did she ask it?

###

Macy used a Phillips screwdriver to unscrew and remove the base of his landline phone to search for a bug. He saw a round metal object that looked like it didn't belong. He touched it. It fell easily into his hand. He realized a magnet had been holding it in place. The listening device. He placed it on the coffee table.

Somebody knew he was going to jack Grimes's lottery ticket, Macy decided. He didn't have time to figure out who. He needed to use the wiretap to his advantage. The bug had been his enemy when he didn't know about it. Now that he knew, he could convert it into his friend.

The eavesdropper thought Macy was going to rob Grimes at nine o'clock tonight. Was whoever it was going to lie in wait for Macy to show up? Was it the cops' bug? Why would the cops be bugging his phone? wondered Macy. He had done his time, and that was the end of it. Maybe they wanted to make sure he didn't go back to his old ways. Why bother? They could care less what he did with his future. They had plenty of other things to keep them occupied.

Somebody else could have planted the bug, he decided. It didn't matter. What mattered was the eavesdropper knew Macy was going to do Grimes tonight at nine. Macy could exploit that knowledge by altering his plans. Instead of hitting Grimes's place at nine, he would go in two hours earlier at seven. The break-in would be over by the time the eavesdropper showed up at Grimes's in whatever capacity. Macy still had no idea what the eavesdropper was planning to do with his ill-gotten knowledge.

Macy walked away from the landline phone into his bedroom, produced his cell phone, closed the bedroom door, and called Porter. "Change in plans. We're going in at seven tonight. OK?"

"No problem," said Porter. "Why the change?"

"Somebody tapped my phone."

Porter took it in. "Maybe we should put it off, if the cops are staking you out."

"Grimes will have time to cash the ticket if we put it off."

"I dunno."

"You don't want that winning lottery ticket?"

"I do, but I don't wanna go back to the joint—"

"Maybe I should do this on my own."

Macy didn't want to do it alone. He had plans for Porter. Porter was used to the rough stuff. Macy wanted Porter to take Grimes out to eliminate any witnesses. Porter might even have to rough Grimes up a bit if Grimes refused to tell them where he had stashed the lottery ticket.

Macy had never beat the crap out of anyone. He was a check kiter, not a torpedo. Maybe that was why he hated his current job as a rent-a-cop. Still, he owned a piece and wasn't afraid to use it.

"I want in," said Porter.

"Bring a piece."

"You think we'll need it?"

"You can never tell. In any case, we gotta convince Grimes it's in his best interest to cooperate with us and tell us where the ticket is. You can bet he's not gonna leave it out in plain sight, not if it's worth a million bucks."

"I can put out a few of his teeth easy enough. It gets them talking most of the time. Or pistol-whipping can be convincing. The steel muzzle of a Glock 19 can be pretty persuasive."

"And, you never know, he might be armed."

"It's best to be prepared."

"Do you have a suppressor for the Glock?"

"I got an Osprey 9. Makes the gunshots sound like clicks. Cost me a grand."

"Then we're all set."

"Dude, you sure your skinny is on the level?"

"Don't call me dude."

Macy hated it when people called him "dude."

"Regardless, my question stands," said Porter.

"He told me himself he had won. Why would he lie?"

"It sounds too good to be true."

"My dear deceased papa, though he wasn't a saint, used to tell me, don't look a gift horse in the mouth."

"What the hell's a gift horse anyway?"

"I'm saying is, guys win the lottery all the time. Most of 'em keep mum, 'cause they're worried about a mugger separating them from their winning ticket. I happened to be in the right place at the right time, living across the street from a lottery winner who wanted to brag about his win. Not all luck can be bad. When opportunity knocks, you gotta go for it."

"My luck is crap."

"You can't go around thinking your luck is always bad and do nothing. If you don't take charge of your life, your luck will always be bad. This is a good deal. We can't lose."

"Stated in that manner, it sounds like the true gen."

"See you at seven."

Macy terminated the call.

He consulted the time on his cell phone. Six fifteen.

He returned to the living room and gazed outside the picture window to make sure Grimes's BMW was still parked in the drive. It was.

###

Porter arrived at Macy's at ten after seven. No taller than five nine, Porter was stocky and muscular from daily workouts at the gym. He was also working on a tan. He had a tattoo of a frog's head on his forearm.

He parked his fluorescent lime Camaro behind Macy's metallic apple red Mustang in the driveway and headed toward Macy's front door.

Macy opened the door before Porter reached it. "You're late."

"There was a traffic accident on the 10. You're not gonna start the party without me, are you?" said Porter with a half smile.

Macy walked outside onto his stoop, a six-pack of Stella in his hand.

"Where's the Bud?" said Porter.

"Let's go."

"Right now?"

"As good a time as any. You got your piece?"

"In my ankle holster."

"Good you're not wearing shorts, then."

"I never wear shorts. I don't wear a beanie either. Why not pop a Stella first, get the edge off?"

"No time. The sooner we do this the better."

"You know how to hurt a guy," said Porter, eying the six-pack wistfully.

"Trust me on this."

"We're just gonna sashay over there and knock on his door?"

"We're being neighborly with our Stella," said Macy, holding up the six-pack.

"I'm not a neighbor." Porter paused. "What's our share?"

"Between you and me?"

Porter nodded yes.

"Fifty-fifty," said Macy.

"Grimes ain't gonna be happy."

"His happiness is of no concern. He's nothing but the courier of our lottery ticket."

They crossed the street to Grimes's property.

"What if he don't wanna play ball?" said Porter.

"Don't worry about it," said Macy.

"How we gonna handle this?"

"Follow my lead."

Macy strode up the cement driveway to Grimes's mint-colored stucco bungalow and knocked on the aluminum screen door.

"Vince," said Grimes, appearing at the door. "What brings you here?"

"We want to celebrate your win," said Macy.

Grimes didn't open the screen door to let Macy in. "I'm sort of busy."

"Busy? This is the weekend, and you just won the lottery. Time to kick back and party."

Macy displayed the six-pack.

Grimes shrugged. "Maybe you're right."

"Of course, I am."

Grimes opened the screen door and let them in.

"This is my friend Porter, by the way," said Macy. "Let's pop open some Stellas."

Porter entered after Macy and shut the door behind them.

The three of them made for the living room.

"Mind if we take a look at the winning ticket?" said Macy.

"Why?" said Grimes. "It's just a piece of paper."

"But it's a winner. I never saw a winning lottery ticket before."

Grimes halted in midstride, becoming suspicious. "It doesn't look any different than a losing ticket. Take my word for it."

"Seeing is believing."

"Look, maybe you better leave."

"Ain't you gonna offer us pretzels for our beer?" said Porter.

"Take your buddy with you," Grimes told Macy, "and let's do this some other time."

"Is that any way to treat a neighbor that brings you a six-pack?" said Macy, raising the six-pack to eye level.

Fidgeting, Grimes adjusted his bifocals. "Another time, another place."

"We wanna celebrate with you."

"I'll celebrate alone."

"Party pooper."

"We want pretzels," chanted Porter. "We want pretzels. We want pretzels."

Macy approached Grimes and shoved him back onto the sofa. "Where's the lottery ticket?"

Somebody knocked on the door.

Macy froze, wondering what was up.

"Come in," said Grimes, eager for company.

The door opened.

Clad in café-au-lait stretch pants and an emerald green blouse, her hair done up, Katherine entered, closing the door behind her, astonished to see her husband with Grimes.

Macy was just as surprised. He analyzed the situation. He put two and two together and did a slow burn.

"Oh, I get it," he said. "You're seeing Grimes on the side. Is that it?"

"I just wanted to say hello to Edward," she said. "What are *you* doing here?"

"You didn't plan on that, huh? You and Grimes. I never woulda figured."

"What are you talking about?" said Grimes from the sofa. "Nobody's seeing anybody."

He made a move to get up.

"Don't," said Porter.

In a matter of seconds he bent forward, retrieved the Glock from his ankle holster, withdrew the Osprey suppressor from his waistband, screwed the silencer onto the Glock's muzzle, and trained the muzzle on Grimes.

"Sit down," said Porter.

Grimes's eyes widened at the sight of the Glock. He remained sitting, clenching his teeth.

Macy swept his gaze from Katherine to Grimes. "You two were planning on running off with your winnings."

"You're insane," said Katherine. "I—I—I came over to borrow a cup of sugar."

"That's a good one." Macy turned to Grimes. "Where's the ticket?"

"Yeah, where is it?" said Porter, glaring and aiming his piece at Grimes's head.

"I don't have it," said Grimes, his eyes glued to the Glock. "I already cashed it in."

"Then where's the cash?"

"I don't believe you," said Macy. "You didn't have time to cash it. I was watching your house the whole day. You never left your house."

"I—I—did it over the phone," said Grimes.

"That won't fly. You can't claim a jackpot over the phone. They want proof."

"I—I—texted them a photo of the ticket."

"I'm not buying it. Photos can be doctored. They're not gonna accept a photo in place of the real thing."

"We're not kidding around," said Porter, stepped toward the sofa, and pressed the tip of his Glock's Osprey suppressor against Grimes's forehead.

Grimes flinched. He held his hands up in surrender. "Don't."

"Where is it?"

Grimes lowered his hands. "I'll share it with all of you. But don't kill me."

"That's only a little over three hundred grand for us," said Macy.

"What about me?" said Katherine, approaching Macy.

"I thought you only wanted sugar," said Macy with a smirk.

"If you cut me out, I'll tell the cops."

"You'd testify against your own husband?"

"I want my share, honey."

"Your threats won't work. A wife can't testify against her husband."

"That's not gonna stop me from testifying against your buddy," she said, eying Porter.

"Did you forget he's the one with the piece?"

"That leaves only a quarter of a million for each of us if she gets an equal whack," said Porter, sneering. "I vote no."

"You heard him," Macy told Grimes.

"You shouldn't get anything," said Grimes. "It's my money. I won it fair and square."

"Shut up, and fork over the ticket," said Porter, his Glock aimed at Grimes. "I'm tired of dicking around."

"Only if we split the winnings."

"Cut him up," said Macy.

Porter pistol-whipped Grimes's face. Grimes screamed in pain and covered his split cheek with his hand. Blood streamed down his face and neck.

"Hand it over or there's more where that came from," said Porter, brandishing the Glock.

Macy pulled a SIG P226 handgun out of his rear waistband and trained it on Grimes. "Start talking."

Macy had brought the piece because he didn't trust Porter. Not only didn't Macy trust him, he didn't like Porter. Porter might decide he wanted the whole nine yards and skip out on him. The SIG would deter Porter. Porter was muscle, and nothing else. Cloaking his thoughts, Macy didn't aim his pistol at Porter, keeping it leveled at Grimes.

"How do I know you won't take it all for yourselves and leave me with nothing?" said Grimes.

"There's only one way to find out," said Macy. "Hand it over."

Grimes hung fire.

Porter got ready to take another swing at Grimes's face.

Grimes didn't want any more of it. "All right. We split it equally four ways."

He reached under the sofa cushion next to him.

Porter pressed the tip of the Osprey suppressor against Grimes's cut and bleeding cheek.

Grimes froze. "I'm getting the ticket."

"Let him," said Macy.

Porter pulled back his piece. "Do it slow."

Grimes withdrew the lottery ticket from under the sofa cushion.

Porter snatched the ticket from Grimes's fingers.

"Don't tear it," said Katherine. "They might not redeem it if it's torn."

Porter examined the ticket, said, "Looks fine," and shot Grimes in the face.

"What'd you do that for?" said Katherine, taken aback.

Grimes slumped on the sofa, a bullet hole in his right eyebrow. He didn't move, his limp legs spread open.

"Because he's an ignoramus," said Porter. "Idiots deserve to be shot on principle. Did he really think we were gonna share the dough with him?"

"Why not? It was his ticket. You didn't have to kill him."

"He woulda ratted us out to the cops."

"Nobody would've believed him. Whoever possesses the winning ticket gets the pot."

"It's a lot easier with him out of the picture. Nobody's gonna complain now when I cash in the ticket."

"You?" said Macy. "Who elected you?"

"I don't want anything to do with murder," said Katherine.

"Then glue Grimes back together," said Porter, snickering.

"That's not funny."

"Does that mean you don't want your cut?" said Macy.

"No, no, no. I didn't say that," said Katherine.

"Changing your tune, huh?" said Macy, with a wolfish grin.

"Why do we have to give her anything?" Porter asked Macy. "This is our scheme. She only got in on it by accident."

Macy thought about his tapped phone. "I wonder."

He had thought it might be the cops that had tapped his line. It could just as easily have been Katherine. But that explanation didn't track.

"Why did you come here at seven instead of nine?" he asked Katherine.

"What are you talking about? I came here when I realized I was out of flour."

Macy searched her face. "You said before you were out of sugar."

"Uh—uh—flour *and* sugar. I'm baking a cake."

"You didn't mention flour before."

"What difference does it make when she came here?" said Porter. "She has no right to any of our dough."

"Why not? I'm here with you two," said Katherine.

"So is Grimes. And look at him."

Worry lines creased Katherine's face. "What's that got to do with me?"

"The original plan was for nine, not seven," said Macy. "That's what you heard on the tapped line. I guess you thought you'd be clever, get the jump on us, and swipe the lottery ticket before we got here. Or were you and Grimes cheating on me and running off together?"

"You're crazy. You're the one that's cheating on me. Do you think I'm stupid?"

"Which is it? Were you gonna jack the ticket for yourself or split the winnings with Grimes?"

"I told you, I came over here for a cup of sugar."

"You mean, a cup of flour."

"Sugar, flour. I came over both of them," said Katherine, irritated.

"Empty your purse."

"What?"

"Do it."

"Why?"

"Shoot her," Macy told Porter.

"Wait a minute," said Katherine, gripped with fear.

She flipped over her purse and emptied it on the carpet. A pink comb, a pink hairbrush, a compact, a plastic contact lens case, lipstick, a tampon in a paper wrapper, a wallet, and a Ruger LCP .380 ACP tumbled out.

Macy chortled at the sight of the piece. "You had the same idea as us. You weren't planning on sharing with Grimes, either. What's wrong? Did your affair go sour?"

"There wasn't any affair, and I always carry that gun for self-protection."

"Shoot her," said Macy.

"My pleasure," said Porter.

"Vince," pleaded Katherine. "If you shoot Porter, there's only you and me to share the pot. And like you said, I can't testify against you. Why cut Porter in?"

Porter didn't like what he was hearing. He shot her in the left eye.

She fell backward against the side of a leatherette recliner knocking it sideways and lay in a heap on her back.

"That's better," he said. "Now we each get half a million bucks." He eyed the lottery ticket in his hand.

"A half million bucks is a lot of dough," said Macy.

"You better believe it."

"But a million bucks is a lot more," said Macy, and shot Porter in the forehead.

Porter crumpled with a heavy thud to his knees, his hands in front of him, like he was praying, then fell onto his face.

Macy had to hunker down and pry Porter's body up to retrieve the lottery ticket from his inert hand trapped under his stomach. Macy's face beamed at the sight of the ticket he now held between his forefinger and thumb.

A ticket to a new life, he decided, straightening up. A good life where chronic unemployment wouldn't matter, not with a million bucks in the bank, most of which he would invest in stocks. He would consult a lawyer, of course, before he did anything with the cash. But then again, how could he trust a lawyer? Nobody was greedier than a lawyer. What if the lawyer decided to chisel him?

He would figure it out later. Now it was time to collect his winnings.

He left Grimes's place, climbed into his Mustang, and drove to the nearest liquor store where they sold lottery tickets. He got out of his car in the parking lot and scoped out the store to make sure it wasn't crowded. He didn't want anyone to overhear him when he collected his winnings from Pablo, the cashier.

Two casually dressed guys—one in his twenties, one in his sixties—were deciding which beer to select in the refrigerated section of the store, which was on the wall opposite the cashier's counter.

They wouldn't be able to overhear him, decided Macy, who entered the shop. A small bell tinkled above him as he pushed open the plate-glass door and headed for Pablo. Despite his thirtyish age, Pablo had deep worry lines carved into his forehead that belonged on the head of a fifty-year-old. Five eight, sporting a buzz cut, he was wearing black jeans and a black T that said AC/DC.

Holding out the lottery ticket Macy kept his voice down. “Pablo, I got a winner.”

Pablo flashed a toothy grin. “Then we both win. The ticket seller gets a percentage.” He paused, losing the grin. “I don’t remember you buying a ticket here.”

“Uh—it was your day off.”

Nodding, Pablo inserted the ticket into the cash register.

Macy figured he would get some kind of voucher for the million bucks. There was no way Pablo would have that kind of dough on hand. Macy would take the voucher or cashier’s check or whatever to the bank. He didn’t know the exact mechanics of it, because the most he had ever won in a lottery was three bucks, which a cashier had handed him from the till.

He would soon find out. His mouth watered at the prospect of a cool million in his hands. Adrenaline coursed through his system, ramping up his heartbeat.

He held out his sweaty hand in expectation.

Smiling, Pablo handed him a hundred-dollar bill. “It’s a winner.”

Macy gazed at the Ben Franklin in stunned disbelief. “Where’s the rest of it?”

Pablo shrugged. “That’s all she wrote.”

“What are you talking about? You owe me a million bucks,” said Macy, becoming angry and grabbing Pablo’s T-shirt. “What are you trying to pull? I won the full monty, a million-dollar win.”

Annoyed, Pablo brushed Macy’s hand away, got out his iPad, and checked the lottery winners on the Internet. He inspected Macy’s lottery ticket.

“You got five out of six numbers right,” he said. “The sixth number is a nine, not a four. You got a four on yours.”

“Lemme see that,” said Macy, and spun the iPad around on the glass counter to check out the winning number.

The blood drained from Macy’s face as he realized Pablo was right.

That idiot Grimes was blind as a bat, decided Macy, seething. Even with his glasses on, the moron couldn’t read the numbers on a lottery ticket. And the guy was a CPA, no less. If anyone should know, *he* of all people should know the difference between a four and a nine. He must have been lousy at his job.

A measly hundred bucks. What good was a measly hundred bucks?

The bell tinkled above the door.

Macy screwed his head around to see who was entering.

Wearing leather driving gloves Brody appeared beside Macy with his outstretched left hand. "I believe this is yours."

Macy gazed at Brody's open hand. On it lay a spent brass cartridge.

"Nope," said Macy. "And who the hell are you?"

"Brody. I'm a private investigator hired by your wife. I watched you leave Grimes's. I thought I'd heard a gunshot while you were inside. I took a look-see." Brody held his hand up with the cartridge. "This brass doesn't match the two handguns I found next to the three stiffs you plugged, a Ruger and a Glock. The Ruger hadn't even been fired."

"You're coming at me from outer space."

Brody snaked his right hand behind Macy's back before Macy could react, whipped out the SIG he had spotted in Macy's rear waistband, and sniffed the muzzle.

"Fired recently," said Brody. "The cops are gonna wanna have a word with you."

Snorting with bitter amusement, Macy flicked the C-note at Brody and watched it flutter to the floor. "Take a gander at what a million bucks looks like."

Macy burst out laughing. He laughed. And he laughed. And he laughed. He didn't think he'd ever stop laughing.

Death Hunt

"I'm thinking this will be the last book I do with you, Fred," said Barry Riley over the phone as he sat in the small living room of his Redondo Beach casita all of five miles from the beach.

"We've been over this before," said Frederick Gommers. "You'd be nothing without me. Like you were before we teamed up on our first thriller together."

Fred was right about that, decided Riley. Riley had been self-publishing thrillers for ten years, none of which sold more than three copies on Amazon, before Fred had contacted him with a book deal as one of his ghostwriters.

Gommers's thrillers always hit the best-seller lists and he raked in the cash.

The problem was, Gommers didn't like the hard work of writing. He would rather bask in the limelight of being a best-selling author than actually sit down at a desk alone and grind out words.

Riley had leapt at the chance to work with Gommers when Gommers offered him a deal to ghostwrite a new thriller for him, even though Riley got only a flat rate for writing the book while Gommers earned all the royalties that poured into his coffers as his novels routinely cracked best-seller lists.

The other problem was, Riley knew Gommers was raking in cash from the books he was writing for Gommers and Gommers was paying him a small fraction of that sum. Riley wanted to strike out on his own and write thrillers under his own name—like he used to before he met Gommers. The thing that held Riley back was the paltry income he earned writing novels under his own name.

But maybe he had learned something along the way, maybe he had become a better writer, i.e., a more commercial writer from his working for Gommers. Maybe now Riley could rack up better sales if he set off on his own. Maybe . . . Or maybe anyone who used Gommers's name could write a best seller, decided Riley, since it was Gommers's name and name alone that sold his books. Maybe the quality of the writing counted for nothing. If Gommers began attaching his name to dreck, would he still remain atop the best-seller lists? The thing was, Gommers *did* seem able to spot good writing when he saw it. In which case, he wouldn't attach his name to junk for fear of debasing his brand.

Riley didn't know for sure if his books would sell without Gommers's name. However, he thought he had matured as a writer working for Gommers and now he was willing to take the risk of returning to writing on his own and let the chips fall where they may.

Gommers had done everything in his power to persuade Riley otherwise, telling Riley it was his, Gommers's, expert editing along with the Frederick Gommers name that had made Riley's works wildly popular. Nobody knew Riley had ghostwritten the recent Gommers thrillers, other than Riley's literary agent and a few others in Gommers's elite retinue, and they, to a man, had signed NDAs swearing they would never tell anyone that Riley had actually written the last five of Gommers's best-selling thrillers.

To wit, Riley couldn't legally publicize the fact he had written Gommers's books to promote himself if he struck out on his own as a novelist. To do so would be to violate the NDA and open himself up to massive lawsuits by Gommers and his battalions of lawyers.

With all this in mind, Riley had been reluctant to break away from Gommers during his stint writing five thrillers for the famous "author."

In the end, though, Riley decided enough was enough. He had enough self-confidence now that he believed he could make it on his own as a writer. He had told Gommers his decision yesterday. Gommers, of course, had tried to talk him out of it. Gommers considered the act of writing difficult scut work that he had no wish to resume.

He had, indeed, penned two thrillers by himself and they had hit the best-seller lists thanks to an expensive publicity campaign and his telegenic personality. He came to dread the drudge work and solitude of writing, vis-à-vis appearing on TV talk shows like *Oprah*, bragging about what a great writer he was in front of millions of adulating viewers, and seeing his name on best-seller lists all over the world. In his mind, nothing could compare with the thrill of being on TV and the huge followings he ginned up with his appearances, certainly not the barren, moldy confinement of the solitary act of writing. He was fond of quoting Gore Vidal: *Never pass up a chance to have sex or be on television.*

"Have you decided to change your mind and stay with me?" said Gommers over the phone.

"No," said Riley. "My decision stands. We need to go our separate ways."

Riley could picture Gommers at the other end of the line, a clotheshorse puffing on his meerschaum pipe, vain and self-possessed. On TV he wore nothing but the priciest bespoke suits purchased from Saville Row.

"You'll never make it on your own," said Gommers. "Without my name on your books, they'll become instant remainders. You'll become a nobody and a hack again. Your books will be consigned to the ash heap of all the other self-published janky novels that die on the vine."

"I'm still a nobody and a hack, except I'm *your* hack. You're stealing all the glory for every book I write."

"But now you're getting a decent paycheck."

"Not as decent as yours."

"Is that what this is all about? Greed?"

"Not at all. A ghostwriter is a ghost. I don't want to be a ghost anymore."

"Not to put too fine a point on it, you're a ghostwriter because you're a drip. You have no personality. On your own, you'll never be able to hawk your books. Charisma is what sells books. All the greats have it. Hemingway. Fitzgerald. And me."

"Those guys could write, too. They weren't just Hollywood-manufactured celebrities with picture-perfect smiles like you."

"Wake up and smell the coffee, Riley. Without my name, you're a legend in your own mind. Nobody else's."

"If that's true, my books shouldn't sell, even with your name on them."

"You don't understand the reading public. They only read what they're told to read by the mainstream media. They're sheep. They can't think for themselves. It's all about the media, and the media love me. I'm their darling. You? You're something the cat dragged in, as far as they're concerned. You're not even that. You're nothing."

He had a point, decided Riley, as much as he hated to admit it. The media could make or break a writer. Certainly, they had made Gommers the celebrity best-selling novelist he was today. But Riley wasn't going to let Gommers or the media who adored him dictate his life.

"My mind is made up," said Riley. "Nothing can change it. We're splitsville."

"Look, I've got a great idea for a new thriller, and I want you to write it. I'm sure you'll agree once you've heard it. Wanna hear it?"

"Not really."

"It can't miss. You know my ideas are diamonds in the rough. You wouldn't agree to do the hard work of writing them and bringing them to life if they weren't."

Gommers wasn't far off the mark, decided Riley. The guy did have good ideas for thrillers, and he was a good editor. He knew how to juice up material to make it come alive. But he lacked the patience, the will, and the stamina to commit a book to paper and see it through to the end.

"I dunno," said Riley.

"That's more like it. I saw this ad on Facebook. It said they wanted to hire someone to see the world and experience a life full of adventure and fascinating assignments. The first assignment will start immediately." Gommers paused, letting his words sink in. "I'm certain the CIA placed the ad, even though they didn't publicize their name. I know they advertise on social media as well as at universities."

"I don't see how I fit in."

"You answer the ad. You take this first assignment and you come back with a ton of great background material as research you can use on our next blockbuster thriller."

It did sound interesting, decided Riley. He had to admit he was bored with sitting in his musty home office all day grinding out words or trying to come up with an idea for a story. He would like to acquire some firsthand knowledge of the CIA. It would give his thrillers verisimilitude.

"Maybe," he said.

"I'll make a deal with you. You work on this book with me, and this will be our last collaboration together. How's that sound?"

One more book for Gommers, decided Riley. He figured he could handle one more and then cut loose on his own. It was hard to believe Gommers would be willing to let him go. This didn't sound like the Gommers who thought he ruled the roost because he sold more copies of his thrillers than anyone else in the world. Riley had been thinking he might have to file a lawsuit to break free from Gommers's ironclad hold on him. He had expected Gommers would do everything in his power to maintain their arrangement.

Riley was relieved to find out otherwise. Maybe the guy didn't want to become embroiled in a protracted lawsuit that would generate publicity despite the involvement of NDAs. In no way did Gommers want to risk being exposed as a literary fraud. Lawsuits were expensive, Riley knew, and he would go out of his way to avoid one with Gommers, since Gommers could afford the best lawyers money could buy.

If he could split from Gommers with no bitter recriminations and threats, Riley was all for it. Anything to avoid a lawsuit.

"Sounds good," he said.

Whatever else you could say about Gommers, he did have good leads that came to fruition as novels, decided Riley. This one sounded like it had potential. Maybe the CIA was recruiting to overthrow a dictator like Venezuela's Maduro. Yes, this could be a very interesting and productive assignment.

"Do you have a passport?" said Gommers.

"Of course."

"Take it with you. You'll need it for ID, according to the ad."

"How can you be sure it's the CIA who's advertising?"

"It has to be them. You know how secretive they are about everything. I want you to find out if it's them and what they want."

"What if it's not them? Do you still want me to accept their assignment?"

A pause of two beats. "I do. Should make for an interesting story, whoever it is doing the hiring."

Gommers gave Riley the number to call to set up the interview and hung up.

Riley called the number and arranged a meet.

###

It turned out to be located in Marina del Rey.

A steady onshore breeze sweeping off the ocean rocked the boats moored at the marina.

Riley managed to find a parking space for his Mustang GT at a one-story robin's-egg blue café not far from the slip where the interview was scheduled. Wearing black jeans and a grey polo, he climbed out of his car and beheld a forest of white sailboats with naked masts docked and bobbing in the marina.

He stood on the wharf and watched the crying gulls wheel overhead and swoop down riding the wind currents among the masts. He marveled at the gulls' agility at avoiding crashes despite the force of the wind.

He wondered if he was making the right move. Maybe he should just pull the plug on his career with Gommers right now.

Then he thought of the red tape and humongous expenses of drawn-out legal proceedings with Gommers and decided to write one more book for him.

He walked along the wharf till he found slip number thirty-three, where he was to meet the job interviewer. A twenty-foot launch named the *Ariadne* was docked at the slip.

The wind tousled his hair as he made for the launch. He felt the force of the wind thrusting against his back as he watched the launch floating. He didn't see anybody on the deck. He wondered if he was at the right slip.

"Hello," he said.

Nobody answered. Maybe the noisy wind and the creaking sailboats in the vicinity were drowning out the sound of his voice. He tried again, yelling this time.

A portly fortyish guy with a receding hairline and three days' growth of black beard climbed up the companionway to the main deck. Riley sniffed the Cuban cigar the guy was holding with his thumb and forefinger at his side. The wind dissipated the unfurling tobacco smoke as soon as it left the cigar tip.

"What can I do for you?" he said, walking onto the deck.

"I'm Barry Riley. I'm answering the ad you placed on Facebook."

"Welcome aboard. I'm Raoul December. Watch your step."

December was wearing a flower-print Hawaiian shirt, khaki Bermudas, a rope belt, and espadrilles.

The cigar smoke's pungent aroma clung in the wind.

Riley climbed onto the launch.

"Follow me," said December.

He descended the companionway to the cabin, Riley in tow.

December sat behind a desk and motioned for Riley to sit opposite him. "Have a seat."

The launch rocked gently beneath them, as Riley took a seat.

A black attaché case lay on the desktop in front of December.

"I'm not clear on the name of your company," said Riley.

"I work for the CIA, and we're looking to hire a candidate who wants to see the world and live an adventurous life. Are you that candidate?"

"I am."

December extended his hand over the desktop. "I need to see your passport."

Riley dug it out of his trouser pocket and handed it to him. December flipped through it, inspecting it.

"You haven't been out of the country lately," he said, looking up at Riley.

"No, I haven't."

"You don't like to travel?"

"I've been working."

December returned Riley's passport. "Can you speak Spanish?"

"I can."

"Excellent. Are you patriotic? Would you like to work for the CIA?"

"I am, and I would."

Riley wasn't exactly a flag-waving jingoist. He agreed with Churchill that democracy was a lousy form of government, but it was better than all the rest. Nevertheless, he wanted to know more about this CIA job. It sounded exciting.

"That's what I want to hear," said December. He flipped open his attaché case and withdrew sheets of legal-sized paper stapled together. "I need you to sign this NDA. If you break the NDA, the agency will prosecute you for violation of the Espionage Act. Do you understand?"

Riley started getting cold feet when he heard December say "NDA." Not another NDA, Riley decided. He had signed one for Gommers, and now December wanted him to sign one for the CIA.

December handed the NDA to Riley.

"Could I have my lawyer look at it?" said Riley.

"I'm afraid not. That would violate the NDA. This is between you and the CIA. No one else must know, or it's a violation of the Espionage Act. Which is a felony that could carry a penalty of life in prison for committing treason."

Riley tried to plow through the dense legalese of the document. It wasn't easy for a layman with no legal background.

He ended up skimming through it. If he took the job, he wouldn't be able to tell anyone about it without risking a prison sentence. However, he could still write a fictionalized account of it without breaking the law, he figured.

"How about a drink?" said December, standing up and parking his smoking cigar in a round cut-glass ashtray on the desktop. "Just sign on that line on the last page of the document."

"Do you have a pen?"

December plucked a ballpoint from a penholder on the desktop and handed it to Riley.

Riley hated signing NDAs, but he smelled a good story, and since he was going to write a novel, he didn't see how the CIA could censor it. Still, he didn't like signing legal documents without his lawyer present.

"How long is this offer good for?" he said. "I want to contact my lawyer."

"You don't have the time."

"If I don't sign, then what?"

"Then we hire someone else. There are plenty of fish in the sea when it comes to applying for a job with the CIA."

Against his better judgment, Riley signed the NDA, with December watching over Riley's shoulder.

"Now about that drink," said Riley.

"Coming right up. How's whisky sound?"

"Fine."

"How do you want it?"

"Neat."

December disappeared into the cramped galley, returned with two glasses of Scotch, one with ice and one without, and handed the latter to Riley.

Riley took a pull on the whisky.

"What's the nature of this assignment?" he said.

"We want you to infiltrate a Mexican drug cartel in Guadalajara. The Jalisco New Generation cartel, to be precise."

"It sounds dangerous."

"I'm not gonna lie to you. It is. But that's what makes it so exciting. And you signed on for excitement, didn't you?"

"That doesn't mean I have a death wish."

December laughed. "It's not that bad. As long as you're convincing, they'll accept you as a new recruit. We've got it all arranged."

Riley was entertaining second thoughts about this assignment.

"Cartels don't fool around," he said. "If they don't like you, they shoot you."

"After they torture you first."

"You're not winning me over."

Smiling, December winked at him. "I'm messing with you. We're giving you a bulletproof cover story. The narcos will never see through it."

"Bulletproof?"

"A figure of speech," said December, still smiling.

"What am I supposed to do after I infiltrate the cartel?"

"We need to know their leader's identity. Find out his name then we'll exfiltrate you."

"Piece of cake," Riley deadpanned. "Should I make out a will before I go?"

December laughed. Riley found something sinister about it.

"You have a great sense of humor," said December.

"I wasn't joking."

"Rest assured we'll take care of everything," said December, sitting down with his whisky in one hand. He winked again. "We're good at arranging funerals."

Riley gave him a look. He didn't find December's gallows humor amusing.

December knocked back his whisky, lifted his cigar from the ashtray, puffed on it, and blew out a smoke ring with contentment. "Nothing better than a fine Havana cigar and a glass of Scotch whisky."

Riley wasn't feeling too good. He felt woozy. Maybe it was the rocking of the boat that was causing his illness. He hadn't been on a boat in ages. Then again, maybe it was the smell of the cigar smoke. Or the combination of the rocking launch and the cigar smoke. Thinking about his assignment wasn't raising his spirits, either.

"We don't send our agents into death traps," said December.

"That's encouraging," muttered Riley.

"We got your six at the agency," said December, tapping cigar ash into the ashtray. "Otherwise, we wouldn't have any field agents left."

Riley was feeling worse by the moment.

"You OK?" said December. "You look kind of peaked."

"A touch of seasickness, I think."

"Relax. You'll be OK. You got an exciting adventure ahead of you," said December, and chewed the end of his cigar, saliva dripping out the corner of his mouth.

"I need to take a walk."

"By all means."

Riley stood up, angled across the rocking cabin groggily, lost his balance, and collapsed.

2.

Riley came to in the dark. He smelled smoke. It wasn't the sweet acrid odor of cigar smoke. It was wood smoke.

Was the *Ariadne* burning? he wondered, panic seizing him.

He snapped open his eyes. He saw a campfire burning ten-odd feet from him, kindling crackling in the golden flames. Overhead, stars stippled the sable black night sky, glittering like shards of ice. He was lying on his back on the ground.

The temperature was comfortable, warmed by the campfire. He wasn't wearing a jacket.

He discerned individuals sitting on the ground in fluttering shadows around the campfire as the flames danced under the faint moonlight.

He smelled meat like a hamburger cooking. One of the men was holding a spit of cuts of meat over the campfire, his face glowing with hungry anticipation in the lambent light thrown by the flames.

The ground was sloped, Riley noticed. They were on the side of a hill or mountain with pine trees scattered on it. He could make out the dark jagged outlines of the pines against the night sky.

"Awake, Gustavo? *Finalmente*," said someone sitting near him.

Gustavo? thought Riley. Was the guy talking to him? The guy was looking at him. Maybe that was the name the CIA had cooked up for him when he went undercover, part of his cover story. Riley reached for his wallet in his trouser pocket. Maybe it had his fake ID in it. With sinking spirits he found his pockets flat and empty.

Riley decided not to say anything until he figured out where he was and what was going on. He saw no sign of December or his launch. He had no idea where he was or who these characters were sitting with him.

"You come highly recommended," said the man. "And we understand you speak Spanish and English."

Riley snuck a closer look at the guy. In his thirties with a pencil-thin black mustache, he was wearing jeans and a black T-shirt that said Ferrari in white letters. Barrel-chested, he had swarthy features and hairy muscular arms covered with tattoos that you could barely see through the forest of hair.

The campfire crackled and popped.

"*Sí*," said Riley.

December must have infiltrated him into the Jalisco New Generation cartel, decided Riley. He had no idea how, since he had been unconscious until moments ago. The last thing he remembered was talking to December on the launch in Marina del Rey.

Was he now in Guadalajara? wondered Riley. Had he been unconscious during the entire flight here?

He realized his head ached and his eyes burned. He began to suspect December had slipped him a mickey in his whisky. For the life of him Riley couldn't figure out why December would drug him. Maybe December didn't want to take the chance of Riley's chickening out at the last minute.

Unconscious wasn't a great way to embark on a perilous mission, decided Riley.

"*Cómo se llama*?" he said.

"Ricardo."

Ricardo produced a cooler, rooted around in it, and withdrew two cold bottles of beer.

"How about a Dos Equis?" he said, handing a beer to Riley.

Riley sat up on the ground, accepted the beer, unscrewed the twist-off cap, and took a pull on the beer. He nodded with pleasure.

"And how about food?" said Ricardo. "You must be starving."

Riley nodded yes. He heard his empty stomach growling in agreement.

"Pass around the meat, Pablo," Ricardo told the fat man with the spit.

A lanky man with long dark hair down to his shoulders approached Pablo and held out a paper plate to him. Pablo removed a chunk of charbroiled meat skewered on the spit and deposited it on the plate. Pablo proceeded to fill eleven plates each with a single cut of meat. The lanky man distributed the plates to everyone.

Riley's mouth watered as he smelled the charbroiled meat he held up in his plate.

"Dig in," said Ricardo.

Riley took a big bite out of the meat. At first he thought it was beef, but it tasted more like chicken.

"Are you ready for your test?" said Ricardo.

"Test?"

"First, have some more meat," said Ricardo, seeing that Riley had cleaned his plate.

"Thanks," said Riley. "It tastes good. What is it? Tastes like chicken."

Ricardo offered Riley a paper plate with a charbroiled human hand on it.

Riley retched at the sight of the hand in front of him.

"Go on, amigo," said Ricardo. "Eat up. It's the rest of the Zeta *cabrón* we killed."

Riley thought about the meat he had just eaten and felt sick. White-faced, he got to his feet, staggered behind a bush, and threw up.

He returned to the campfire on wobbly legs.

"*Qué pasa?* You ate too much?" said Ricardo. "It's kind of rich, but it'll make a man of you."

The men around the campfire chuckled and snickered at Riley's malaise.

Riley took a pull on his beer to help settle his stomach and drown out the rank odor of vomit drool that streaked the edges of his mouth. He wiped the drool from his mouth with the back of his hand. *I ate human flesh?*

The mere thought of it made him want to puke again.

What was he doing sitting around a fire breaking bread with a bunch of cannibals? he wondered. He had thought his job for the CIA was to infiltrate a cartel. December hadn't said anything about cannibals.

"You were saying something about a test," Riley managed to say.

"If you want to join CJNG, you need to pass a test."

CJNG, decided Riley. The Jalisco New Generation cartel. Then he was in the right place. The cartel members just happened to be cannibals. He had no idea.

"Fine," he said, wondering with apprehension what kind of test it was. December hadn't told him anything about taking a test.

"When the sun rises, in about an hour, we'll give you the test."

Riley had thought it was nighttime. He realized the sky was lightening as the sun commenced its implacable rise in the east.

"You passed the first part of the test already," said Ricardo. "You ate a Zeta."

Riley didn't want to think about it. He dreaded what he would have to do for the second part of the test.

He had no idea what kind of a test he had to take. He wished December had prepared him better for this assignment. The guy hadn't told him much of anything, hadn't even told him his false identity, his legend, as the CIA called it.

"Don't worry about it," said Ricardo, knocking back his beer. "It's a cakewalk. You'll probably get a kick out of it."

By the time Riley had finished his beer and his stomach was settling down, the sun had cleared the horizon and was peeking through the pine needles overhead. He was relieved to have washed the taste of human flesh out of his mouth.

"Bring in the Zetas," said Ricardo, getting to his feet.

Riley noticed Ricardo had a Glock 19 tucked in his waistband.

Two twentysomething gangbangers in baggy jeans, Ts, and sneakers marched two guys their age dressed in similar attire toward Ricardo. The two anxious hostages had their hands bound behind their backs with black plastic zip ties.

Ricardo pulled one of the hostages away from the group, handed his Glock to Riley, and said, "Kill the Zeta."

Riley didn't take the pistol.

"This is your test," said Ricardo, continuing to hold out the Glock for Riley. "You don't want to find out what happens if you flunk it."

Riley didn't know what to do. He had never killed anyone. He doubted he could kill a defenseless man in cold blood.

"They are enemies of CJNG. Take the gun," said Ricardo, his tone steely.

His heartbeat jackhammering, Riley accepted the Glock. He didn't aim it at either of the hostages that stood six-odd feet in front of him.

"Don't you know how to use a gun?" said Ricardo, needling Riley.

Riley counted at least ten cartel members circled around him, not counting the hostages. He knew from writing numerous crime thrillers that a Glock 19 had a standard magazine that held fifteen rounds. But he had no idea if the magazine was full. He couldn't tell from the weight of the gun. He couldn't tell if he had enough ammo to blow away all of the cartel members.

They weren't going to stand idly by watching him shoot them. They were all armed to the teeth with either AK-47s or Tec-9s, as well as handguns. He saw no way he could blow away all ten of them before at least one of them took him out.

Ricardo withdrew another Glock from his rear waistband and trained the muzzle on Riley. "Whack the Zeta or we deny your admission into the cartel."

Riley aimed his pistol at the Zeta, whose eyes widened in fear.

Riley couldn't squeeze the trigger. Breaking into a sweat he stood staring at the Zeta, his gun trained on him. He heard the fire crackling behind the Zeta.

"I got news for you," said Ricardo. "Flunking the test is a lot worse than passing it. All you have to do to pass is whack the Zeta. Am I getting through to you?"

Riley clenched his teeth, chewing over what to do. He might be able to take out Ricardo, but the other gangbangers would make short work of him. Riley saw no way to proceed. He would have to flunk the test and suffer the consequences—no matter how dire.

The hostage was shifting nervously on his feet.

"Stand still," said Ricardo. He turned to Riley. "You don't have all day to complete the test. Kill him now."

Shaking his head Riley lowered his Glock.

"Bad decision," said Ricardo.

The hostage turned tail. Ricardo shot him in the back of the head before the Zeta took two steps. The Zeta's head exploded into pink mist. He crumpled on the ground, dead.

"I'm disappointed in you, Gustavo," said Ricardo. "You came highly recommended, and look what a mess you've made. *Malo, muy malo. Qué pasa? No huevos?*"

"He had his hands tied behind his back," said Riley. "Killing a guy with his hands tied doesn't take *huevos*."

"Don't question my orders." His face stern, Ricardo paced back and forth, deep in thought. He came to a halt in front of Riley. "I'll give you one more chance. Maybe you don't understand the gravity of this test. If you fail it, you become one of our enemies—and one of our victims. *Comprendes?*"

Ricardo motioned for the gangbangers to bring forward the other hostage.

"Kill him," Ricardo told Riley.

"This makes no sense," said Riley.

"Sense? What's sense got to do with it? He's the enemy. I gave you a direct order. *Mátalo*."

Fearing the alternative, Riley trained his Glock on the second hostage. He told himself if he didn't pull the trigger, he was jeopardizing his life. It didn't do any good. He couldn't shoot the second hostage with bound hands. Riley lowered his gun.

"He's gonna die whether you shoot him or not," said Ricardo. "You might as well do yourself a favor and whack him out."

Riley couldn't do it.

Ricardo shot the Zeta twice in the forehead.

A second corpse lay on the ground.

"You're gonna be next, Gustavo," said Ricardo, seizing the Glock from Riley's hand in a fit of anger mixed with disgust.

"I didn't hire on as an assassin."

"All cartel members are *sicarios*. Assassins. It goes with the job. You're a big disappointment."

Ricardo aimed his Glock at Riley's forehead.

Riley swallowed hard. "What's the point of killing me?"

"You failed your test. You flunked out. I'm not a heartless man, though," said Ricardo, lowering his Glock. "I'll give you a fighting chance. Mainly because it's boring to shoot you while you're standing there."

"You didn't give the Zetas a chance."

Ricardo spat on the ground. "I hate Zetas. All they deserve is a bullet to the head."

Ricardo snapped the magazine out of Riley's pistol, ejected the remaining rounds into his hand, slapped the magazine back into the butt, and handed the empty gun back to Riley. Riley was right. The magazine hadn't been fully loaded. It had held only two rounds. Now it held none.

"What good is an empty gun?" he said, holding up the Glock.

"If you shut up, you'll find out."

"Is it supposed to allay your conscience if you shoot me while I'm holding a gun?"

"Conscience? What's conscience got to do with anything? I want entertainment. I'm bored. It was dull enough whacking out the Zetas. Now I gotta do you. I need to make it interesting."

Riley considered making a run for it. He figured he stood as much chance as the two Zetas if he chose to cut and run. He held his ground.

"Pablo, come here," said Ricardo.

The chef, a thirtysomething short fat guy in charcoal grey trousers and an olive drab T, approached him. Pablo had a double chin, a nose like a blob, and black curly hair that hung over his ears. He grinned with nicotine-stained teeth.

Ricardo handed him a bullet he had taken from Riley's magazine.

Ricardo pointed. "You see that pine over there? The short one between the two taller ones."

"*Sí, patrón*," said Pablo.

"Take that bullet and lay it next to the tree trunk."

"Any reason?"

"Not that you need to know."

Chastised, Pablo nodded. Bullet in hand, he jogged toward the indicated pine at least a half mile away, cutting across the rock-strewn ground.

Riley watched him with puzzlement.

"You understand now?" said Ricardo.

"No," said Riley.

"On my say so, you take that gun in your hand and fetch that bullet to load in your magazine."

"Why?"

"Because we're gonna hunt you down and kill you. I'm giving you a sporting chance. I'm giving you that gun and one bullet. If I thought you were a Zeta, you'd be dead now, splayed out beside those other two Zetas."

"I'm trying to join your cartel as a member, *not* as target practice."

"You should've thought of that before you failed your test. Failure has consequences in CJNG. If you fail, you suffer the consequences."

"One bullet? That's not much of a chance against ten guys with loaded guns."

"It's all the chance you're gonna get. I shouldn't even give you that much. I oughta just blow your head off where you stand," said Ricardo, raising his Glock and training it on Riley's face.

Pablo returned from the pine tree on the run, huffing and puffing.

"You eat too many Cheetos," said Ricardo.

"*Sí, patrón*," said Pablo, wiping his blubbery purple lips with the back of his hand, mistakenly thinking he had orange Cheeto crumbs on his mouth.

Lowering his piece Ricardo turned to Riley. "When we catch you, I won't kill you right away. I'll string you up by your wrists from a tree, gut you, strew your entrails along the ground, and feed them to a starving crocodile as you watch in agony. Think Hansel and Gretel. Your guts will be like the breadcrumbs they dropped on the ground to find their way out of the forest. The crocodile will follow your guts to find his way to you, gobbling them all the while, licking his chops. Like you, I'll be watching the whole thing. But, unlike you, not in agony."

"There's nothing on Netflix?"

Ricardo snorted in annoyance. "Eventually the croc will eat all your guts and start eating the rest of you as you're hanging dying from the tree, starting on your feet and working his way up. Hopefully for you, you'll be dead before he gets beyond your legs. But, I have to tell you, dear Gustavo, it usually doesn't work out that way. When I slit open your belly, I don't plan on injuring any major organs. You can live a long time with your guts hanging out. Of course, that's without a croc munching on them. When he starts working on your legs, you can say sayonara. You'll die from bleeding out when he severs your femoral artery."

Ricardo looked amused.

"All this for failing a test?" said Riley. "What do you do to guys that screw your wife behind your back?"

Blowing a fuse, Ricardo landed a right hook to Riley's jaw. "Don't ever drag my wife's name through the mud."

Riley rubbed his aching jaw.

"I don't want to have to beat you to death before we start our game," said Ricardo.

Where was December? wondered Riley. When was the CIA extraction squad going to exfiltrate him? If ever there was a time for them to get their act together, the time was now. He scoped out his surroundings. He saw no sign of them. This whole fiasco was beginning to reek of a setup. The way it started, with him unconscious, and now the way it was going to end, with him as a stiff—unless he could figure out a way of surviving Ricardo's death hunt.

Riley decided December and the CIA had hung him out to dry. He wasn't obligated to do anything for them.

"Let me walk out of here, and we'll never see each other again," said Riley.

"Promises, promises."

"I mean it."

"You flunked your test. The grade for flunking is *D*—for Death. I'll give you a ten-minute head start to get your bullet and run. Then we come for you."

Ricardo glanced at his gold Rolex wristwatch.

"This is pointless," said Riley, palms sweaty.

"You flunked. Good-bye. You're wasting time," said Ricardo, still eying his watch. "One minute gone. Now you have only nine minutes."

Riley gazed in the distance at the pine where he had seen Pablo leave the Glock's bullet.

One bullet was better than nothing, Riley decided, and broke into a run for the pine, his heartbeat racing.

Arriving at the pine, breathing hard, his lungs burning, he cast around for the bullet in the duff around the trunk. He had trouble focusing his eyes because he was breathing so hard. Where was it? he wondered. He had seen fat Pablo run to this pine, but, thanks to the long distance, he hadn't been able to discern where exactly the guy had deposited the round. It had to be around here somewhere.

He tried not to walk around too much lest he step on the bullet and bury it in the duff and never find it.

Regaining his breath and breathing normally, he hunkered down and combed through the fallen sere pine needles for the bullet. He cut his eyes toward Ricardo.

It looked like Ricardo and his cartel members were going to start their hunt any second.

Riley glanced at his wristwatch. Only five minutes at most had passed since he had left the campsite. So much for the ten minutes Ricardo had promised. Riley couldn't waste time thinking about the SOB's lies. He had to find that bullet.

He saw something glinting in the pine duff a foot in front of where he crouched. He brushed the duff away with his hand and saw that it was the round's brass cartridge that was glinting. Standing up he withdrew the Glock 19 out of his waistband, ejected the magazine, loaded the bullet into it, and jammed it back into the Glock's butt.

Ricardo and his men were already coming for him, Riley could see.

Jamming the Glock into his waistband, Riley fled into the woods.

One bullet, he decided. Should he save it for Ricardo when he was in range? What would prevent the other cartel members from killing him in reprisal? They all knew he had but one bullet.

As Riley saw it, a gun with one bullet wasn't going to do him much good. To survive he had to prevent the narcos from catching him.

Then he heard something that sent a frisson of fear down his spine. Dogs barking.

The narcos had dogs tracking him.

He ran faster up the slope.

He had to find a river to lose the baying hounds.

He caught a glint ahead through the trees and bolted toward it. It might be water. As he neared the glint, he made out the water that was reflecting it. A narrow creek wound down the mountain. He charged into the creek and waded through it to lose his scent. The water wasn't more than a foot deep. Probably runoff from recent rain, he decided.

He had waded through the creek for the better part of two hundred feet before he heard the baying hounds getting closer. His shoes and trouser legs dripping wet, he climbed out of the creek onto the opposite bank and sprinted along the bank away from the narcos.

He considered hiding up in a tree. But if the hounds found him, he would be dead. They would bark at him till their masters arrived.

He had better keep running, he decided, not pausing to rest and refill his lungs. Throat burning, he kept running along the creek bank. He had no idea how many dogs the narcos had. If they had four, they could split into four groups and comb both sides of the creek in both directions till the dogs picked up his scent again. If they had less than four, the narcos would have to guess which direction he had taken before their hounds could again pick up his scent.

After running another mile, he forded the creek again and headed away from it till he spotted a stand of oak trees with thick boughs. Pausing to catch his breath, he looked up at the branches and thought he could climb out on a limb onto another limb on a neighboring oak. Then he could climb down that oak's trunk. The dogs would think they had treed him. He could gain valuable time while the narcos figured out they didn't have him at bay and the dogs would have to pick up his scent again.

He climbed the oak and walked out on a sturdy bough toward the neighboring oak. He hoped the bough would support his weight. As he kept walking along it, balancing himself by clasping the branch above him, he heard the branch he was standing on start to crack. As it snapped and fell, he held onto the limb above him.

He swung along it like a monkey till it, too, began to crack. As it gave way, he swung onto the nearest bough of the neighboring oak. Unable to stand and balance his weight on it, he slipped off it and swiped at it with his outstretched hands as he fell. Scratching his arms on nearby smaller limbs, he managed to get a grip on the main bough and stop his fall. Hand over hand, he swung along the bough to the oak's trunk and climbed down to the ground.

His arms scratched and bleeding, he broke into a run away from the creek and down the mountain.

He came upon some outcroppings and, exhausted, took cover behind them. He realized he was getting thirsty. He heard a dog baying in the distance behind him. Had one of them picked up his scent after he had forded the creek? He couldn't tell how far away the hound was. Maybe it was still sniffing along the creek bank, and it might be on the wrong side of the trail he had left, in which case it wouldn't pick up his scent. There was no way he could tell the hound's exact whereabouts from here.

He wondered where he should head. If he kept bearing down the mountain, he would no doubt encounter people eventually. Maybe someone would help him—unless everybody around here belonged to the cartel.

Who was he trying to kid? It was hopeless. He was alone in a foreign country. Somewhere in Mexico, he supposed. Maybe Guadalajara, if he could believe anything December had told him. Narcos armed with AKs and Tec-9s were chasing him guided by hounds. And all he had to defend himself was a Glock with one bullet.

Now he realized what the one bullet was for. It wasn't for killing the narcos. It was for killing him. One shot to the head, to be exact. If he shot himself, Ricardo wouldn't be able to torture him by disemboweling him and feeding him to a crocodile.

The hound's baying sounded louder.

It had picked up his scent, decided Riley. Ricardo and his narcos were closing in. Riley had no chance of escape. He imagined a crocodile eating his uncoiled intestines as he hung by his wrists from a tree. The cold terror of watching himself devoured to death one bite at a time consumed him. The pain would be beyond belief. He couldn't take it. He had to get this over with.

Breaking into a sweat he withdrew the Glock from his waistband and pointed the muzzle at his temple. Beads of sweat popped out of his forehead, as his forefinger brought pressure to bear on the Glock's trigger. One squeeze, and it would be over.

Gazing down the mountain he discerned a cloud of dust.

A motor vehicle driving on a dirt road? he wondered. A means of escape. From this distance and vantage point he couldn't make out anything other than the rising dust cloud. He had to find out what was stirring up the dust.

All thoughts of blowing his brains out vanished from his mind.

He snugged the Glock back into his waistband and bolted away from the outcropping down the mountain. He ran full tilt. He had to intercept the vehicle before it vanished. It didn't appear to be going very fast. He had a chance if he pushed himself to his limits.

Gasping for breath he scrambled down the rock-strewn slope.

He could see it now. It was a stake truck chugging along a winding dirt road. He could cut the truck off if he could reach the road before the truck rounded the bend. Scrabbling down the slope he waved frantically at the driver and bounded onto the road.

"*Hola*," he yelled. "*Ayuda. Ayuda.*" Help.

The stake truck slowed, but didn't stop.

He scampered out of the way, as it passed him.

"*Necessito ayuda*," he yelled after it, his hopes dashed. "*Alto. Alto.*" Stop.

Maybe his Spanish wasn't any good, he decided in dismay.

The stake truck slowed to a halt thirty feet beyond him.

Overjoyed, Riley dashed after it. It had a worn silver and black Raiders sticker pasted on its rear bumper, which didn't have a license plate. They even liked the Raiders in Mexico, he decided.

He reached the passenger's-side window, which was open, and stuck his head in.

"*Ayúdame, por favor*," he said.

The thirtyish female driver frowned at him with puzzlement.

"*Narcos quieren matarme*," he said.

He heard the hound baying louder.

"Narcos what?" said the Hispanic driver.

She had a café au lait complexion, full lips, and large brown eyes. Her long black hair cascaded down her shoulders. She was wearing a taupe button-down blouse and stonewashed jeans.

"Can you speak English?" she said.

"Of course," he said, his face sweaty. "Narcos are trying to kill me. They're gonna feed me to a crocodile. I need a ride."

"A crocodile? They don't have crocodiles around here," she said, eying him suspiciously.

Riley glanced back over his shoulder. He could glimpse figures higher up the mountain making their way downward. He turned back to the driver.

"I'll explain later," he said. "Can you give me a lift?"

"All right. Climb in."

"*Me llamo* Barry."

"I'm Bianca."

He clambered in beside her and shut the door.

The stake truck lurched forward. A large strawberry-shaped air freshener swung on a string dangling from the rearview mirror.

"I'm glad you speak English," he said.

"I know hardly any Spanish."

He turned to stare at her. "How can you live in Mexico without knowing Spanish?"

"I'm not Mexican. I was born in Los Angeles."

The stake truck shuddered, driving over the uneven dirt road.

"Then you moved to Guadalajara?" he said.

She looked at him like he was crazy. "What are you talking about? What's Guadalajara got to do with anything? If you don't stop talking crazy, I'm gonna kick you out. I don't give lifts to psychos."

"No, no. Don't do that. Aren't we in Guadalajara?"

"Whatever gave you that idea?"

Riley changed the subject. He could be anywhere in Mexico for all he knew. "I need to get to the border. Can you help me?"

She gave him a look, but said nothing.

"I don't have a passport. The narcos stole my passport," he said.

"You been smoking weed? Are you jiving about narcos? And we don't have crocodiles in California."

"I'm telling you the truth. They're trying to kill me," he said, frightened. "You gotta believe me."

"Take it easy. Maybe you need a doctor."

"California?" he muttered. "Did you say California?" *What the hell is going on?*

"It's that big state next to Nevada."

"I know where it is. I'm from LA."

"Then why do you keep speaking Spanish?"

"I thought you were from Guadalajara."

"I've never been there. I've never even been to Mexico."

Riley shook his head in confusion. "I don't understand. Was I hallucinating?"

"All I can tell you is this is sunny California."

His head down, Riley sniffed the odor of wood smoke impregnating his shirt. He hadn't dreamed the campfire. A dream didn't leave an odor on your shirt. Ricardo and his cartel weren't figments of his imagination. They were real, and they wanted to kill him.

"*A dónde vas?*"

Bianca shot him a blank look.

"I mean, where are you going?" said Riley.

"LA."

"Perfect. Could I go with you?"

She scoped him out. "As long as you don't act crazy again and flip out."

"I promise."

He was too fatigued from running for his life to flip out. He would use the ride to catch some Zs. Then he was going to pay Raoul December a visit. The son of a bitch.

###

When a cab dropped him off in Marina del Rey, he checked slip thirty-three for December's launch.

The *Ariadne* wasn't moored, the slip empty.

He had told the cabbie to wait for him. He returned to the cabbie.

Truth be told, he wasn't surprised. He figured December wasn't the mastermind of this scam. Gommers must have dreamed it up. It had his fingerprints all over it. A revenge ploy to retaliate against Riley's threat to go solo and dissolve their "writing team." Writing team, indeed. It was Riley that did all the writing.

Riley took the cab back to his casita in Redondo Beach, where he scrounged up some cash from a strongbox in his closet to pay the cabbie.

After the cabbie left, Riley called Gommers with his landline. Riley had no idea what had happened to his cell phone. Either December or Ricardo and his narcos had jacked it, along with his wallet and everything else in his trouser pockets.

Riley's mind was made up. He knew what to do. He waited for Gommers to answer his phone.

"Hello," said Gommers.

"Hello, Fred. It's me."

Riley could have heard a pin drop for the silence on the line.

"Don't you recognize my voice?" said Riley.

"What kind of a gag is this?" demanded Gommers, his voice edged.

"No gag. This is Barry Riley."

Silence.

"Kind of surprised to hear my voice, huh, Fred? Dead men tell no tales, and all that."

"Is that you, Riley? If this is supposed to be funny, it isn't."

"You're damn right it isn't. Your trying to have me killed isn't funny at all."

"What are you talking about?"

"You and your buddy Raoul December cooked up this CIA scam to get rid of me because I'm dissolving our so-called writing team."

"Nobody dumps me, buddy. *Nobody*. Certainly not some washed-up hack who couldn't sell a book with his name on it if his life depended on it. I'm the one that does the dumping. Me, Frederick Gommers. When a deal is over, it's because *I* say it's over, not because anybody else does. And that includes you, you bottom-feeding scribbler."

"I got news for you. It's over. I'm pulling the plug on it. I'm not gonna be your galley slave any more. And listen to this. I got a new story to tell. Maybe the cops are gonna wanna hear it. You think? It's about a famous in-name-only writer who hired a cartel to whack out his ghostwriter, because said ghostwriter refused to grind out any more best-selling thrillers for him. You think the cops'll dig that story?"

"You can't prove a word of it. I'll sue your ass off."

"Doesn't matter. Your career's gonna be in ashes when I start talking. The media are gonna have a Roman holiday with you. It's called *schadenfreude*."

"What?"

"The great wordsmith," Riley scoffed. "You don't even know the meaning of words. I'm gonna reveal you for the fraud you are and relish every minute of it."

"You bastard. Say one word of this to anyone, you're dead meat."

"Is that the best line you can come up with? I thought you were a great writer."

"You lowlife. You'll regret the day you ever tangled with me."

"Save it for the papers after they get my story and you're saying good-bye to your 'writing' career."

"Why you—"

Riley hung up beaming with satisfaction. It was time to start a new career—as the writer Barry Riley.

Violated

Somebody was trying to kill her.

That was all she knew.

She didn't know why.

She had just turned thirty and she had almost died.

The first attempt on her life took place that morning when a silver Land Rover swerved into another lane while she was walking in the crosswalk and tried to run her over. She had managed to dart out of the crosswalk and onto the sidewalk in the nick of time, almost dropping her black nylon art portfolio tote strapped over her shoulder. The Land Rover had screeched its tires, fishtailed, and rocketed away.

Gasping for breath, smelling burnt rubber, her heart beating like it was on steroids, Ashley stood on the sidewalk in her heels, one of which was broken, she noticed, as she stood unevenly and tried to make out the fleeing assailant's license tag. As near as she could make out, he didn't have one. Which meant the vehicle could have been leased. Leased cars didn't need license plates in Los Angeles County. Or maybe the driver had removed the plates to avoid being identified.

It had all happened so quickly she hadn't had time to get a look at the driver's face. One minute the Land Rover was heading toward the intersection on San Vicente Blvd. while she was in the crosswalk. The next it was swerving and accelerating toward her in an attempt to break every bone in her body.

A middle-aged bald man, clad in a dark suit and carrying a briefcase, scurried over to her to make sure she was all right.

"Did he hit you?" he said with concern. "Should I call 911?"

"No. I'm OK," she said, limping on her one good heel.

"Your leg? Did he hit your leg?"

"My heel's broken. That's all."

"My God, you poor thing. I'll call for an ambulance."

"It's just a heel." She hastened to add, "*On my shoe*. Well, it used to be on my shoe."

"Oh," he said with relief. "Your shoe."

"I'm not hurt. It scared me to death, though."

"I bet. He must've been drunk. A wino in a car is an accident waiting to happen."

She didn't believe the driver was drunk. She believed he had deliberately tried to kill her. He swerved out of his lane right at her. She wished she had seen his face, but when the Land Rover swerved toward her, her reflexes took over. They told her to run for her life. All she could remember of her view of the driver was the sun visor pulled down in front of the guy's face.

She couldn't believe how wired she was.

"I think it was deliberate," she said, having difficulty talking through a dry, tight throat.

"What did you say?"

"I—I—uh—I can't talk," she husked.

"That's no surprise. You just missed getting run over. You need to relax."

She was too keyed up to relax. Adrenaline was still shooting through her system, fraying her nerves.

"I need to go home," she managed to say.

"Are you sure he didn't hit you? Your face is white as a sheet, and you're limping around."

"I told you. Just a broken heel."

"All right," he said, but didn't look convinced.

"He missed me. Not by much. Less than an inch, I'd say. All I could see was his car's grillwork bearing down on me, inches away from me, closing fast, and I jumped out of the way."

"I thought for sure he hit you." He paused. "I better be going. I'm already late. My wife must be going nuts worrying about me. I stopped in a Starbucks for a cup of mocha, and now she's going to give me a ride to work. I ended up staying longer than I had planned. I started working on my project and lost track of the time—"

"Go ahead. Don't worry about me. He missed me."

She wondered where her broken heel had gone. From the sidewalk she inspected the crosswalk, trying to locate the heel with no luck. Another car must have run over it and knocked it who knows where.

It wasn't important. These shoes were ruined. She would have to throw them out. She was the one that looked drunk, stumbling and lurching around on her uneven shoes as she tried to negotiate the sidewalk.

"Did you get his license plate?" she asked the businessman.

"No. I didn't really see what happened. I heard tires screeching, looked in your direction, and saw you lunging toward the sidewalk as the Land Rover plowed through the crosswalk. I thought he hit you, so I ran over to you."

"Should I call the police and report this?"

"Uh—I—uh, that's up to you. I doubt they'll do anything. No harm, no foul. That sort of thing."

"Even if it was deliberate?"

The man strode away from her, all arms and legs and a briefcase swinging rapidly. "I have to be off. What did you say? *Deliberate*? I doubt it. Just another DUI," he said over his shoulder. "Why would anyone want to kill you?"

He rounded the corner and vanished.

Why, indeed? she wondered. Nevertheless, she was certain the driver *had* tried to kill her. He was aiming right at her as he changed lanes at the last minute in front of the crosswalk and would have struck her if she hadn't bolted out of his way.

She needed a drink to calm her nerves.

She walked, more like *hobbled*, in her broken heel the next two blocks to her apartment. At least she hadn't sprained her ankle. Considering what had just happened to her, she had escaped in remarkably good condition.

Her apartment house was a Spanish-styled Mission Revival affair with apricot stucco walls, black grills in the windows, and a red tiled roof. A common style in this neck of the woods in

Southern California. And then there were the requisite birds of paradise in the front garden along with bright fuchsia bougainvillea that clung to a white, peeling trellis parallel to the façade to the right of the entrance. The residence even had its own grapefruit tree growing on its frontage.

Home, sweet home.

Only it wasn't.

Sweetness had nothing to do with it.

She couldn't believe her eyes.

Someone had broken into her apartment and ransacked the place.

Doorknob in hand, she gawked at the mess. Cushions from her sofas and books from her bookcases strewed the carpet. The intruder had tossed helter-skelter the glossy magazines that had been lying on her coffee table.

Now there was no doubt in her mind the driver had tried to run her over. Somebody was targeting her.

Was it a run-of-the-mill burglary? she wondered. Or were they looking for something in particular? She didn't own any fancy paintings or statues. Why would they target her middle-class apartment? Other residences in Brentwood were more expensive than hers—namely, the houses on the other side of San Vicente Boulevard.

Or maybe it wasn't a burglary. What if someone had broken in with the intent to kill her? Or could the trashing of her digs have been a threatening message meant to terrify her?

She rubbed her head. She had to calm down. She was reading too many crime thrillers. Then again, it could be her job as a court artist that was stressing her out. All she saw at her job day in, day out was the evil side of the human race, a parade of malefactors that marched by her seat as she sketched—mostly criminal—witnesses that testified on the stand.

Sometimes when she was bored, she even sketched members of the audience, besides the judge, of course, as demanded by her job, along with the prosecutors, lawyers, bailiffs, and defendants.

A graduate of the Rhode Island School of Design, armed with her BFA degree in Illustration, she had ended up at a carnival of criminals, otherwise known as a courthouse, pursuing her dream of becoming an artist.

Her job gave her a bird's-eye view of mankind at its worst, lowering her opinion of human nature every day. Listening to the nefarious acts of crime lords, corrupt politicians, murderers, robbers, and rapists all day long could turn you sour on life if you let it get to you.

And now this. She wasn't just listening to evil deeds as a spectator. She was the victim of them—an attempt to murder her in the crosswalk and the ransacking of her apartment, both on the same day.

Was the driver who had targeted her in the crosswalk the same guy that had trashed her apartment? Was that why the guy was in the neighborhood? Because he had broken into her apartment?

There was no way around it now. She needed to call the cops.

The near miss in the crosswalk could have been dismissed as an accident. Such a case would be hard to prosecute. But a ransacked apartment was evidence of a crime. There was no other explanation.

She called the cops and filed a report with them. They said they would send an investigator to her apartment.

Meanwhile, she wandered around her rooms, trying to notice if anything was missing. The cop on the phone had told her not to touch anything or move anything around before the police arrived.

Nothing was missing as far as she could tell.

Her study was as messed up as her living room.

Items like her stapler, pencils, erasers, and pencil holder that had been on her desktop littered the carpet. Several of her courtroom sketches lay strewn among her upended office supplies. The invader had yanked drawers from bureaus and scattered the contents on the floor.

Was the guy just trashing the place or looking for something? She couldn't tell. But why would someone enter her apartment with no other intention than to trash it? To show it was no problem for him to break into her digs and violate her? To scare her?

Or was it to rob her?

She kept looking around, examining the mess, careful not to step on anything, but didn't notice anything missing. She could think of one explanation. He didn't find what he was looking for. But what *was* he looking for?

She heard knocking on her door.

She negotiated her way through the mess and answered the door, expecting to see a cop.

Instead she saw her sister Clarice standing in the hall, looking dressed to kill in her canary yellow dress and Jimmy Choo black heels, a Givenchy Antigona leather purse in her hand exuding the power of money.

Extroverted, attractive, and envied by most everyone, Clarice, who had married well, was the polar opposite of Ashley, who was introverted, unmarried, average in the looks department, and uncomfortable around people. Ashley would rather spend her time clad in jeans and a sweatshirt drawing sketches than getting tricked up and socializing.

Clarice saw the mess on the carpet behind Ashley and burst into the room.

"What the hell happened here?" said Clarice, surveying the shambles.

"The maid didn't come in this week."

Clarice whirled around to confront her. "Seriously?"

"No. Somebody broke in."

"This is awful," said Clarice, surveying the room. "Crooks are everywhere these days. Nobody's safe. Do you know who did it?"

"No idea. The cops'll be here any minute."

"What did the crooks take?"

"I dunno. I haven't noticed anything missing."

"What about your bedroom? That's where they usually hit."

"That's the funny thing. They didn't go in there. Everything's in order, such as it is, in my bedroom."

"That's weird. Maybe they were interrupted before they got there. The bedroom's where most people hide their valuables."

Valuables, decided Ashley. As though she had any valuables to speak of.

Somebody rapped on the door, which hung ajar.

Ashley answered it.

A middle-aged LAPD cop with hair cropped so short it glittered like steel filings stood in the hall in black slacks and a shepherd's check off-the-rack blazer without a necktie. He was five nine with wide shoulders. He had a port-wine stain on his forehead that reached onto his scalp under his hair.

"Hello. I'm Detective George Macready of the LAPD. You reported a break-in?"

"Come in, please," said Ashley.

Macready took in the disarray, showing no reaction.

"Anything stolen?" he said.

"Not that I know of."

"Odd."

"Not when you combine it with what happened earlier."

He eyed her with interest. "I don't understand."

"Somebody tried to run me over in the crosswalk while I was walking back to my apartment."

"Did you get his license tag?"

"He didn't have one."

Macready nodded. "Could have been leased or even stolen. Did you get a good look at him?"

"It happened too fast."

"Type of vehicle?"

"Land Rover, I think. It was silver."

"I hate to sound suspicious, but are you sure it wasn't an accident?"

"He swerved right at me while I was in the crosswalk. I broke my heel running out of his way."

"Did you call 911?"

"No point."

Macready raised his eyebrows.

"Doesn't it hurt?" he said, glancing at her feet.

"The heel of my shoe."

She needed to be more precise in her answers, she realized, especially when she was talking to a cop.

"Ah," he said. "Did you file a police report about the attack?"

"I—I—haven't had time."

Macready nodded, his face blank.

He returned to assessing the clutter in the apartment. "Are you sure nothing was stolen?"

"I'm not positive. It's hard to tell if something's missing, especially with everything strewn around the room. My laptop's still in the study." She glanced in the laptop's direction. "That would be the most expensive thing I have."

Macready wandered toward the study, his eyes roaming around taking everything in.

"Did you find any urine stains or feces?" he said.

"Excuse me?" said Ashley, unsure she had heard him correctly.

"Burglars frequently leave their mark. Like dogs marking a fire hydrant. In the case of burglars, though, it's a sign of contempt for the owner of the residence they hit."

"I haven't seen anything like that. Thank goodness."

"The things you learn," said Clarice, pulling a face.

"Why would they be that stupid?" Ashley asked Macready. "Wouldn't it leave their DNA at the scene of the crime?"

"Actually, it's quite difficult to get DNA out of urine. In any case, burglars aren't known for being smart."

"I don't know why these creeps keep targeting Ashley," said Clarice.

"Hunh? What do you mean?" said Macready. "Has this happened before?"

"Ashley said she was pursued by a stalker last year."

"Oh? Who was it?"

"Some guy she dated. He thought she liked him and they would have a long-term relationship. She didn't share his feelings. He got mad. You know how that goes."

Macready cleared his throat. "The story of my life, unfortunately."

Clarice stifled a brief laugh.

"What happened to him?" said Macready.

"What did happen to him, Ash?"

"He stopped stalking me after I finally got through to him that I wanted to end it," said Ashley, not wanting to think about it.

"What if he *didn't* stop stalking you?" said Macready.

"You think he's the one that trashed my room?"

"We can't rule him out."

"He denied the whole thing," said Clarice in a throwaway remark.

"What?" said Macready.

"The stalking. He said Ash was making the whole thing up and that he never stalked her."

"He was lying," said Ashley. "He's very convincing. It's one reason I broke off our relationship. He lies all the time."

"Maybe that explains why he's so successful," said Clarice, archly.

"I don't like liars."

"What's his name?" said Macready.

"Ricky. Ricky Sanders."

"Maybe he's starting up on you again for some reason."

"I can't imagine why. I haven't seen him in a year, and he's made no attempt to contact me. Why would he decide to attack me out of the blue?"

"You never know what sets these guys off. Maybe he saw your name in the paper or on the news. What is your job?"

"I'm a court artist."

"You don't say? Are you the one that draws those sketches of defendants and lawyers during trials?"

She nodded yes. "Guilty as charged."

"I've always marveled at how accurate court artists' sketches are. It's like I'm at the trial when I see those sketches."

"Thanks, Detective."

"I admire anyone with creative talent. You must be good if the courts hired you."

"She's always had the talent in the family, and I've always had the looks," said Clarice, smiling. "Nature's way of compensating for her lack in the looks department."

Clarice loved throwing out that backhanded compliment about her, Ashley decided, putting a lid on her anger. Ashley couldn't count the number of times Clarice had said the exact same thing.

"Talent is a wonderful thing," said Macready.

"She also has imagination," said Clarice. "Don't forget her other specialty. Ricky went so far as to accuse her of making up the whole thing about his stalking her. Imagine that."

"He was trying to make me look like I was a nut job so nobody would believe me when I accused him," said Ashley.

"If you don't mind my asking," said Macready, "what trial are you working on now?"

"Sure. The trial of a guy accused of being a cartel narcoterrorist hit man. Some guy named Cuchillo."

"Ah. Good old Cuchillo. He's on our Most Wanted list. Those narcos got tons of money and can hire high-power lawyers who can drag out court proceedings like you wouldn't believe."

"You're telling me."

"You gotta have a strong stomach to listen to a hit man's litany of crimes at a trial."

"And then she comes home to a ransacked apartment," said Clarice. "She can't win for losing." She faced Ashley. "Some court artist is gonna end up sketching *your* face at *your* trial if your life doesn't improve, Ash."

"What am I supposed to do?"

"We'll take care of it," said Macready. "I'll talk to this Ricky Sanders you're talking about. What's his job?"

"He's an ad executive. Quite successful at it. He has many clients. He doesn't like losing any of them. That's why he blew up when I called off our relationship. That's how he sees relationships—in terms of winning or losing."

Just thinking of Ricky made Ashley's skin crawl. His idea of fun was slicing her wrists with razor blades to make it look like she had tried to commit suicide. Anything to make her look bad when she opposed him. His harassment of her never stopped till she told him to get lost.

Then the stalking began.

Until she showed him some spine.

“He messed up Ash’s brain,” Clarice told Macready. “She had to go to an asylum. She tried to off herself.”

“No, I didn’t,” said Ashley.

“Then what about those scars on your wrists? Any fool can see they’re from a razor.”

“He did that,” said Ashley, turning over her wrists so nobody could see the thin white scars. “He cut me. I didn’t do it.”

“You *did* go to the asylum. You can’t deny that.”

“It was the only place I felt safe from him.”

“I’m not putting you down. I’m just trying to explain to the detective what happened between you and Ricky.”

Clarice was making her out to be a full-blown loony, decided Ashley with resentment.

Thanks, Clarice. With sisters like you . . .

Ashley reined in her anger.

“The fact is, somebody trashed Ashley’s apartment,” said Macready.

“And tried to run me over in the crosswalk,” said Ashley.

“Did you take down the names of any witnesses at the crosswalk?”

“Uh—no. I was too upset. I didn’t think to take names. I talked to a businessman after I escaped injury, but I didn’t get his name.”

“All right. That’s OK. The CSI team will be here any minute and search for fingerprints and DNA.”

Macready angled toward the open front door and inspected its locks. He also inspected the doorjamb.

“I don’t see any signs of jimmying or any other forced entry,” he said.

“Then how did he get in?” said Clarice.

“He didn’t enter through the windows. We’re on the third floor. Unless he’s a cat burglar. But I doubt it. Frankly, this looks like amateur hour with all the mess he made.” Macready turned to Ashley. “Are you sure you locked your door?”

“Positive,” she said.

“Maybe it’s a friend of yours that entered.”

Friend, thought Ashley. What friends? The only friends she had, if you could call them that, were a couple of her coworkers. What did that say about you, if your only so-called friends were coworkers?

"I—"

"She doesn't have many friends," Clarice cut her off.

"Nobody you gave a spare key to?" Macready asked Ashley. "What about this Ricky character?"

Ashley frowned in thought. "I can't remember. I don't think I gave him one."

"If the B&E man had a key, it would explain the lack of jimmy marks on your door. Technically it wouldn't even be a B&E because he didn't break in."

"Maybe the guy used a lock pick," said Clarice.

Macready nodded yes. "It's possible. Some burglars know how to pick a lock without leaving a trace. To do so, he'd have to be a professional."

"How many professional burglars do you know, Ash?"

"None," said Ashley, biting her lower lip.

"If I was you, I'd have the locks on your door replaced," said Macready. "To be on the safe side."

"I can't believe somebody has my key. It's scaring me."

"We don't know that for sure. It's just a precautionary measure."

"None of it makes sense. I don't have anything worth stealing."

"Which doesn't rule out harassment. Ransacking your room could be a terrorist tactic. Do you have a lot of enemies?"

"She doesn't have friends. She doesn't have enemies," said Clarice in a singsong voice.

"I can speak for myself," said Ashley.

Clarice shrugged. "You know the type, Detective."

"What about you?" he asked. "Do you have a key to her apartment?"

"Me? No. Why would she give me one?"

"You're sisters."

"I don't go around handing out keys to people," said Ashley in an access of irritation. "Is that what other people do? What's the point of even having a key, if you give all your spares away?"

"We're trying to find out how the intruder got into your apartment," said Macready. "No offense meant."

"I'm not taking offense. I just need to rest. It's not every day someone tries to run me over and burgle my apartment." Ashley felt a shiver run down her spine. "I feel violated."

"I understand. We have enough to go on for now."

The CSI unit arrived in their protective gear and commenced photographing her apartment and dusting for fingerprints.

"What do you have in your shoulder tote?" Macready asked Ashley.

"Recent courtroom sketches," she answered.

"Ah. People with talent are so fortunate. I wish I had some artistic talent."

Talent compensates for not having a life, she thought, not without a trace of bitterness.

"I'm not fortunate today," she said with a forced smile.

"Do you need your psychiatrist?" said Clarice, frowning with concern.

"No. It's just stress."

"You don't want to have another breakdown."

"I'm not."

"Well, I gotta run," said Clarice, watching with rheumy blue eyes the forensics team dust the coffee table near her for prints. "I'm allergic to dust."

"Good-bye," said Ashley, relieved to see her go.

She turned to Macready. "Is there some way I can get police protection, Detective?"

"Not in this instance. We don't have the manpower to post officers around every residence that gets burgled."

"But somebody tried to run me over, too."

Macready considered it. "Have you actually been threatened by anyone? If we had evidence of a threat . . ."

"No verbal threats, if that's what you mean."

"It doesn't have to be verbal. It could be written or some action perceived as a threat."

"Like waking up with a horse's bloody head in your bed?"

"Yeah. I saw that movie, too."

"Trying to run someone over is threatening."

"But what's the purpose of the threat? What we're lacking here is motive. Why did this driver try to run you over?"

"I have no idea."

Macready shrugged. "I'll look into it. Don't be concerned."

I almost got killed today, but don't be concerned. Right.

# # #

She didn't sleep well that night. She kept dreaming someone was opening her apartment door and walking in while she watched paralyzed in bed.

She took her sketch pad in her tote bag to work and felt irritable thanks to her lack of sleep. She sat at her desk in the courtroom and tried to concentrate on the trial, instead of on who was out to get her.

The narco hit man Cuchillo was on the stand declaring his innocence to his lawyer.

She tried to sketch the hit man, but her attention kept wandering. She kept yawning as she sketched him as he testified that he had never killed anyone. Thick dark hair, round face with big cheeks and a low brow, large, haunted black eyes. She needed to get some sleep.

She hadn't called her psychiatrist Dr. Kretchmer. Why should she? A shrink couldn't protect you from a hit-and-run driver, nor from a burglar. Nobody was going to protect her. She had to fend for herself. The cops only did their job with earnest after blood was spilled and the bodies were cold. Their focus was on solving a crime, not preventing one.

It was driving her nuts trying to figure out who was targeting her. It might be Ricky, but the truth was she hadn't spoken to him in over a year. What would prompt him to recommence harassing her? What had changed in that year? Nothing that she could see. Ricky, the hard-charging ad executive with the combustible temper who thought he had the world on a string. Controlling and abusive. Yet he couldn't control his own life, abusing drugs, snorting booger sugar, so he had to control hers. She hoped he wasn't on her case again. She didn't see why he would be, since they had kept out of each other's sight after their breakup.

She looked at her sketch.

It was terrible. The product of an exhausted mind.

The sketch bore only a remote resemblance to Cuchillo. She hadn't gotten his eyes right. That was the main problem. They were wary, haunted, and belligerent at the same time, but she hadn't caught that with her sketch. In her drawing his eyes looked like the wide black eyes of a deer, instead of a stone killer's. She had caught his awareness and suspicion, but not his propensity for violence.

She was thankful when the judge adjourned the trial for a recess. Hopefully, she would come back to the trial feeling refreshed and inspired.

During the break she was sitting outside the courtroom in the hall on a cement bench on the jade green marble floor under the watchful gaze of a guard in a grey uniform thirty-odd feet from her with his chest thrust out, his thumbs hooked under his belt. Was he singling her out? she wondered. No, he was just doing his job checking out people in the hallway.

He wandered down the hall away from her, his head cocked up, his thumbs still hooked under his belt, observing people.

She was trying to unwind when her cell chimed.

She took the call.

"Hi, Ashley. I understand you need my help," said her psychiatrist, Dr. Kretchmer, with his high-pitched voice that grated on her nerves.

She could see Nathan Kretchmer now with his beard, horn-rimmed glasses, and scarlet cardigan with only its top button buttoned. He liked to walk around his office with a large aquamarine and orange macaw on his shoulder. He said the bird relaxed him and his patients.

"What are you talking about?" she said, baffled.

"Clarice phoned me and told me you're upset."

Clarice, thought Ashley angrily. What right did she have to call Kretchmer?

"Somebody broke into my apartment yesterday," said Ashley. "How would you feel if someone broke into your house?"

"She said you're experiencing episodes."

"Episodes? If getting burgled is an episode, yeah, that's true."

"That's not what we're talking about. You know better, Ashley. Clarice said you think someone tried to run you over."

Clarice running her mouth again.

"I don't *think* it," said Ashley. "I *saw* it."

"Are you sure you're not having one of your episodes? Feeling persecuted?"

"I know what I saw."

"I can make room for you tomorrow, if you'd like."

"I wouldn't like. This has nothing to do with you. Tell Clarice to mind her own business."

"Are you having problems sleeping? You sound irritable."

"How'd you guess?"

Ashley tightened her grip on her cell phone, miffed that Clarice had contacted Kretchmer of all people about the break-in. Was he supposed to be an expert on break-ins? Clarice could be such a pain. Who the hell else did she call?

"I think you should come in," said Kretchmer. "I don't want you to have a relapse."

"I have to return to work."

She terminated the call.

She saw someone staring at her. Short, in his thirties, with tousled black hair, wearing black jeans, suede tan cowboy boots, a charcoal grey blazer, and a bolo tie with a turquoise clasp. His chin was so narrow it was almost pointed. She could tell from the half inch of peach fuzz growing on the scruff of his neck that he needed a haircut.

Had she been talking too loud on her mobile? she wondered. Why else would he be staring at her? She didn't recognize him, yet he looked familiar. Was she getting paranoid again, imagining people were out to get her?

But somebody *was* out to get her. The guy that had tried to run her over.

Bolo Tie looked away from her.

She must have been talking too loud. That was why he had been staring at her, she decided. Now that she wasn't talking he wasn't looking at her.

Idly, she watched him make for the men's room, his boot heels clomping on the marble.

Had she seen him somewhere before? she wondered.

He might have been a spectator in the courtroom. Sometimes she sketched spectators. The TV newscasts rarely broadcast them, since their audiences were interested in trial defendants, lawyers, and witnesses. Occasionally a celebrity would be sitting among the spectators, and her sketches of them would air on the local TV news.

Her cell chimed. She checked the caller ID. It was Clarice.

Ashley groaned. She decided to take the call.

"Hi, Ash. Do you want me to talk to Ricky to tell him to leave you alone? It might be better if I did it instead of you. Your talking to him might trigger one of your episodes."

Ashley rolled her eyes. "I can take care of this. You don't need to do anything."

"Dr. Kretchmer was worried—"

"Why did you tell him anyway? He's a shrink. He doesn't know anything about people who try to run over other people."

"That's the point. This might be one of your episodes."

"There's no connection," said Ashley with annoyance. "Look, I know what you're trying to do."

"I'm trying to make sure you're OK. I know what happens to you when you're under duress."

"You also know that if I'm locked away in an insane asylum, you can declare me not of sound mind and inherit all of Mom's millions when she dies. Which is probably going to be pretty soon because of her lung cancer."

Dead silence.

Ashley could picture Clarice at the other end of the line appalled by her candor. Clarice had it coming, decided Ashley.

"Phew," said Clarice. "Listen to you. You and your persecution complex. You really do sound paranoid. And I resent your accusations. To think your own sister would hatch such a diabolical scheme."

"My mind's as sound as yours."

"I care about you, Ash. I don't want you to have another one of your breakdowns. And this is how you treat me? With horrible accusations about how selfish and greedy I am?"

"I have to go back to work."

Ashley terminated the call and felt like hurling her mobile to the floor. The demanding sound of the chime stayed her hand.

If it was Clarice, she wasn't going to answer it.

The caller ID said Private.

"Hello," she said.

"Where is it?" a voice whispered.

"Where's what?"

"Where is it?"

"I don't know what you're talking about. Who is this?" she said on the verge of terminating the call.

"If you don't hand it over, you'll regret it."

She hung up, her pulse pounding.

Was it Ricky? she wondered. She couldn't tell because the guy was whispering. It could've been anyone. The guy who had tried to run her over and burgled her apartment? It must have been him. Which meant he hadn't found what he was looking for in her apartment and he would continue to torment her.

For that matter, it could have been Clarice's voice. It was possible it had been a woman whispering on the phone. Clarice could own two phones with different numbers.

Ashley started when her cell chimed in her hand.

Clarice.

"Are you sure you don't want me to call Ricky for you?"

"I'm sure, Clarice." Ashley paused. "Did you just whisper to me on the phone?"

"*Whisper* to you? Are you hearing voices whispering to you?"

"Just answer the question."

"No, I didn't whisper to you on the phone. This is getting out of hand, Ash. You *must* make certain you see Kretchmer."

"Can we talk about this later? I have to go back to work."

"I've been thinking. How do we know you didn't trash your own apartment?"

"What?" said Ashley, taken aback. "Why would I do that?"

"You know how starved you are for attention."

"This is no joking matter, Clarice."

"I'm serious."

"Why would I want all this attention?"

"Maybe you're trying to get back at Ricky."

"I never said Ricky trashed my room. *You're* the one that brought up his name."

"You're confused. This is why I want you to see Dr. Kretchmer—"

"Answer me. Was that you whispering threats to me over the phone?"

Silence.

"I'm worried about you, Ash. What in the world makes you think I'm whispering threats to you? You're hearing things. Dial Dr. Kretchmer now and set up an appoint—"

Fit to be tied, Ashley terminated the call. She couldn't believe Clarice would dare suggest she was making the whole thing up. She glared at her cell phone like it was Clarice's face.

Most of the time her cell never rang. Now it was ringing nonstop. With unwanted calls, no less.

When she looked up, she saw Macready striding down the hall in her direction, wearing a mauve tie with his blazer this time.

"Hello, Ashley," he said with a smile.

"Hi. I was getting ready to call you. What are you doing here?"

"I have to testify at a trial this afternoon. Are you OK? You look pale."

"I was talking to my sister. Just an argument."

"Oh. What brings you here?"

"My job. I'm working the trial of a narco hit man, doing sketches."

"Oh, yeah. You mentioned you were a court artist when we first met. Cuchillo's trial, right? Why were you getting ready to call me?" he said, coming to a halt in front of her.

"Somebody called me and threatened me."

"Did you recognize who it was?"

"No. He was whispering. It could've been anyone."

"What exactly did he say?"

"He said, 'Where is it?'"

"Where is what?"

"I have no idea."

"Is that all he said?"

"He said—let me see if I can remember his exact words—'If you don't hand it over, you'll regret it.'"

"All right. I'll check out his number and see if we can trace it to him. Did you recognize the number he was calling from?"

"No. My caller ID just said it was an unknown caller from Los Angeles. I bet it was the same guy that trashed my apartment."

"Tell me the number, and I'll check it out."

She read it to him off the list of incoming calls on her cell. He withdrew his cell from his blazer's inside breast pocket and typed the number into his Notes app.

"My memory's a sieve," he explained.

She chuckled. "I can't even remember my own number sometimes."

"I've been trying to get in touch with Ricky Sanders, but he hasn't answered his phone. I left several unanswered messages for him on his voicemail."

"OK."

"Clarice called me and told me you're not handling the break-in well."

"Not *her* again." Ashley rubbed her eyes in distress. "I wish she would mind her own business. Don't listen to her."

"I'll call in this phone number to headquarters and see if they can trace it to the caller."

When he got off the phone, he glanced at his wristwatch.

"I still got some time to kill before my trial. Mind if I take a look at your sketches?" he said, picking up on the portfolio tote strapped to her shoulder.

"Of course," she said, smiling. "Artists always need praise. It goes with the territory. We're very insecure."

He gave her a look.

Does he think insecure *means* psychotic? she thought, beginning to regret her choice of words.

He sat down beside her on the cement bench.

She removed her sketchbook from her tote and leisurely flipped through the sketches she had drawn this morning so Macready could take a gander at them.

"These are good," he said. "Very lifelike. You capture the essence of their personalities in their faces."

"Well, I don't know if they're *that* good. But thanks for the compliment."

"And who is this character?" he said, gazing at her sketch of a man with a pointed chin. "This doesn't look like Cuchillo."

"Why, no." It was Bolo Tie, she realized. "That's . . . hmm . . . He must have been a spectator in the audience. Come to think of it, he was here yesterday, too. I remember sketching him. He has an interesting face. When I'm bored I sometimes sketch spectators, though they hardly ever show the sketches on TV."

Macready frowned. "I feel like I know this guy."

"Just some guy."

"I guess it's because your sketch is so realistic that I feel like I know him."

Ashley smiled.

"Flattery will get you nowhere," she said, though she didn't mean it.

His cell buzzed.

"Macready here." He listened intently. His eyes widened. "Are you sure?"

He bolted to his feet, cell in hand.

"What's wrong?" said Ashley.

"That phone number you gave me belongs to a payphone in this courthouse," he said, scoping out the pedestrians in the hallway.

"He's here?" she said, fear tightening her voice.

"How long ago did he call you?"

"Not long. Ten minutes. Maybe less."

"He probably left the payphone by now, but I can check it out. I know the layout of this place because I've been here so often. I know where all the payphones are. And there aren't that many anymore because nowadays everybody has a cell phone."

"Why did he use a payphone?"

"Because he doesn't want to be traced. We can trace the payphone, but not who called from it. I'm gonna check out the payphones."

"Am I in danger?"

"I doubt he'd try anything in the courthouse." He cursorily checked out the people in the hall, casting around for anyone threatening. Satisfied, he turned to Ashley. "You wait here."

Macready jogged down the corridor, his open blazer flapping around his hips.

Out of the corner of her eye, Ashley caught sight of Ricky Sanders bustling toward her from the other end of the hall. He looked upset. She braced for a confrontation.

Clad in jeans, a white polo, and a pair of ornate brogues he favored, he charged up to her. In his midthirties he was clean-shaven and had an air of authority about him.

"I thought I'd find you here," he said.

"What do you want, Ricky?"

Was he the one who had threatened her from the courthouse payphone? she wondered, adrenaline coursing through her system.

"Where do you get off telling Clarice I tried to run you over and trashed your apartment?" he said, full of piss and vinegar, looming over her as she sat on the cement bench.

"What are you talking about? I didn't tell Clarice that."

"She called me and told me you did."

Clarice again. Damn Clarice. Why didn't she mind her own business?

"I never told her any such thing," said Ashley. "Don't listen to Clarice. She's a gossipmonger. You can't believe a word she says."

"She said you told the cops I tried to run you over."

"I didn't say it was you. I couldn't see who did it."

"Then how come a cop keeps calling me demanding to talk to me? Some guy named Macready."

"He just wants to talk to you. That's all."

Where was Macready? she wondered. What was taking him so long? Maybe it *was* Ricky who had tried to run her over. And if he *had* been the one on the payphone, she didn't want to think about what he might do next. He didn't seem to care one bit he was surrounded by people in a courthouse. He always had a hot temper, and he was making no effort to keep it in check.

"Do you know how many times he's called me?" said Ricky, exasperated.

"Well, why don't you answer your phone and he won't call you anymore?"

"Because I want to discuss with you these accusations you're making about me before I talk to any cop."

"I told you, I didn't accuse you of anything."

"Clarice said—"

Ashley fetched a loud sigh. "Forget Clarice." She paused. "Were you the one that phoned me?"

"What? When?"

"The threat on the phone."

"There you go again making accusations against me."

"I'm asking, not accusing."

"Are you having one of your episodes?" he demanded, his voice strident.

Ashley groaned. "Now you sound like Clarice."

Behind Ricky she saw Bolo Tie striding down the corridor in her direction, his black eyes homing in on her like lasers. In his hand he held a silenced pistol, which he was raising and leveling at her.

She screamed.

"Give it to me," he said, his eyes wild. "The sketch you drew of me."

A shot rang out.

No. Not like this.

"I could've been killed," said Ricky, aghast, his eyes riveted to the body sprawled at his feet with a bloody chest.

Her heart stopped. Was she still alive?

Rubberneckers gathered around the bloody body crumpled on the floor.

I can't believe this is happening.

"Stand back," said Macready, charging up to them, his face hectic. "LAPD."

Holding up his Glock 17 he waved with his other hand for them to move away. The crowd backed off in shocked confusion.

"Are you hit?" he asked her.

Her heart was starting to beat again as she picked up on Bolo Tie's body splayed on the floor, the chest of his shirt saturated with blood.

"No," she said with relief.

"Now I recognize that guy," he said, casting a glance at the crumpled figure on the floor ten feet away, a silenced pistol lying beside his boot. "He calls himself 'El Glotón.' The Wolverine. He's a cartel *sicario*. He must have been at your trial listening to hear if Cuchillo ratted him out. Maybe he was there in the audience in order to intimidate Cuchillo into holding his tongue about him."

Ashley's cell chimed.

Still dumbfounded, she answered it.

"It's me, Ash."

Not Clarice again.

Beside herself, Ashley leapt to her feet and flung her cell across the hall.

An Unfortunate Little Habit

Quint went to the Authorcon in Fort Worth, Texas, not because he wanted to but because he had been told by other writers that appearing there would help boost sales of his thrillers, which inevitably ended up dying on the vine when they went on sale. In his late forties, having self-published for five years he was tired of the poor sales of his books.

At times he wondered if he didn't get any sales because he wasn't an academic. A lot of the authors at the convention were teachers, who moonlighted as writers. Quint had worked at FedEx in San Diego for ten years and had quit, using his savings to pursue a writing career.

During most of the convention he felt ill at ease, not sure what he was supposed to do.

When it was his turn to sign his book, he went to the capacious room where authors autographed their books for fans. He dutifully sat on the metal folding chair at his table, which abutted a series of other tables forming a straight line along one side of the room. A rectangular white piece of paper with his name on it in a Magic Marker's large black block letters had been folded in half lengthwise and tented on the tabletop in front of his chair, his name facing outward.

He took his seat behind the sign. And wished he was elsewhere, as he watched with envy other authors sitting at their tables signing autographs for long lines of adoring fans. Nobody waited in line for an autograph from Quint.

Feeling humiliated, fidgeting, he didn't plan on sitting at the table much longer. Fans were milling about the large room purchasing books from booksellers at tables set across from the autograph tables. He saw none of the fans so much as glance in his direction.

He drummed a tattoo on the tabletop, wondering how much longer he could stand sitting there behind his name, which branded him for everyone to see as The Writer Without Any Fans.

And then there was the writer at the adjoining table, who had a long queue of adoring fans clutching his book standing in front of him. He kept looking over at Quint and gloating, his face smug. Quint felt like dislocating the guy's jaw. Or was he imagining it? Why would the guy pay the least bit of attention to him?

The guy was better looking than him, too, decided Quint with resentment. Of average height with a receding hairline, Quint was growing a spare tire around his middle and would never be mistaken for a matinee idol.

He was an idiot to show up. It was an exercise in masochism.

He couldn't sit there any longer. It was too much. He felt like people were staring at him out of pity. He had to beat it.

He was preparing to get to his feet and get a drink at the bar when a blonde in her late twenties with large liquid hazel eyes walked up to him carrying a trade paperback clutched to her chest with both arms obscuring the book's title and author. Surprised to see anyone approach him, he sat back down on his chair.

Dressed in jeans and a white blouse with the top buttons unbuttoned, she wore her hair in a pageboy, a half inch of dark roots visible.

"Are you Riley Quint?" she said.

"I've been accused of worse," said Quint, wanting to shrink and disappear, feeling alone and naked at his assigned seat.

She looked puzzled.

"It was supposed to be a joke," he said.

"It would help if you had your picture on your book cover. Otherwise, we can't be sure it's you."

"The sign on the table—"

"Anybody could be sitting behind that sign."

She had a point, decided Quint. He could be one of the convention volunteers who happened to be taking a break for all anyone knew. That gave Quint an idea. Maybe he should pretend he was someone else. No. Why was he thinking such crazy, self-defeating thoughts?

"It really is me," said Quint, and offered an awkward smile. "Do you want to see my driver's license?"

She smiled. She had a bright smile with nice teeth. "I believe you."

After all, why would anyone pretend to be him, an unknown author who had penned ten self-published thrillers that nobody had ever heard of? he decided.

She unveiled the book in her arms and held it out to him.

Taken aback, he stared at it.

Had this woman actually read one of his thrillers? he wondered in disbelief.

He looked at the book's title. *Haywire*. About a psychotic serial killer and the female journalist Charmian who writes an article about one of his murders. Seeking his identity, she becomes his prey when he finds out what she is up to. She puts up a heroic fight as he stalks her in a deadly cat-and-mouse game, but in the end he murders her as a dozen cops shoot him in a hail of gunfire. The Kindle e-book was ranked number 9,800,000 and had no reviews on Amazon the last time he had looked.

"I read your book," she said.

"Oh, you're the one."

"I would like your autograph," she said, bending forward, smiling, revealing cleavage.

"My pleasure," he said, turning the book around and flipping it open so he could sign the front page as if he wasn't in the least surprised she had asked for his autograph. "What is your name?"

"Sondra."

"Nice to meet you, Sondra."

"I guess I got here just in time," she said, scoping out the other writers busy signing autographs sitting before long lines of fans.

"What do you mean?"

"I got here before the crush of autograph hounds formed at your table."

She had no idea she was the first and only fan who had sought his autograph, he decided with self-deprecating amusement. He wasn't going to disabuse her.

"Perfect timing," he said. "In fact, I was getting ready to leave and grab a bite to eat just as you showed up."

He scribbled his name on the title page.

"Then why don't we do lunch at the bar?" she said, leaning forward again and grasping his book with a coy smile.

"Uh, I have to meet with my agent." Which was a lie. He had no agent, but he wanted to sound important.

"Oh," she said, disappointed.

"But," he said, standing up, noticing the tightness of her jeans, "he can wait. Let's go."

They walked out of the cavernous, bustling room together.

"I can't imagine how exciting it must be being a famous novelist," she said, her hazel eyes getting dreamy.

"I can't either."

She eyed him with bafflement.

"Another one of my jokes," he said.

"I guess writers have a strange sense of humor."

They reached a pub and sat at its polished dark mahogany bar.

She made sure the countertop was clean and dry before laying his book down on it in front of her and arranging it just so.

"What's your poison?" he said.

She giggled. "I haven't heard that expression in a long time. You crime writers. Everything with you is poison and guns and knives."

"I guess we're obsessed with death."

He ordered a Guinness Black Lager from the thirtyish, swarthy bartender with a man bun.

Sondra placed her purse on the bar, withdrew a pillbox, opened it, took out two pale green pills, and placed them beside his book.

"A Michelob Ultra," she said, getting up. "I have to powder my nose."

She headed to the ladies' room, as the bartender retreated to fetch their drinks.

A five-nine guy with curly white hair and a short white beard, glasses with thick black plastic frames perched on his Roman nose, walked past her empty barstool and picked up on the pills.

"Getting the roofies out, huh, Quint?" he said.

It was the crime writer and ex-journalist Hudson Baker Quint had run into last night at the bar. Pushing sixty Baker was dressed in jeans and a peach polo. Quint figured the guy was three sheets to the wind. But with Baker it was hard to tell. The guy could hold his liquor, as Quint had discovered last night.

"Those aren't mine," said Quint, glancing at the pills Sondra had left behind.

"Then whose are they?"

"A fan I met at the book signing put them there."

"She goes to the bar with you and leaves two roofies at her seat? You expect me to believe that?"

"I don't care what you believe. It happens to be true."

"Now you're getting all touchy."

"How would you feel if somebody accused *you* of trying to date-rape someone?"

"I call 'em like I see 'em."

"How do you know those are roofies?" said Quint, eying the pills.

"I'm a writer. It's my business to know these things. Especially a crime writer when it comes to roofies. I thought you were a crime writer. How could you not know those are roofies?"

The big difference between Quint and Baker as writers was that Baker actually made money from his writing, decided Quint. He felt jealous of Baker.

"You have an overactive imagination," said Quint.

"Your date isn't the right woman to victimize," said Baker.

"Oh, yeah? How would you know? And who the hell said anything about victimizing her?"

Baker snickered. "That's Jack Cardiff's daughter."

"Jack Cardiff? Am I supposed to know who that is?"

"You should if you're a thriller writer. He's a crime boss in the Big D. Dallas's answer to Boston's Whitey Bulger. Cardiff controls narcotics' trafficking in these parts. And loansharking. And prostitution. He's got his hand in the till in everything illegal."

"What's he doing here?"

"I thought you'd never ask. He's promoting his new autobiography *My Way or the Graveyard.* I don't know how many guys he's had whacked." Baker laughed. "Maybe the answer's in his book."

"I don't want to know."

"I plan on buying a copy for research. I suggest you do the same. A crime writer needs to keep his writing chops up to date. You know what Hemingway used to say: writing is the one craft nobody can ever master. Or something like that. The guy was full of portentous-sounding bullshit."

Baker wiped his mouth with the back of his hand.

Quint shrugged. "Maybe I will."

Baker leaned toward Quint confidentially, giving Quint a whiff of whisky breath. "I'd walk out of this bar right now if I was you."

"It wouldn't be good business to walk out on a fan."

"I'm not talking about a business decision. I'm talking about a life-or-death decision."

The only person to want his autograph was the daughter of a trigger-happy crime boss, decided Quint with dismay. Maybe he was better off with no fans. Could it be true Sondra was Cardiff's daughter? Baker must be putting him on. Quint wasn't buying it.

"Is this your idea of a practical joke?" he said. "How naïve do you think I am?"

"Life is a bad joke, or haven't you woken up to that fact yet? Why do you think I drink?" said Baker, taking a swig of Quint's Guinness.

Quint gave him a dirty look.

"Thanks for sharing," said Baker.

"Do you know how hard it is to get fans in this business?" said Quint.

"In this country if you're not the best at your profession, you're nothing."

"When you say the best, you mean, make the most money."

"Damn straight. The two go together like peanut butter and jelly. The best gets the most shekels."

Baker commandeered the barstool beside Quint, almost sliding off it.

"You need to sleep it off," said Quint.

"What if I told you I would overlook those two roofies and not tell Jack Cardiff that you're trying to rape his daughter?"

"I'd say your sense of humor is wanting," said Quint.

"I'm not a greedy man. Um . . . I'd settle for twenty grand."

Quint laughed. He couldn't help himself. "Now I know you're plastered. Trying to blackmail me? Oh, sure. You honestly believe I have twenty grand on me? That's the first funny thing you've said all day."

"I really don't think you want Cardiff to find out about those roofies," said Baker, his face grave.

"The joke's over," said Quint, beginning to get nervous. "Maybe you better leave."

"Forearmed is forewarned," said Baker, standing up. "Or is it the other way around?" He paused, making a show of looking thoughtful. "You have one hour to pony up. Well?"

"You're soused to the gills."

"Well?"

"Well what?"

"Just pay me now and we're even."

"This isn't funny anymore." Quint waved good-bye at him. "Go and sleep it off."

"I'm warning you."

"That's enough," said Quint, turning away from him in disgust.

Baker staggered away.

Swiveling around on his barstool, Quint watched him leave. He couldn't make Baker out. Could the guy be on the level about telling Cardiff about the roofies? Quint hadn't left them on the counter in the first place. Sondra had. And were they really roofies, as Quint claimed? They could be anything. How many millions of different kinds of pills were there?

He heard rustling behind him and, turning around, saw that Sondra had returned to her seat.

He took a pull on his Guinness, trying without success to forget Baker had drunk from his mug.

"Did you miss me?" she said.

"I was beginning to think you stood me up."

"I wouldn't leave without getting my purse first. Why would I want to leave anyway? I'm doing lunch with my favorite author. It's not like that happens every day."

Quint found himself beginning to relax. Baker had disconcerted him. He was glad the guy was gone. What kind of a writer would threaten to blackmail a fellow writer? he wondered. He didn't know Baker that well. He had met him once at another authors' convention in Miami. If he never saw Baker again, it would be too soon.

Quint noticed that the two green pills on the countertop were gone. Sondra didn't mention them, so he kept his mouth shut.

"What were we talking about when I left?" said Sondra.

"I don't recall."

He took another pull on his Guinness.

"Is this where you ask me up to your room?" she said.

Quint raised his eyebrows in surprise.

"I . . . ," he trailed off.

"What if we do it differently? I'm a modern woman. What if I ask you up to my room instead? I have a room with a view."

"Sounds good."

That was the problem, decided Quint. It sounded too good to be true. Like a scene from a porno flick. A confirmed cynic, he didn't believe in good luck. Especially *his* good luck. Experience had taught him otherwise. Maybe he should lighten up and go with the flow.

He felt the beer going to his head. Puzzling. That never happened with half a bottle. Maybe it was because he hadn't eaten all day. Lightheaded, he stood up.

"Let's go," said Sondra.

Quint paid for their drinks.

Sondra led him to the elevator to her room.

He wheeled around, suspecting Jack Cardiff might be watching them. He didn't see Cardiff anywhere. Then again, he didn't know what Cardiff looked like. The guy was a local crime boss Quint knew only by reputation. Quint didn't see anyone watching him. Was Sondra really Cardiff's daughter? Or had Baker been pulling his leg? The whole episode with Baker had left him uneasy.

"What's wrong?" said Sondra.

"Nothing," said Quint, still not believing his good fortune at receiving an invitation to her room, as they entered the elevator.

The elevator hummed upward, came to a halt, and discharged them.

The corridor's maroon carpet seemed to be undulating like a running river as the elevator opened. He took a tentative step out, feeling seasick. Wobbling forward he couldn't find his sea legs. He didn't know if he was going to make it all the way to her room.

She led him down the hall to her door, dug her key card out of her purse, slipped it into the lock, which beeped, and let him in.

He staggered to her bed and passed out.

# # #

He woke up lying on his back on a strange bed. He stared up at a light fixture in the middle of the white stucco ceiling. His head ached. He tried to massage it with his hand and discovered his hand was cuffed to the bedstead's cast-iron leg. He tried his other hand. Same deal. Only it was cuffed to the bedstead's opposite leg. He looked down at his body. He was spread-eagled buck naked. His ankles had cuffs on them that secured them to the bedstead's leg nearest each of them.

A young blonde with her hair in a pageboy left the bathroom and approached his bed, naked save for her lacy lime bikini panties.

He felt his brain getting foggy. Her image blurred. The room started to spin. He shook his head to clear it.

"Are you into BDSM?" he said.

"No," she said.

"Then let me go. I'm not either."

"I don't want to let you go."

"A little foreplay first? Fine with me."

He wondered who the woman was. Was he supposed to know her? He got the feeling there were blanks in his memory. He didn't know how he had got here in this unknown blonde's room. He couldn't focus his thoughts, like a record player's needle that couldn't find the groove.

He was a writer who had gone to an authors' convention. He remembered that much. He must be at the convention. But how did he get up here in this room?

"You don't understand," she said.

He shook his head in puzzlement. "I guess not. Why don't you explain—after you release me first," he said, rattling the handcuff on his right wrist.

"That's not gonna happen."

"Look, this kind of thing doesn't turn me on," he said, discomfited. "Release me and then we can make out."

Make out? he wondered. With a total stranger? Why did he say that? He must know her.

She raised her hand, which was holding a razor blade between her thumb and forefinger.

He broke into a sweat. "None of that."

She held the razor in front of his face, where it caught the light and gleamed, flashing in his eye, sun-bright. He was having trouble concentrating.

He struggled to break free from his bonds. To no avail.

"Put that razor away," he said. "I'm not into BDSM. How many times do I have to tell you? It turns me off."

"I can see that," she said, glancing at his crotch. "And that's the way it should be."

"What the hell is this all about?" he said, feeling sweat bead above his upper lip.

"What do you think it's about?"

"This kind of thing turns you on?" he said, at a loss. "This is how you reward me for writing a book you like?"

Yes, he remembered that much. Now it was coming back. She was the fan who had asked for his autograph. They went to the bar together. His mind went blank after that. What happened after they were at the bar?

She thought about it. "What makes you think I liked your book?"

"You wanted me to autograph it for you, for Chrissake."

She turned around and walked away from him. "I did like it—until . . . ," she trailed off.

"Until?"

She slewed around in her high heels, her expression angry. "I liked it until you killed off my favorite character Charmian."

"I didn't enjoy killing her off. It's a thriller. People have to die by violence. The serial killer has to have victims."

"She was the hero."

"My thrillers are dark. They don't have happy endings. That's what makes my books so realistic. They could be called horror stories."

"I hate you for killing Charmian," she said, stalking toward him, her face twisted with rage.

Arriving at the bed she lifted the razor blade in front of her face and reached deliberately toward his eye.

He writhed in fear, trying to escape from his chains, his face working, sweat oozing from every pore.

"I'm gonna cut your eyelids off so my face and this razor are the last things you'll ever see, the way it looks now as I slice away at you, wreaking vengeance on you for Charmian's murder."

She was insane, he decided, his eyes wide, his heart pounding hell for leather. He had met his only fan, and she had turned out to be a bloodthirsty maniac.

"You'll never get away with this," he said, racking his brains trying to figure out a way to prevent her from maiming him. "There were witnesses at the bar. Somebody saw you with me before we left."

"There aren't any witnesses now."

"They saw you pick me up at the bar."

"Are you sure?"

His memory was fuzzy. He thought there had been witnesses. Wasn't he talking to someone at the bar about her? He couldn't remember. His mind wasn't functioning.

"Did you spike my drink?" he said. "I can't think straight."

She smiled. And that smile froze his blood.

"Flunitrazepam," she said.

He looked baffled.

Her next words brought his heart to a full stop.

"How did you know I'm gonna kill you after I cut off your eyelids?"

"What do you mean?" he managed to say with a dry throat.

"You mentioned witnesses. You must know I plan on killing you, which means you can't testify against me, and other witnesses will have to implicate me."

"That's not what I meant. I—I—don't believe you're gonna commit murder."

"Why not? You murdered Charmian. Why can't I murder you?"

"The story demanded it. She had to die. That doesn't mean I wanted her to die."

"My story demands you have to die," she said, edging the razor closer to his eye. "After I slice your eyelids off, I'm gonna slit your throat."

Her expression intent, she took practice swipes with the razor in front of his face.

"My book is a tragic thriller," he said. "It must conform to the rules of tragedy. Charmian had to be murdered."

"Now it's your turn to be murdered."

"You can't blame me for fate."

"Fate?"

"Fate had it in for Charmian."

"Fate didn't write the book. You did. You could have kept her alive, but you didn't. You killed her."

"I can't let my personal feelings get in the way of the dictates of the story. I liked Charmian, too. Like I said, my book is a tragedy. She had to die. Remember Thomas Hardy novels. The characters are all controlled by fate. Like Tess of the d'Urbervilles. No matter what the characters do, fate determines how they end up."

"I don't know any Thomas Hardy. This isn't about him. It's about you and your murder of Charmian. You're not gonna get away with blaming this on some guy named Hardy."

As though he could persuade a psycho with literary theory not to kill him, decided Quint, feeling like an idiot, sweating more profusely now, desperate to figure a way out. He doubted he could reach her with a discussion of belles-lettres.

"Nobody died," he said. "Charmian is an imaginary character. It all happened in your imagination."

"She was more real to me than anybody else in my life."

Ordinarily he would consider her comment a compliment, but in this instance it was his death sentence, decided Quint.

"Life is cruel," he said. "People die whether they're good or bad."

"It was you that killed her. Not life."

"Art mimics life. I need to make my stories realistic to make them believable."

"You're not getting out of this. *You* killed her. She was your creation, and *you* killed her."

She leaned closer to Quint and placed her razor blade at the top of his eyelid directly beneath his eyebrow, preparing to slice off the lid. Writhing on the bed, Quint darted his eyes around the room frantically, as he turned over plans of escape.

"Stop moving or I'll cut your eyeball," she said, holding the glinting razor over his eye, concentrating on beginning her cut. "You don't want to go blind, do you?"

"Wait. How do you know Charmian's dead?"

Sondra paused. "Because it's in your book. The psycho stalker killed her."

"Maybe she's really still alive. How do you know she's not gonna return in my next novel?"

Which was a lie, he decided. He had made no plans to resurrect Charmian. But his life was at stake. He would say anything to go on living.

Sondra thought about it then shook her head. "I don't believe you."

"You can't be sure till you read my next novel."

"Stop pretending you didn't kill her. I'm not gonna fall for your lies."

She inserted the razor's edge into his eyelid, drawing blood, which poured into Quint's eye, blinding him. He screamed in pain. She commenced sawing away at his eyelid, gripping and pulling his eyelashes stretching his lid with her fingers in one hand as she wielded the razor with the other.

The door burst open.

Starting, Sondra wheeled around, bloody razor in hand.

It was her father Jack Cardiff, all six menacing feet of him. A barrel-chested, fortyish man with a large head with greying temples, he stood in a black blazer framed in the doorway.

"Are you torturing another writer?" he said.

He stalked toward the bed, snagged a pillow, smashed it down on Quint's blood-streaked agonized face, and smothered him. Quint squirmed, trying to free himself.

"Why do I always end up cleaning up your messes?" said Cardiff.

"He tried to drop roofies in my drink and rape me," said Sondra.

"How could he rape you chained to this bed?" said Cardiff, continuing to press the pillow down on Quint's face suffocating him.

"I took his roofies at the bar so he couldn't spike my drink. I used them on him and cuffed him to the bed after he passed out."

"You said the same thing about that other writer you tortured at the Vegas writers' con last month."

"I can't help it if men want me."

Cardiff realized she was half naked.

"Get dressed," he said. "We need to get you out of here."

"I didn't want to get any of his blood on my clothes," she explained.

Quint stopped struggling under the pillow.

Sondra disappeared into the bathroom, shutting its door behind her.

The phone on the lacquered wooden nightstand rang.

Cardiff eyed it suspiciously. He decided to answer it. He lifted the handset, while he kept pressing the pillow against Quint's face with his other hand.

"Jack Cardiff? It's me Baker."

"What do you want?" said Cardiff, his voice gruff.

"Wasn't my intel about Quint's plan to date-rape your daughter worth twenty grand?"

"You got your money. Now bug off," said Cardiff, on the verge of hanging up.

"I think it's worth another ten large. What do you say?"

Cardiff squeezed the handset till his knuckles turned white, clenching his teeth. "Come on up to her room."

"You got it," said Baker, and hung up.

Cardiff cradled the handset and realized Quint wasn't struggling beneath the pillow anymore. Cardiff released the pillow, reached inside his blazer, and produced a nine mil SIG P220.

Sondra opened the bathroom door and walked out wearing a ruffled salmon chiffon minidress, white stockings, and shiny white patent-leather stiletto heels, smiling, holding the blood-smeared razor at her side dripping on the carpet.

"How do I look, Daddy?"

"Like a million bucks, honey," said Cardiff, returning her smile, remarking how much she resembled a child in her Little Bo Peep outfit with her beaming face.

She picked up on the semiautomatic in his hand. Her smile morphed into a pout of concern.

He ejected the SIG's magazine, checked to see that it was full, and, satisfied, slammed it back into the rod's butt. He racked the slide, jacking a round up the spout.

"I need to take care of some business before we leave," he said, waiting for Baker to show up. He paused, glancing at Quint's motionless body on the bed. "And then I think we need to pay another visit to your psychiatrist because one of these days

I'm not gonna be around to clean up your unfortunate little habit with writers."

Fever Pitch

Cindi Rockwell didn't know who was knocking on the door of her Manhattan Beach condo and would have been better off never knowing. All she knew was that her tabby cat Bungee didn't like them. Bungee scurried into the bedroom at the sound of the knocks.

It should have tipped Cindi off on the spot.

Bungee usually didn't run away from people at the door, decided Cindi. Wondering what was up, Cindi peeked through her condo door's peephole and saw two men standing in the hall. She didn't recognize either of them.

A former criminal investigator with a GS-13 pay grade in the US Marshals Service, Cindi tended to be suspicious of people. Pushing forty, she had learned through experience that individuals were capable of anything, even the most heinous crimes. She had personally dealt with some of these individuals when she had apprehended fugitives. Suspicion was second nature to her profession. Though she had to admit, these two looked harmless enough.

Wearing a black blazer, a cream button-down, jeans, and white sneakers, the older guy looked to be in his early thirties with dark hair and salt-and-pepper temples. He had a confident assurance about him that would put most people at ease, she decided. A used car salesman, perhaps.

His partner was some three inches shorter, had slicked black hair with a part in the middle, and a smooth round face with a pasty complexion that gave him a childish appearance. He wore jeans and a black Metallica T.

Cindi cracked the door, but didn't undo the chain lock.

"Hello," she said.

"Ms. Cindi Rockwell?" said the tall guy with an easy smile.

"Who wants to know?"

"I'm Douglas Merchant. You can call me Doug. And this is my brother Cal."

"Hello," said Cal with a cordial nod.

They didn't look like brothers, she decided. But then again they could have different mothers.

"And?" said Cindi, bracing the door with her toecap, in case they tried to barge in without permission.

Maybe she was paranoid. But it was part of her training as a US marshal. It had a become a reflex. She always prepared herself with a defensive maneuver whenever she met strangers. She had met a raft of thugs in her line of work transporting fugitives to jail.

"We have reason to believe you know where our brother Rex is," said Doug.

"I don't know anyone named Rex," she said.

"He had some troubles with the law. He tended to use an alias."

Doug seemed to be apologizing for his brother Rex with an embarrassed demeanor.

"I don't know anyone by the name of Rex Merchant," said Cindi.

"You may think you don't know him," said Doug. "And that's understandable, because he didn't get along with the law. A friend of ours told us you're a US marshal." Doug looked around the corridor apprehensively. "Could we talk inside? I don't want to wash our dirty laundry in public. My brother's the black sheep of the family. I'd feel better if we had some privacy."

"I don't work for the Marshals Service anymore."

"No need to explain."

"I wasn't offering to."

An uneasy silence fell between them.

"Will that be all?" she said.

"Can't you understand our dilemma? We haven't seen Rex in ten years. We want to know if he's OK. You're the only one we know that can help us. Do you have any idea what it's like not to see your brother in ten years? How do we know he's not dead?"

"I'd like to help, but I don't see how I can."

Doug neared the crack in the door and lowered his voice. "I don't want to endanger his life by talking about it out here. I don't want anyone else to overhear his new address. If we could just have a few minutes of your time—in private."

He seemed on the level, she decided. Maybe the quickest way to get rid of them would be by letting them inside and having their say. And, besides, she wanted to help them if she could. She could understand why they would be worried about their brother since they hadn't seen him in so long.

She undid the chain lock and let them in.

"We're grateful to you," said Doug.

"Have a seat on the couch," she said. "But I don't see how I can help."

"Rex is in the witness protection program," said Doug, sitting down. "We don't know what name he's going under or where he's living."

Cal sat beside him, looking mournful.

"That's for his own good," said Cindi, sidling toward a highboy whose top drawer had a Glock 22 .40 S&W cached in it.

She considered them harmless, but her training had taught her nobody was harmless.

"We found out at the USMS headquarters in downtown LA near city hall that you were the one in charge of putting Rex in the witness protection program," said Doug.

Cindi felt annoyed. What was headquarters doing revealing the names of people she had put in WITSEC? That intel should be confidential.

"That's a violation of protocol," she said. "Who told you this?"

"We can't reveal our sources. We're desperate to contact our brother."

Cindi thought about it. "I don't remember anyone named Rex being in the program."

"Maybe they changed his name before they handed him over to you."

"Possible."

"All we want to know is where Rex is hiding under an assumed name."

"I'm not allowed to divulge that information."

"Not even to his own kin?" pleaded Doug.

"He's flesh and blood," said Cal. "He's all that's left of our family. Our mom and dad died of the flu last month." He bowed his head. "May they rest in peace. We need to tell him. Don't you see?"

"I understand your problem and I find it touching," said Cindi, "but we take an oath of secrecy in the service never to reveal anyone's true identity or whereabouts in the program."

"His mom and dad died, Cindi," said Doug. "Our beloved parents. There must be extenuating circumstances in a case like this. And"—he paused for effect—"we promise not to tell anyone else where Rex is living."

"I'm not a US marshal anymore."

"Then your oath of secrecy with them is no longer valid."

"Actually, it is. It's valid for the rest of my life. I could go to the slam for a very long time if I violate it."

"Do you have any idea what we're going through? He could be dead for all we know. How do we know he's still alive, if you won't allow us to see him? He needs to know Mom and Dad died."

"I told you, I don't work there anymore. I don't know what your brother's situation is at this time."

"But you could find out."

She demurred. "Maybe."

"That's not good enough. We need to see him in the flesh." Doug paused. "I didn't want to bring this up, but there's a little matter of the will."

Cindi rested the crook of her arm on the highboy, her piece well within reach.

"Will?" she said.

"My father left a will with provisions for Rex, but he specified that Rex had to be present at the reading of the will in order to receive his share of it."

"I see," said Cindi, chewing it over. "You do understand his name was legally changed by the service, as part of witness protection protocol. The government even gave him a new Social Security number."

"That's why we need you to tell us where he is and what his new name is."

"But his new name wouldn't be mentioned in the will."

"Of course not. My father had no idea what Rex's new name is."

"Are you sure the will would be valid for Rex under his new legal name?"

"Rex Merchant is Rex Merchant no matter what name he's using now."

Rex Merchant, she was thinking. Now she remembered him. He was involved in a jewelry store heist, which had netted $20 million. He had avoided a jail term by ratting out the store owner, his ex-employer, for being a money launderer for narcoterrorists. Rex had justified his jewelry heist by claiming there was nothing wrong with robbing a crook. The owner had got ten years in the joint as a result of Rex's testimony. Fearing retaliation by the narcos, Rex had entered the witness protection program. If her memory served, only half of the loot was ever recovered. Rex had said he gave the other half to the money launderer to keep his mouth shut about Rex's involvement with the heist. The money launderer had denied it.

"I sympathize with you, but I can't reveal the name or whereabouts of anyone in WITSEC," said Cindi.

"Not even to his own brothers?" said Doug. "That's cruel and unusual punishment."

"There are no exceptions to the rules."

"But you don't work with the marshals anymore. You don't have to obey their rules."

"Like I already said, marshals are sworn to secrecy for the rest of their lives when it comes to witness protection."

"If you don't mind my asking, why did you leave the service?"

"I do mind," said Cindi, becoming defensive.

It was none of their business that the service had terminated her for a nervous breakdown, she decided.

"You're too young to have retired," said Doug.

"Maybe it's time for you two to leave."

"Which means you either quit or they shitcanned you. In either case, you can't be too happy about the way they treated you."

"It's none of your business. The door's over there," she said, pointing at it.

Doug stood up. The couch's springs squeaked at the shift in weight.

"You don't owe them a thing," he said. "There's bad blood between you. It's obvious. You can get back at them by telling us where Rex is. I promise we'll never tell another living soul you told us."

Cal stood up. He looked at her with a weird smile pasted on his boyish face.

"I can't help you," said Cindi.

"I'll let you think it over," said Doug, retreating toward the door.

"Once a marshal, always a marshal. It stays with you forever."

Doug lingered at the door. "He's our own flesh and blood. Can't you understand? What if it was *your* brother?"

"An oath is an oath."

"Blood is thicker than water. You've heard that saying, haven't you? It happens to be true. Blood is the only thing that really matters in this rotten meaningless world. You gotta help us."

"My hands are tied."

Doug opened the door. "I'll give you time to think it over. I'm sure you'll come around. You put on a good act that you're tough as nails. But I can see through you, Cindi Rockwell. You got a heart like the rest of us. And you'll do the right thing."

He nodded good-bye and walked out. Smiling at her with that off-kilter smile of his, Cal shrugged and followed him.

Cindi relaxed. She had no idea how wound up she was until they shut the door behind them. She strode over to it, locked the dead bolt, and breathed a sigh of relief.

Why was she so keyed up? she wondered. Nothing had happened. It was just an uncomfortable situation she would rather not have had to deal with. She wasn't a marshal anymore. Her career with the government was over.

Sure, she was angry at the service for firing her. She didn't think she had deserved it. She had some emotional issues and she went to a psychiatrist. So what was wrong with that? A lot of people went to shrinks. It wasn't a firing offense in other professions. But in the service you couldn't allow yourself to be seen as weak. Someone who had a breakdown had to be canned. Such a person couldn't be trusted to have the six of her fellow marshals. Such a person was unreliable. Such a person had to go. So she was told in no uncertain terms.

She supposed she could get back at the service for firing her by telling the Merchants where their brother was. And it *would* be the humane thing to do. But that wasn't her. She didn't nurse a grudge. As for being humane, she compartmented her life. She thought she was pretty successful at keeping her business life separate from her personal one.

She wanted to forget about the Merchants and their problems and move on.

She peeked out the peephole in the door. The carpeted hallway was empty. The two Merchants were gone.

She did feel sorry for them, she had to admit. She wasn't a machine. She had feelings.

But if Rex wanted to get in touch with his brothers, he could do it on his own without her help. Why did they have to go through her? Rex must have known where they lived and had their phone numbers. Was it her fault he hadn't called them? She wasn't responsible for anyone in the program after they entered it. What they did thereafter wasn't her concern. The only thing she was required to do was keep her mouth shut about any witness that had entered the program.

Bungee crept out of the bedroom, peeked around the corner of the doorjamb, made sure the coast was clear, and padded into the living room. His green eyes looked at her with curiosity.

"They're gone, Bungee."

Bungee meowed and rubbed against her leg.

###

The next morning she was awoken in bed by her chiming phone.

She blinked her eyes awake and snagged her cell from the nightstand.

"Hello?"

"Good morning," said Doug. "Have you decided to help us?"

"No. I told you I can't."

"I'm saddened to hear that."

"I have to obey the rules. I can't give you special treatment."

"I'm messaging you a video. I think you'll change your mind."

She had thought she was rid of these two characters. Nothing was going to change her mind. Didn't they realize that?

She was about to put her cell down when it beeped and vibrated. She opened the incoming message, which contained a video.

She played the video.

She bolted upright in bed, terror-stricken, not believing her eyes.

It was a video of her shooting a fortysomething woman with long, curly, dirty blonde hair in the head. The woman was sitting in a chair on the cement floor of a room that looked like a basement. When the bullet hit her forehead, her head snapped back and she went limp with her head lolling forward on her chest.

The blonde was dressed in a button-down white blouse, a modest navy blue skirt, and brown flats. She wore auburn plastic-framed glasses. When her head hung forward, they slid off her nose. A rope was tied around her stomach and the seat back, her wrists lashed behind her.

Cindi replayed the video.

The camera, which was placed behind the blonde and looking over her shoulder, showed her profile and Cindi's face clearly as Cindi aimed the automatic, squeezed the trigger, and fired. There could be no mistake. It was her.

But it wasn't her.

She hadn't shot anyone. Not totally true. She had been forced to defend herself and use her weapon on several occasions during her job. But she had never killed anyone.

This wasn't just a matter of killing someone. It was far worse. It was cold-blooded murder. Shooting a woman tied to a chair. It was a flat-out execution.

She had never seen that blonde in the video before. She had no memory of shooting her.

What the hell was going on? she wondered.

She replayed the video several times.

That couldn't be her in the video. It must have been someone that looked like her. Or maybe the video had been doctored.

She admitted she had had a nervous breakdown. She had a case of dissociative identity disorder and she experienced lapses in her memory. But she didn't go around committing murder in cold blood. That was the work of a homicidal sociopath. It had nothing to do with dissociative identity disorder.

They wanted her to believe she committed murder during her memory lapses?

No, this was all wrong. Even though the shooter looked just like her, it couldn't be her. It was an actress impersonating her.

Her cell phone vibrated and chimed in her hands. She dropped it on the bed in surprise. Frozen in terror, she watched it keep chiming. The caller wasn't going to hang up.

She decided to take the call.

"We tried being nice to you," said Doug, "and it got us nowhere. We thought you would do the decent thing and help two brothers seeking their lost brother. But you refused. How would you like this video to be sent to the US Marshals Service LA headquarters on Spring Street?"

Cindi gripped her cell in fury.

"Now listen to me and listen good," she said. "That's not me in this snuff video you shot. And you know it's not me. I never saw that woman tied to the chair before in my life. The service will never believe that's me doing the shooting."

"It *is* you, Cindi. We know your dirty little secret. You have multiple personalities. And one of them is a murderer."

"You expect me to believe this cock-and-bull story you dreamed up and this phony movie with an actress pretending to be me in it? How stupid do you think I am?"

"Seeing is believing. You blew away an innocent woman. The proof is on the video."

"I would never do such a thing."

"Your shrink would say otherwise."

"What? What are you saying about my psychiatrist? You have no idea who I'm seeing."

Silence on the line.

Which lasted an eternity, it seemed to her.

She was afraid Doug had hung up.

"Hello?" she said.

"We have a mole in the marshals headquarters. That's how we found out you were the one in charge of hiding our brother Rex. The name of your shrink is in their files on you."

"You're lying," she said, tentatively, not believing her words wholeheartedly but wishing they were true.

"Videos don't lie. Your committing homicide was caught on video. It's there for the entire world to see."

Cindi slumped her shoulders in despair. This couldn't be happening. And yet it was. She played the video again. She paused it when it gave the clearest view of her face. It was her. Even if it really wasn't her, the video said otherwise. How could you argue with a video recording?

"Videos can be doctored," she said. "You photoshopped it."

"You're in denial, Cindi. You have a split personality. Your other identity is a homicidal maniac."

"Lies. All lies."

"Do you think that's what headquarters will say when they see the video? I don't."

"What the hell do you want from me?" she said, fit to be tied, flushing with rage.

"You know full well what we want," said Doug in a maddeningly calm voice. "We want you to tell us where we can find our brother Rex."

"And that's why you shot this fake video?"

"It's not a fake video, and you know it. That's why you're scared out of your wits we'll show it to someone and they'll find out your terrible secret."

Cindi felt the walls closing in on her. She had to figure a way out of the Merchants' frame.

"They'll never believe this video when they see it downtown," she said.

"Seeing is believing, Cindi. Take your time and think about it. We don't want you to do anything rash. We'll give you one hour to make your decision. Take your time and think this through. We're sure you will come to the decision that your only choice in this matter is to agree to our terms. At that time, if you act like a fool and refuse to help us"—Doug sighed—"we'll be forced to send the video to the marshals. And . . ." His voice trailed off.

"And what?"

"And I hope you have the best lawyer money can buy if it comes to that."

Doug terminated the call.

Cindi was at sixes and sevens. She saw no way out of the Merchants' blackmail scheme. She had to destroy the video. Impossible. Doug must have had copies of it. How would she ever know if all of the copies had been destroyed? If she couldn't destroy it, she had to discredit it. That was her best move. But how?

She needed to get an expert to examine it to determine its authenticity. But that would involve implicating herself in a crime. The expert would see the video of her committing murder. But if he was an expert, he would see that the video had been doctored and he wouldn't believe that she had killed anyone. But what if he didn't see that it had been doctored? *He'd have to see it because she hadn't killed that woman.*

Lying on her bedcovers, her cell chimed.

She jumped at the sound. She didn't want to talk to Merchant anymore. She glanced at her wristwatch that lay on the nightstand. It hadn't been an hour since his previous call. Why would he be calling now?

She checked the caller ID on her cell. Private.

She took the call.

"Hi, Cindi. This is Dr. Blaise's office. We're calling to reconfirm your appointment with Dr. Blaise tomorrow at 10:00 a.m."

"Oh. Yes. Fine."

"Thank you," said the receptionist and hung up.

Her psychiatrist, decided Cindi. No problem. If she wasn't thrown in jail and given a life sentence for committing a murder she didn't commit, she'd be able to keep her appointment. Dr. Blaise was the least of her worries.

She racked her brains trying to figure out how to prove the video was phony.

She knew a professional photographer, Dan Symanko, who did freelance work for the Marshals Service authenticating photographs. Maybe she should get in touch with him and hire him on a personal basis. She was convinced he would be able to prove the video had been doctored.

Without the video, the Merchants had no hold over her.

But how in the world could she have Dan analyze the video within an hour? The Merchants would send it to headquarters if she didn't agree to their demands. There was something about those two brothers that rubbed her the wrong way. She couldn't put her finger on it. Just a feeling, she guessed. She had no doubt they would make good on their threat to send the video to headquarters if she refused to cooperate with them.

There was no resemblance between the two. Was that what bugged her? Two brothers that bore no resemblance. But the explanation was easy, as she had decided earlier. They must have had different mothers.

She was wasting time.

Cell in hand, she punched out Dan's name on her contact list.

Could she trust him to keep the video secret? she wondered. Hiring a complete stranger would make her even more anxious about the revelation of the video's contents. Her best bet was to go with Dan.

She called him. Still uncertain, she listened to her cell ringing on his end.

Of two minds, she was tempted to terminate the call before he picked up. Was this the right thing to do? The more people that saw the video, the worse it was for her. But Dan was a professional. He knew a fake video when he saw it. No doubt he would know right away the video of her had been doctored. So why was she worried?

What if it wasn't doctored? *Impossible*, she thought.

Still, she *did* experience memory blackouts. Could she have killed someone during one? A complete stranger, no less? That flew in the face of plausibility. Why would she tie up a stranger and blow her away?

Insane. It could not be true.

"Yeah?"

"Dan? This is Cindi Rockwell. I've got a favor to ask you."

Too late to turn back now, she decided.

"I heard you don't work for the marshals anymore," he said.

"This is a personal favor. Where are you?"

"In my office. I just got here. I'm on my cell."

"Great."

"You know my rates."

"Right. Could you examine a video for me and tell me if it's been doctored?"

"Sure. I could tell you in a couple of days."

Cindi tightened her grip on her cell. "That's too long. I need to know within an hour."

"An hour? Jeez. That's gonna cost you double."

"It's an emergency. I'll pay whatever you want."

Like she was rolling in money, she decided. *Ha.* Especially since the service had canned her. She would worry about it later.

"It depends on the quality of the doctoring," he said.

"What depends?"

"The amount of time it takes me to authenticate the video. If it's an obvious fake, I'll know right away. Otherwise . . . How fast can you get it to me?"

"I can e-mail you the video right now."

"Fine." He cleared his throat. "I don't want to get your hopes up. The quality of fakes these days can be exceptional. It could take a while for me to be sure one way or the other."

Cindi fetched a long sigh. Not what she wanted to hear.

"I don't think the guys that shot the video are pros," she said. "You can probably see it's a fake as soon as you watch it."

"All right. It's your money. Send it over."

She heard a snick and a drawer opening over the phone.

"What are you doing?" she said.

"If you must know, I'm reaching for a bottle of whisky I keep in my filing cabinet."

A short burst of laughter erupted from her. "The perks of being your own boss."

"Just a shot to warm me up. It jump-starts my batteries. I don't plan on getting stewed, if that's what you think."

"Of course not."

Did she really want to expose herself to Dan? she wondered, hesitating to attach the video to an e-mail and shoot it to him.

"Promise not to let anyone see this video," she said.

"No problem." He paused.

Was he suspicious? she wondered.

"Unless it's the recording of a crime," he said. "In which case, I would have to report it to the authorities."

Why did he have to say that? decided Cindi, agonizing over her decision to send Dan the video. Her index finger hovered above the Send button on her cell.

The video was fake. It had to be. Dan would be able to see it as a sham right off the bat. She had nothing to worry about.

Nevertheless, she ground her teeth, trying to make the right decision. She was in control. What she decided mattered. So what if she had been fired? So what if she had a shrink? She could still make her own decisions.

She pressed the Send button.

She heard a whooshing sound on her receiver.

"Got it," said Dan. "I'll get back to you as soon as I finish analyzing it."

He rang off.

Cindi felt the blood drain from her face. Had she done the right thing? She had opened herself up to being blackmailed by yet another person. Was she *that* paranoid? Dan did a lot of work for the LAPD as well as the marshals. He was on the up and up. He didn't go around blackmailing his clients. He would lose all of thcm if he did.

And the most important thing was the video was fake. He would see it for what it was right away.

To think that she would shoot a harmless, tied-up woman. No way, she decided.

But the blackouts. What had she done during the blackouts?

Nothing. She hadn't done anything. Which was why she couldn't remember doing anything. She had probably slept the entire time. But how could she be sure? Her memory was no help. Trust the video? The video showed her murdering a woman she had never met. She'd have to be a fool to trust a doctored video.

She got out of bed and paced around her bedroom in her nightgown.

Now was the hard part. She had to wait for Dan to get back to her. What was she supposed to do in the meantime? Grind her teeth flat? Bite her nails to the quick? Wear a beaten path in her rug with her pacing? Tear her hair out?

She got dressed instead.

What the hell was wrong with her? Why was she going to pieces because of a phony video?

She paced around some more. Bungee meowed at her feet. He wanted breakfast.

She told herself to chill out. Dan would call back soon and tell her the video was a sham. Or was he reporting her to the police even now after watching the video? She massaged her forehead. She was stressed out. Her mind was racing.

She consulted the electric clock on her nightstand. How much time had passed? What time had Merchant called her? She couldn't remember. Was the hour he gave her close to being up? Where was Dan? Why was he taking so long? He was better than that. Nobody was better at his job than Dan.

He was reporting her to the cops.

No.

She scoffed up her cell from her bed and fumbled it in her hands. She was tempted to call him to see what was what. Maybe she should tell him not to call the cops. Or had she already told him that?

She had to think about something else.

She walked to her bedroom's picture window and watched the sun rising, ladling out cold light on her beachside neighborhood. A tired fortysomething jogger in a navy blue tracksuit passed under the arching palms on the sidewalk in front of the lime stucco condo on the other side of the street, breathing with his mouth open. Behind him a twentyish woman in a cerise down jacket walked her two dachshunds on leather leashes on the buckling sidewalk.

It was just another day, Cindi told herself, trying to get her blood pressure down. She would solve the problem, and everything would be OK.

Her cell vibrated in her hand, sending an electric shock through her system.

Dan. It had to be Dan, she decided. Not Merchant. Please not Merchant. It had to be too soon for Merchant's call.

And what if it was Merchant?

Would she give him the intel he wanted about his brother Rex to prevent him from sending the video to the marshals? There was no way she was going to give out Rex's address and assumed name. She had taken an oath in the service never to reveal an address of anyone in the witness protection program. Even if they *had* fired her, she wasn't going to renege on her oath.

But revealing the info was for Rex's own good, she decided. He stood to benefit from an inheritance. Didn't that fact make it OK to reveal his address to his brothers? No. Her oath didn't provide for extenuating circumstances.

Her cell vibrated insistently in her hand, wrenching her out of her thoughts.

"Hello?" she said, raising the cell to her ear, wishing it really *was* just another day.

"Hi, Cindi. This is Dan—"

"You've got the proof?"

He cleared his throat. "I'm not gonna be able to determine the authenticity of the video in the time frame you wanted."

Cindi's heart missed a beat. "But it's obviously fake."

"That's the problem. It's *not* obvious. My analysis can't prove it's fake at this point. The video isn't blurry. Fakes are frequently blurry. And I checked the shadows. Shadows on fakes are out of true a lot of the time. The shadows in your video look like the real deal."

"That's impossible, Dan. Didn't you watch the video? It has to be doctored."

"I can't say for certain whether it's real or fake. I need to do more tests. If this video was doctored, it's a deepfake—"

"What the hell's a deepfake?"

"Deepfakes are almost impossible to distinguish from authentic videos."

"Is that possible?"

"Unfortunately, the answer to your question is yes. The technology exists today to create fake videos that are indistinguishable from the real McCoy."

Cindi gasped. Now what was she going to do?

"Dan, you know me," she said, lowering her voice and trying to sound restrained. "You know I wouldn't shoot someone in cold blood."

"I do, Cindi. But that doesn't alter the fact that I can't prove this video is fake. Maybe with more time I can—"

"I don't have more time."

"What? Why not?"

"Never mind."

She didn't want to tell him about the Merchant brothers.

"Are you in some kind of trouble, Cindi?"

Yeah. Sort of.

She didn't want to go into it with him.

"Who shot this video, Cindi?"

"I'll take care of it, Dan."

"I can't believe this is real. But I can't prove it's not. The AI these days can do anything. What they can create with it is as real as reality—even to the trained eye. It's downright scary is what it is."

"Whatever you do, don't let *anyone* see that video."

"I understand. I got your back. And I'm gonna keep working on this."

He terminated his call.

Cindi refused to stand around letting herself fall apart at the seams waiting for Merchant's call, which was hovering over her head like a guillotine blade primed to fall. There had to be a way out of this. All she had to do was find it.

She needed more pieces to the puzzle. Research. She decided to get on her laptop and research Rex Merchant. She didn't remember the case very well.

She found a newspaper article that covered Merchant's trial. She didn't find anything in the article that could help her out of her dilemma. She did further hunting and looked up Merchant's father, whose first name turned out to be Nathan. He had passed away last month, as Rex's brothers had told her. He had been a professional electrician.

The obit didn't say anything about his having married twice, failing to explain the dissimilar-looking brothers Doug and Cal. She read to the end of the obit. Nathan had only two survivors. Rex and his sister Lisa.

Cindi started. The two strangers that had accosted her weren't Merchants after all.

They were running a scam. They had tried to pull the wool over her eyes about their true intentions. Who were they really and why did they want Rex's address? she wondered.

She heard a rap on the door and all but jumped out of her seat, her nerves wired tight as catgut on a tennis racket.

She bolted to the door and peered through the peephole. Doug and Cal stood in the corridor outside her door. Pretending not to be present, she decided not to acknowledge them.

"We know you're there," said a smothered voice behind the door. "We heard your floor creak."

She stole away from the door to her highboy keeping mum and wondered how far they would go if they called her bluff.

She didn't have long to find out.

The door exploded in its frame, splintering the jamb as it flew open under the impact of Doug's kick.

Standing beside the highboy she could reach her Glock if she had to. Eyes wide with apprehension, she watched Doug and Cal enter her room. She dissimulated her fear as soon as she realized what was happening. She knew these two thugs could smell fear. They had to be thugs. There was no other possible explanation.

"I thought so," said Doug, seeing her. "Your pretending not to be home isn't gonna stop us from getting your intel."

"I suggest you walk right out of here before I call the cops," she said, trying to sound resolute, her expression grim.

"We're not going anywhere without your intel. Remember our deal? Where's Rex living?"

"I didn't make any deal."

"Do I take that to mean you're not gonna cooperate with us? That I should send the video to the marshals?"

Cal kept watching her with his weird smile slanting his chubby boyish face, creeping her out.

"I did some research," she said. "This is a scam. Rex Merchant didn't have any brothers."

Doug exchanged glances with Cal.

Doug returned his gaze to Cindi, shrugging.

"We tried doing this the easy way with you," he said. "I guess you want it the hard way."

"Who are you?" said Cindi.

Cal retreated toward the open door, looking almost sheepish, and deliberately shut it to prevent anyone in the corridor from seeing them.

Cindi's heart was beating like crazy, her palms sweaty. She wondered if it was time to reach for her piece.

"Who are you?" she repeated.

"We may not be Rex's brothers by blood, but we *are* his brothers in crime, shall we say," said Doug. "We were in on the jewelry heist and we want to know where he stashed our loot."

"He was supposed to tell us after the trial, but he vanished into thin air," said Cal.

Even his voice sounded boyish, decided Cindi, but mean, nonetheless.

"We couldn't find him for years," said Doug. "We did, however, find out it was you that placed him in the witness protection program." He paused a beat. "Do you really want us to send the video to the marshals? Somehow, I don't think you do. We tried doing it the easy way, the nice way. But don't kid yourself. We can do it the other way, no sweat."

Still sporting his wacky smile, his eyes on Cindi, Cal nonchalantly withdrew a switchblade out of his trouser pocket and flicked it open.

"Why did you even bother with that stupid video?" said Cindi, her tension mounting, if that was possible.

"Because we're nice guys," said Doug. "We thought you would be reasonable and make the correct decision. Believe it or not, we really don't like being mean."

Cindi didn't believe a word of it. They liked seeing her squirm was what it was, liked playing with her. Two cats tormenting a mouse. She wasn't going to give them the satisfaction.

"I'm giving you ten seconds to beat it," she said.

"Not without Rex's address."

"Don't try me."

"Cal can do things with a knife you wouldn't believe. He's a regular Picasso. It's something you don't want to find out. He can flense you while you're still living. Do you know what the word *flense* means?"

"Do you know what the words *get out of here* mean?"

Doug withdrew his cell phone from his trouser pocket. The screen came to life when it ID'd his face. He tapped and swiped the screen a few times.

"I'm all set to send the video to the marshals," he said, holding up his cell. "It's up to you. Give me Rex's address and I'll delete the video on the spot."

"Nothing's changed," she said, refusing to submit to his threats. "I'm not giving you his address."

She had a duty to protect everyone she placed in WITSEC by keeping their new address and name confidential. There were no exceptions. She would not dishonor her profession by shirking her duty.

"Then you'll spend the rest of your life behind bars," said Doug.

"The video is fake."

"Actually, it's genuine. And you know it."

What was he trying to pull? she wondered.

"I *know* it's fake," she said.

"I have the original. I gave you a copy. The original has a date and time stamp on it, proving it's authentic. It was recorded by a security company's CCTV. You shot your ex-supervisor at the Marshals Service for firing you. We recovered the video at her house."

"Impossible," she said, contorting her face.

"I can't say that I blame you. She had it coming."

She shook her head. "You're gaslighting me. I have news for you. It's not working."

"As I see it, you have three options. Of which the easiest one is to give me Rex's address. Or, two, I send the video to the marshals. Or, three, Cal flenses you where you stand with his switchblade until you howl with pain as he peels your skin off inch by inch with infinite care and deliberation making sure it hurts as much as possible until you start singing like a canary. Which is it?"

Her mind was flying again, trying to come up with a solution. Her thoughts were a jumbled whirl as though caught in a spinning washing machine. She had to pull herself together. There was only one solution—and Doug hadn't enumerated it.

She reached into her highboy's drawer, whipped out her Glock, aimed for Cal's upper body mass, and fired a round. The .40 S&W slug slammed into his chest, jerking him back. He wasn't smiling anymore, his legs folding under him. She shot Doug in the forehead, knowing she had to inflict instant death giving him no chance to tap his cell and e-mail the incriminating deepfake video to the marshals.

The two thugs sprawled on her carpet, one of them still bleeding. Cal. His black T glistening with blood. His eerie smile nothing more than a memory.

Doug's fingers weren't moving, his hand empty. His cell had fallen out of his grasp and now lay on the carpet.

The question was, had he had time to fire off the e-mail?

Somebody knocked on the door.

The gunshots, she realized.

"This is the LAPD."

So fast? she wondered, her heart in her mouth. How could that be?

"Come in," she managed to squawk through a tight throat, the acrid tang of gunpowder in the air. "It's open."

She heard muttering outside the door.

The door burst open.

She didn't see anybody in the doorway.

Someone peeked around the doorjamb, a pistol in his hand trained at her. He was wearing a black uniform.

"Put the gun down," he said.

She realized she was still holding her Glock. She tossed it down.

Two uniformed cops appeared in the doorway, a thirtyish brown-eyed narrow-hipped brunette woman with short hair, hawklike eyes, and no makeup, and a man about the same age with a flattop and a cleft lip, which was currently pulled back in a sneer, their guns drawn.

"It was self-defense," said Cindi.

They kept their guns trained on her.

She couldn't understand how they had gotten here so fast. Even if her neighbors had reported the gunshots as soon as they had heard them, the cops couldn't have gotten here by now. Maybe their cruiser was in the area.

The cops scoped out the bodies on the carpet.

The woman got down on her haunches and felt for pulses in their necks, while the man kept his service pistol trained on Cindi.

"They assaulted me," said Cindi.

The female officer straightened up, shaking her head at her partner.

"Too late for EMTs, Theo," she said.

Cindi saw movement behind them. Somebody was entering her apartment from the hallway, his face shielded from view.

"You're under arrest for murder," said Theo.

Cindi couldn't believe her ears. "They tried to kill me. See that shiv on the floor? It was that guy Cal's," she said, pointing at his stiff.

The female cop noticed Doug's trouser leg was bunched up at his ankle revealing something on his calf. Leaning forward she pulled the trouser leg up high enough to expose a Ruger handgun snugged in a Velcro ankle holster strapped to his leg.

"These guys came loaded for bear," she said, straightening up.

"I told you," said Cindi. "You can put that gun down," she told Theo.

"No, I can't. You're under arrest for murder."

"Murder?" said Cindi, taken aback. "I was defending myself from those two jewel thieves. Check their hot sheets. They're both crooks."

"You're under arrest for the murder of Noreen Murphy."

Cindi stood nonplussed. She couldn't make her mouth move.

The guy behind Theo ghosted into view.

Dan. A shade under five ten, middle-aged, he had tousled chestnut hair, the beginnings of a potbelly, and wore rimless glasses, whose filmy lenses looked like they hadn't been cleaned in months.

"I showed them that video you sent me, Cindi," he said, adjusting his glasses on the bridge of his nose, as if trying to hide his face from her in embarrassment, his head slightly cocked. "I had to. It's authentic. I couldn't let you get away with murder."

"I trusted you."

She was there, but she wasn't there. She didn't know how else to explain it.

"Cindi, you need help."

Cindi looked blank. "Who's Noreen Murphy?"

"Your victim in the video."

"I don't know her."

Dan began to assert himself, standing straighter.

"You can quit the playacting," he said. "She was your supervisor at the service. The Supervisory Deputy US Marshal, to be exact. The one who canned you. I can understand why you would be furious with her. The rage you must have felt. After I watched the video of you and her I decided to check on Murphy. She hadn't reported to her office. I drove to her bungalow in Santa Monica. There wasn't any traffic at that hour. I was there in twenty minutes. She didn't open the door, but it wasn't locked."

Cindi wobbled, feeling her legs turn to rubber. She couldn't believe any of this was happening.

"The video is fake," she said, her voice sounding detached.

"I didn't like the feel of it," Dan went on. "Something was wrong in her house. Call it a sixth sense, but I knew something hinky had happened inside. I entered her house, calling out her name. *Noreen Murphy. Noreen Murphy.* Nobody answered. I couldn't find her anywhere. Finally, I went downstairs and found her body in the basement, a bullet hole the size of a tennis ball in the back of her skull."

"I trusted you with the video, Dan. How could you?"

"It's evidence of a murder. I could go to jail for withholding evidence."

"Fake evidence," she said, her voice flat. "Fake."

She didn't know what was keeping her upright. Her world was tumbling down around her. If she couldn't find something to hold onto, she was sure she would collapse. The only two people that could testify the video was fake were its makers and they lay dead at her feet.

Theo clamped flex cuffs to her wrists behind her back and led her away.

The last thing she heard as she left the room was Bungee's forlorn wail.

Cyberstalker

The son of a hooker and a john, whose identity remained a mystery to him, Kyle grew up proud and disdained—proud as a means of self-defense against the disdain of others. His single mother Patti never told him the name of his father. Perhaps, because she didn't know it.

Not that Kyle cared what the guy's name was. The guy was a creep who had abandoned them. Why did Kyle want to waste his time caring about a bum?

All of twenty, Kyle liked girls, but found out the hard way they didn't like him. The ones he asked out rejected and humiliated him. Infuriated, he found solace in a group of incels on the Internet. Many of them belonged to QAnon, a conspiracy theory group.

Kyle met one of the members by the name of Ron at a Burger King in Culver City. Short and thin with a hatchet face and a chalky complexion, Ron wore thick black plastic-framed spectacles over his beady black eyes. He wore grey slacks and a white button-down with thin blue vertical stripes.

"The important thing is to get back at them, if they reject you," said Ron, sitting opposite Kyle. "You have to make them pay for it. You can't let them get away with it. They trashed you by rejecting you. Now it's your turn to trash them."

"But how?" said Kyle, and sipped his Coke.

Ron munched on an onion ring, warming to the subject.

"Any way you want," he said, "but it's got to put them in their place. Show them who's boss. You're telling them they're not worthy of you, and you only asked them out because you felt sorry for them for being such ugly losers. Tell them that or something like it. You gotta make them pay."

"Mess them up bad. I agree."

"When they reject you they want you to feel so bad about yourself that you'll kill yourself."

"You think?"

"I know. You gotta be tough with them or they'll walk all over you. They'll spread rumors about you to their friends if they see you as being weak."

"How do *you* get back at them?"

"Me? A girl named Linda fucked me over once. I FedExed her a dead rat. The thing was as big as a tomcat. I pried its mouth open with toothpicks to make sure she saw its monster teeth. I never had any trouble with her spreading rumors about me after that. She moved, and I never saw her again. You have to get back at them. Always attack. Otherwise, girls they're always talking. They'll spread rumors that you're a putz or goofy or something bad about you. Then everyone will think you're a jerk."

"That's how they operate, all right."

"You gotta be clever, though. You can't just swear at them and call them whores or something. That's too obvious, and, actually, they expect it. I think they sort of want that. It proves they hurt you. It has to be worse than that. Something they don't expect but hurts them big time."

Food for thought, decided Kyle.

He lowered his voice. "Did you ever whack a girl?"

Ron gave him a look. "You have potential."

Kyle didn't know what Ron meant. Potential for what?

"You know what the problem is?" said Ron. "A lot of girls are raped before their teens. And they take it out on guys who ask them out."

"That so?"

"If not by their father, then by a close relative."

"Hmm."

"And don't forget the pedo rings run by white slavers, you know. The multibillionaire geezers that run the world also run pedo rings so they can buy any girl they want because they know girls are crazy about money. Like that Epstein perv that supposedly hanged himself in his jail cell. Epstein was different because he got caught. Most of them never get caught. They can buy their way out of any problem. And they want 'em young while they got their cherries. The pedos wreck it for the rest of us. They're completely corrupt, and they corrupt the world and everyone in it. They control everybody. You know that movie *The Blob*?"

"Yeah. Steve McQueen."

"Their sleaze is like the Blob. It covers and corrupts everyone with slime. Once that slime is on you, you can never get it off." Ron paused. "But their day is coming."

"How?"

"With their cabal ruling us, we're heading for an apocalypse. The billionaire pedo ringleaders are going down. And they're gonna take us down with them."

"What can we do?"

"Know the truth about them. That's all we can do."

"Bummer."

"It's up to us. We at QAnon are the only ones that know the truth." Ron stood up. "I gotta run. There's a new sci-fi series on Netflix I wanna see. *Devos* or something. WWG1WGA."

"Same to you."

The best idea would be to swear off women, decided Kyle, watching Ron leave. They were more trouble than they were worth.

Kyle drove his old rusted white VW Bug back home. He hoped his mother wasn't turning tricks. He didn't want to have to listen to all the grunts and groans coming out of her bedroom.

Driving down his home street, he spotted a black Toyota Camry parked on his asphalt driveway.

Bad sign, he decided. Probably a trick paying her a visit.

Kyle debated whether to pull in behind the Camry.

As he was making up his mind, his mother appeared in the doorway, smiling.

"Kyle," she said, waving to him to come in.

If she had a john with her, she wouldn't be delighted to see him. Kyle parked behind the Camry and approached her.

"Come on in," she said. "I want you to meet my cousin Natalie Bayer."

Kyle entered the living room after her, not especially eager to meet Natalie. He was expecting a woman his mother's age. When he saw a good-looking brunette in her twenties, he stopped dead in his tracks, struck by her beauty.

"You never told me we had a cousin," Kyle told Patti.

"I lost track of her," said Patti. "I haven't seen her in years."

"You never told me about your son," said Natalie.

"Didn't I?" said Patti. "We haven't seen each other in so long, I can't remember what we talked about. How did you ever find me?"

"I have my ways."

Kyle felt an attraction when he eyed Natalie with her full head of raven hair, her large sparkling blue eyes, her turquoise miniskirt, and shapely figure. As he gazed into her eyes he felt as if he and she were somehow communicating.

"Nice to meet you," said Natalie.

"Same here," said Kyle.

"I've never been to Culver City," she told Patti. "I'm glad I didn't get lost. You know me. I have epilepsy, and I can get disoriented sometimes. If I don't know exactly where I'm going, I can end up lost."

"You were here when you were younger," said Patti. "I bet your subconscious remembered the way."

Natalie shook her head no. "I don't recall."

"Anyway, you made it here safe and sound. That's what counts."

Patti went over and hugged Natalie.

Kyle wasn't a big fan of hugs. Hugs he could do without, he decided. His eyes lingered on Natalie.

"Want me to show you around town?" he said with a smile.

"Oh, no. My boyfriend wouldn't like that. I really can't stay long."

Boyfriend? wondered Kyle. Who said anything about a boyfriend? What's her boyfriend got to do with driving around town?

"Maybe some other time," said Patti, noticing his discomfort. She turned to Natalie. "Let's go to the kitchen and grab a bite to eat."

Watching them leave the living room, balling his fists at his sides, Kyle wanted to explode. He knew he should have sworn off women. This was what he got for not taking his own advice.

His initial impulse was to chase her and scream at her that she was a whore running around in a microskirt. But he recalled his conversation with Ron, who said that was what they wanted you to do, proving they had hurt you. It was difficult, but Kyle managed to bridle the impulse.

The fury bottled up inside him needed an outlet—one way or another.

He stormed out of the house, sprinted to his car, climbed into the driver's seat, fired the engine, and backed out of the driveway, almost crashing into a passing SUV whose middle-aged driver honked irately at him. Kyle honked back at him, his eyes bugging out. The guy must have thought Kyle was nuts or on dope and beat it, his tires shrieking.

Parked in the driveway, Kyle told himself to calm down. It was a bad idea to go driving around town jacked up with rage. He couldn't let Natalie get away with it. He had to get back at her, like Ron had said. Somehow.

Kyle took deep breaths to slow his heartbeat and lower his blood pressure.

Feeling calmer he backed into the street, making sure no cars were approaching, and drove away. He hoped driving would calm him down. On the other hand, it could lead to road rage.

Epilepsy, Kyle decided. What did Natalie mean when she said she had it? Was that why her eyes were so big and luminous, as if lit with electricity? He had heard of epilepsy, but he didn't know much about it. Whatever it was, it wasn't an excuse for her to trash him. She had no excuses.

He pulled into a liquor store parking lot, withdrew his cell phone from his trouser pocket, and consulted a dictionary app. He typed *epilepsy* into the search bar.

# # #

Natalie drove back to her motel room, which she shared with a friend of hers named Susan. Susan had long straight dark hair that went halfway down her back. Of average height, she had a plain face with brown eyes and full lips. She had a determined demeanor, which some found off-putting. She was a graduate student at UC Riverside working on her MBA.

Even though Natalie had no interest in economics, they hit it off. They had met at UCR, where Natalie was pursuing a degree in fine arts.

They had decided to share a motel room and stay overnight in Culver City, where Natalie could visit Patti, and Susan could visit a friend of hers who lived in the vicinity.

"How did it go?" said Susan, as Natalie entered their motel room, a chilled can of diet ginger ale in her hand.

"Awkward," said Natalie.

"That's not surprising. You haven't seen each other in such a long time you were both uncomfortable."

Natalie plunked down in front of the laptop they shared that lay on the desk that faced the window. Susan's Macbook Air needed repairs and was at Apple's Genius Bar. Natalie was kind enough to let Susan share her laptop with her. Apple took weeks to repair Macs because of the long lines at their store. Susan didn't know how long she would be without a computer.

Natalie popped open her cold soda and took a drink. Cars streamed by on the Culver City thoroughfare skirting the motel.

"Checking your e-mails?" said Susan.

"Mostly I get spam, but if I don't get rid of it right away, I'll end up with hundreds of e-mails I'll have to sort through."

"Are you going back to see her?"

"I dunno," said Natalie, examining her score of e-mails on the laptop screen. "I don't know how to act when I'm with her. It's very uncomfortable for me. I think it's uncomfortable for her, too, but she doesn't show it."

"Is this one of those strained relationships?"

"Honestly, she seemed glad to see me."

"We're in town for another day. You might as well see her again."

"I don't know what I'm supposed to say," said Natalie, breaking away from her e-mails and stealing a glance at Susan.

"Just make small talk, like anyone else."

"You don't know her profession."

"What's that got to do with anything?"

"A lot," said Natalie, but didn't go into details.

"I don't get it. I don't care what someone's profession is. Why should that matter?"

Natalie resumed reading her e-mails. "You have no idea what it's like. You're better off not knowing."

"I don't want to tell you how to live your life, but I think you should see her again while you're in town."

Susan disappeared into the bathroom and took a shower.

Natalie opened an e-mail from someone whose name she didn't recognize. She was tempted to delete it, but it might be important. It didn't look like typical spam.

"Have you made up your mind?" said Susan, finished in the bathroom and backing out of its doorway, taking one last look at her face's reflection in the mirror over the sink and prinking her hair.

Natalie didn't respond.

When Susan turned around she saw Natalie sitting frozen in front of her laptop, whose screen had gone black.

"Natalie, are you OK?" said Susan.

Natalie continued sitting motionless, her eyes staring blankly.

Concerned, Susan approached her. "You're scaring me."

Susan shook Natalie's shoulder, trying to get her to react.

Startling Susan, Natalie began shaking her arms and legs uncontrollably. Natalie shook so violently she fell off the chair onto her back on the carpet. She was having trouble breathing.

Susan didn't know what to do.

Terrified, she retrieved her cell phone and called 911.

"What is the nature of your emergency?" said the female dispatcher.

"My friend passed out."

"What was she doing at the time?"

"She was sitting in front of her laptop."

"And what happened?"

"She was sitting paralyzed in front of the laptop. Then she started shaking her arms and legs uncontrollably and fell off the chair onto the floor."

"Is she breathing OK?"

Susan stared at Natalie's face. "I don't think so. Her face is turning blue."

"See if you can pry open her mouth."

Susan hunkered down beside Natalie's head. Natalie stopped thrashing her limbs. Susan tried to open Natalie's mouth, but her jaw was locked.

"I can't get it open," said Susan.

"Give me your address and I'll send help."

Susan had to look up the motel's address. She gave it to the dispatcher.

"How long will it take you to get here?" said Susan.

"They'll get there as fast as they can."

"She's not gonna last much longer," said Susan, eying Natalie's wan face with apprehension.

"They'll do their best to get there in time."

"Please hurry."

Twenty minutes later, two EMTs in navy blue uniforms arrived and found Natalie unresponsive. Unable to detect a pulse, they declared her dead.

"I don't understand," said Susan, sobbing. "She was totally healthy a few minutes ago. What happened to her?"

"Looks like she had a seizure," said the thickset thirtysomething EMT with unruly black hair, who looked to be in charge. "The ME will have to determine the exact cause of death. Do you know what she was doing before she died?"

"She was sitting in front of her computer when I took a shower. When I came out she was paralyzed."

"She looks . . . Do you know if she had epilepsy?"
"That's right. She told me she did."
The EMT nodded. "She could've had an epileptic seizure. SUDEP. But I'm just guessing. The coroner will know for sure."
"SUDEP?"
"Sudden unexpected death in epilepsy."
"I can't believe this. She was so young."
"It can happen at any age, young or old."
The EMTs left to retrieve a gurney from their ambulance.

###

Susan brooded over Natalie's death for hours after the EMTs departed with the cadaver strapped to their gurney. It felt wrong to her. Susan didn't want to call the cops because she figured they wouldn't help. After all, there wasn't any smoking gun to indicate a murder had taken place.

Still, Natalie's premature death struck her as wrong. Natalie was so full of life. How could she just drop dead? Something must have happened at Patti's house that brought this on, Susan decided. She had no idea what, but she couldn't accept Natalie's death as natural. How could sitting at a computer make you die? It made no sense.

At last, she decided to summon the help of the Internet private detective Scott Brody, whose ad said he saved on overhead by not renting an office and therefore could charge his clients reasonable rates.

A big guy with cropped hair, Brody arrived at her hotel room around suppertime, wearing a dark blazer, a grey T-shirt, and jeans.

"I'm glad you agreed to hear me out," said Susan, letting him in.

"You piqued my interest when you mentioned epilepsy over the phone," said Brody.

"Do you want something to drink?"

"Water's fine."

Susan returned with two glasses of water from the bathroom and handed him one.

They sat on recliners opposite each other.

"The EMTs said Natalie died from SUDEP," said Susan. "Sudden—"

"I know what it is. The reason I'm interested in your case is because I'm an epileptic like your friend Natalie. What was Natalie doing when she had her seizure?"

"She was at her laptop."

"Doing what?"

Susan thought about it. "She said she was reading her e-mails."

"Who does she have her e-mail account with?"

"Uh—Gmail."

Brody noticed the open laptop on the desk. He got up, sat down at the desk, and tried to boot up the laptop.

"It's password protected," he said.

"I know. We share it."

Susan stood up, walked to the laptop, typed in the password, and returned to her seat.

Brody accessed Natalie's Gmail account.

"What are you looking for?" said Susan.

"You said she was reading her e-mails when she had her seizure. I'm wondering if something she read triggered her seizure."

"Is that possible? Can an e-mail trigger a seizure?"

"Maybe she got some really bad news that upset her."

Brody read through Natalie's open e-mails. She wouldn't have had a chance to delete the offending e-mail—if there was one. Her seizure would have debilitated her.

"Are you finding anything?" said Susan.

Brody didn't answer. He was staring at the laptop screen as if mesmerized.

"Oh, no. Not again," said Susan.

She bolted from her seat, grabbed Brody's shoulders, and tried to shake him out of his trance. She held her hands in front of his eyes so he couldn't see the computer screen.

Brody came out of his trance. "What happened?"

"You looked like you were paralyzed while you were reading the e-mails."

Brody couldn't see the screen on account of Susan's hands blocking his view of it. He got to his feet and walked around the room, getting his circulation going, clearing his head.

"What's on the screen?" he said, without looking at it.

"I don't want to look at it if it's causing everyone to have a seizure," said Susan, turning away from the laptop.

"It might be just certain people that are affected."

"I don't want to take that risk. Natalie's e-mails paralyzed both of you. Why wouldn't they paralyze me?"

"I need to know what's in that e-mail."

"Can't you remember?"

Brody shook his head no. "My mind's a blank."

"This is spooky."

"There's a reasonable explanation for this. This isn't a horror movie where everyone who looks at a possessed computer screen dies. Just read the e-mail to me."

"Easy for you to say."

"Maybe it only affects epileptics. Are you epileptic?"

"No."

"But Natalie was. And so am I."

"The operative word is *maybe*. You said *maybe*," said Susan, vacillating.

"If anything happens to you, I'll run over to you and cover your eyes so you can't see the screen."

Susan chewed it over. "All right."

Circumspectly, she turned around to glimpse the laptop screen out of the corner of her eye.

Shielding his eyes from the screen with his hand, Brody watched her.

"How do you feel?" he said.

"OK," she said, her voice tentative.

"What do you see on the screen?"

"An e-mail."

"What's it say?"

"I hate you, Natalie. You're a PT. I'm killing you. What's it feel like to die?"

"Somebody was cyberstalking her."

"You're scaring me."

"Is that all the e-mail says?"

"There's a GIF."

"What kind of GIF?"

"Some kind of stroboscope or something. There are a lot of flashing lights."

Brody nodded in understanding. "Who sent the e-mail?"

"Kyle666. Whoever that is."

"You don't know him?"

"Must be someone Natalie knew."

"All right. Close the laptop's window," said Brody, avoiding looking at the laptop screen.

"Why? I don't understand."

"Just close it. I'll explain."

Susan closed the screen's window.

Brody lowered his hand shielding his eyes and looked at the blank screen.

"I believe I know what happened to Natalie," he said. "Kyle666 murdered her remotely."

Susan gasped. "I knew something wasn't right. I could feel it. But how?"

"You said there was a GIF with flashing lights on that e-mail from Kyle666."

"So?"

"Watching flashing lights can trigger a seizure in an epileptic. That's what happened to Natalie and, to a lesser extent, me. I had a seizure, but you blocked the screen and eliminated the cause, so the seizure was minor. Natalie wasn't so lucky."

"That's horrible, but how do you know the sender of the e-mail killed her deliberately?"

"The e-mail said, 'I'm killing you.' The sender knew exactly what he was doing."

"It could have been meant as a threat and that's all."

Brody shrugged. "Possible. But why would someone e-mailing a threat attach a GIF with flashing lights?"

"Unless he knew it would cause her to have a seizure. Is that what you're saying?"

"Most people don't equate flashing lights with murder. Flashing lights aren't scary."

"True."

"Why not attach a GIF of someone firing a gun, hoping it would scare her to death?"

"I see what you're saying. But I doubt any kind of GIF would scare someone to death."

"She wasn't scared to death. The flashing lights triggered a seizure in her which killed her."

"What's your point?"

"I can't think of any other reason for the cyberstalker to attach that particular GIF to a death threat. And let's be clear. It was a death threat."

"How did he know he could kill her with an e-mail? She didn't go around telling everyone she had epilepsy."

"This Kyle666 knew she had epilepsy and knew flashing lights would trigger a seizure in her. He murdered her, as surely as you and me are standing in this room together."

"She never told me anything about anyone named Kyle." Susan touched her chin. "Oh, wait a minute. She told me her cousin she met today has a son called Kyle."

"Did she say anything about him?"

"She tried to be nice to him because he's a relative, I think she said. But he misunderstood and asked her out. She had to tell him she had a boyfriend."

"How'd he take it?"

"Not well. He went off in a huff, she said."

"I better have a talk with him."

"Would a guy kill a girl just because she wouldn't go out with him? It sends a chill down my spine thinking about it."

"Maybe something else went on between them she didn't tell you."

Susan mulled it over. "She did mention she felt uncomfortable with Patti."

"Patti?"

"Her relative she went to see."

"They don't get along?"

"Natalie didn't go into it with me. She just said she felt awkward around Patti."

"Did they have a fight when Natalie visited her?"

"I don't think so. She said she felt awkward around her. Didn't say anything about a fight. I got the impression she felt embarrassed when she met Patti." Susan shook her head in confusion. "I dunno. Strange."

"Why would she feel embarrassed?"

"I have no idea."

"That's another lead I should look into."

"You think Patti had something to do with Natalie's death?"

"Patti's son's name is Kyle, and Kyle666 sent the e-mail that caused Natalie's death."

Breaking down, Susan clasped her face with both hands. "I can't believe anyone would kill Natalie."

###

Brody drove his Mini to Patti's house, a modest white clapboard affair on a street which favored pocket Mission Revival stucco houses with Moorish arches and red tiled roofs. To find a parking place he had to park several blocks away from Patti's.

He knocked on Patti's black iron security screen door.

"Yes?" she said with a tentative smile flickering across her face, not recognizing him.

He had trouble making out her face behind the heavy door's grillwork.

"Are you Patti Hightower?" he said.

"And who are you?"

"I'm Scott Brody. I have some bad news for you about your cousin Natalie."

"Natalie?" she said with puzzled concern.

"Could I come in?"

She hesitated a moment then unlocked the screen door's dead bolt and let him in.

"You said something about bad news," she said, showing him into the living room.

An attractive blonde in her forties wearing jeans and a form-fitting coral batik tube top stood before him. An open bottle of Grey Goose vodka stood on a sideboard behind her.

"There's no easy way to tell you this," he said.

"How are you related to Natalie? She never mentioned you."

"I'm not related to her. I'm a private investigator."

"Why would she need a PI?" said Patti, worry creeping into her voice.

"Maybe you should have a seat."

"I don't want to have a seat."

He fetched a sigh. "Natalie's dead."

"Dead?" said Patti, reeling. "That can't be. I just saw her. She isn't dead."

"I'm afraid she is. And I believe she was murdered."

Brody heard a floorboard creaking in an adjacent room.

"There must be some mistake," said Patti, pacing around the room trying to shake it off.

"No mistake. Her roommate Susan was there when it happened. She was the one that hired me."

Patti halted and faced Brody, the blood draining from her face, at a loss for words. She tried to speak.

"Do you want some water?" he said.

"No."

She turned around, took a pull on her bottle of vodka, and replaced the bottle on the sideboard.

"Want some?" she said.

"No, thanks."

"You said she was murdered?"

"She was."

"By who?"

"That's why I'm here. I'm trying to find out who did it."

"I have no idea. I hardly ever see Natalie. I don't know what's been going on in her life."

"Is your son Kyle here?"

"Why do you want to know?" said Patti, becoming defensive.

"I'd like to talk to him."

"He knows less about her than I do. The first time he ever met her was this morning. He doesn't know anything," she said, agitated.

Brody picked up on her distress. "Has he been having problems?"

"He's—he's a troubled kid, you know. He'll find his way. But now—he spends too much time on the Internet, I think."

"The Internet? How do you mean?"

"It's that QAnon Internet group he's always chatting with."

"The conspiracy group?"

"Is that what they are? He seems angry all the time since he's hooked up with them. And he hangs around with that other QAnon guy Ron. That guy incites him." She paused. "But maybe it's my fault." She clutched her forehead. "I haven't been the best of mothers. I try. It's hard being a single mother."

"Getting back to Kyle—"

"I feel like I've failed him. It's complicated. My life . . . ," she trailed off.

"What happened to his father?"

"He left us." She became angry. "I haven't had any luck with men. I always end up with the rotten apples."

"Would you consider Kyle an incel?"

"Incel? I don't even know what it means."

"It's a celibate man who doesn't want to be celibate, but he can't get a date. Therefore he hates women. Incels join certain groups on the Internet like QAnon and share their feelings of alienation."

"I never heard of anything like that. I can't keep up with all these new things." She paused a beat. "Kyle doesn't hate women," she said, her voice low. "That's crazy talk."

"Do you know what Kyle did today?"

"He drove off somewhere, while Natalie was here. He didn't tell me where. Why?"

"Did they have a problem?"

She became defensive again. "Of course, not. Why would they?"

"You said they never met each other. Maybe they didn't hit it off."

"I wasn't with them the whole time she was here. All I can tell you is I saw no problem between them. Why should there be? After all, they're related."

"I have reason to believe Kyle had something to do with Natalie's murder."

"That's nuts," said Patti, her eyes popping with indignation.

"You said he was having emotional problems."

Patti slumped. "That's on me. Don't blame him for that. I haven't been the greatest mother. I try. But, it's so hard being a good parent. I try to be there for him when he needs me. My life isn't easy."

"Did he know Natalie had epilepsy?"

Patti shook her head in irritation. "I don't know. What difference does it make?"

"It makes a lot of difference. Whoever killed Natalie knew she had epilepsy."

"How could you possibly know that?"

"Because of the manner in which she died. She died of a seizure."

"I thought you said she was murdered."

"Her seizure was triggered by an e-mail she received from Kyle."

Brody heard floorboards in the next room creaking again.

"How can an e-mail cause a seizure?" said Patti.

"It can trigger a seizure in an epileptic who opens the e-mail if it contains a GIF of flashing lights."

"How would the sender know Natalie had epilepsy?"

"There's something else I didn't tell you."

"What?"

"What the e-mail said. It said, 'I hate you, Natalie. I'm killing you.'"

"That doesn't necessarily mean the sender knew she had epilepsy."

"Attaching the GIF of flashing lights to the e-mail proves he did, and he knew her viewing the GIF would kill her."

"So who sent it?"

"Kyle666. I'm betting that's your son."

"That's impossible. He would never do that," said Patti, overwrought. Her voice rose with vehemence. "He would never kill his own sister—"

When she realized what she was saying, she held her breath.

Brody heard floorboards creaking in the adjacent room.

"Sister?" he said in surprise. "You said you were Natalie's cousin."

"I—I—I've had a complicated life, like I said before. Natalie was my daughter by another husband. I never told Natalie or Kyle about it." She sobbed. "I'm not proud of the life I've lived, but I had to make a living. I had to survive. Men are attracted to me. I learned to use the only thing nature gave me. I work for an escort service. I don't go around bragging about it. I never told Kyle or Natalie about their fathers. I never even told them they were brother and sister."

"Then he wouldn't know he killed his own sister. He thought he was killing someone else."

Her face turned ashen. "Oh, what have I done? I can't believe this is happening. I know I haven't been a model parent, but I don't deserve this much misery."

A gunshot rang out.

Brody wheeled around, trying to determine the whereabouts of the shooter. He didn't see anyone. The report had come from the adjoining room.

He bent down, whipped his SIG P365 from his ankle holster, and stole toward the room. Creeping down the hallway, he noticed the room's door was open. He pulled up at the doorway and peeked around the jamb, wary of someone taking a shot at him. He glimpsed a limp arm lying on the bed. Beside the arm lay a man's head with a bloody bullet hole in the temple. At the side of the motionless body on the coverlet lay a Glock 17.

"He was listening to us," said Brody over his shoulder.

Relaxing, he lowered his SIG, entered the bedroom, and approached the body.

Behind him Patti screamed in agony at the sight of her dead son.

Undiscovered Country

Power had Shelby bound and gagged in his black Audi's rear trunk, as he was driving on Ocean Avenue, parallel to the Pacific Ocean shoreline, during the warm summer evening when a CHP motorcycle cop pulled him over.

Bad timing to say the least, decided Power. The CIA inspector general had tasked him, an officer in the IG's Office of Investigations, with a difficult assignment as it was. Now this. His pulse accelerating, Power hoped Shelby wouldn't start kicking the trunk and raising a commotion when he realized the Audi was coming to a halt.

Power had no choice. He had to pull over. If things got dicey, he had a SIG Sauer P365 Nitron Micro-Compact tucked into a Velcro ankle holster strapped to his left calf. As if he would shoot a cop. That would be the day. But he couldn't let the cop know he had Shelby trussed in the Audi's trunk.

There was no way Power could explain away a hostage concealed in his trunk. The cop would run him in for kidnaping and false arrest. No matter what, Power, as a member of the CIA's OIG, could not let that happen. The OIG was as clandestine as the agency for which it worked. Nobody was supposed to know what they did.

This mission was going sideways even before Power had had a chance to interrogate Shelby. The inspector general Hobart Winterboro would never forgive him if the LA cops initiated an investigation of Power and Shelby. Winterboro would disavow any knowledge of Power, and Power would have to take the rap for a kidnaping charge.

The whole point of this mission was to keep the cops out of the picture.

A park on the top of the bluffs that overlooked the coastline skirted the west side of the avenue, while nursing homes and apartment houses skirted the east. As he was heading north, he pulled the twin-scrolled turbocharged V6 Audi S4 over in front of an unassuming two-story nursing home.

Power glanced in his rearview mirror and saw the CHP officer dismount from his Harley Electra Glide, whose flashers continued to blink blue and red in the darkness like maleficent eyes. A scrim of purple grey clouds floated under the full moon, casting ominous shadows on the unfolding scene.

Power couldn't help but notice his thirty-five-year-old face in the mirror. Normally unlined, it was showing too much concern in his forehead. He told himself to dial it back a couple notches and look calm for the cop. At least he had gotten his hair cut yesterday so he looked presentable for his ticket. Ticket for what, he didn't know.

Clad in a butternut uniform and black jackboots, the highway patrol cop approached Power's driver's-side window. As he got closer, Power could see it wasn't a he but a she, a blonde who looked like she had something to prove. The only reason he knew she was blonde was the stray lock of hair that dangled out from under her blue and gold motorcycle helmet.

He didn't know how she could see in the dark with her aviator shades on. She removed them as she approached.

Her flinty blue eyes were sizing him up when she halted beside his open window clacking her boots on the tarmac one after the other.

Power said nothing to her. He just wanted this to be over, so he could get on with his mission, which wasn't going to get any easier after this ill-timed confrontation with the law.

"What's the problem, sir?" she said under her breath.

Power breathed a tad easier. At least, Shelby wouldn't be able to hear the cop's whispery voice.

Power read her name over her breast pocket. C. Beasley. Looked to be in her thirties, decided Power. An icy blonde with a supple figure, probably due to frequent workouts at her nearest Equinox or other favorite gym.

"Nothing, Officer," he said.

"Then why were you speeding?"

"I didn't know I was," said Power, keeping his voice down.

If Shelby heard them, he might start kicking the trunk to alert Beasley. Power's CIA training had prepared him for tense situations, but all the training in the world couldn't prevent his heartbeat from racing in a tight squeeze.

"You were doing forty in a thirty-mile-an-hour zone," said Beasley, stone-faced. "Maybe if you were paying attention to your driving, you would have noticed."

He had thought he was doing thirty-five when she pulled him over. LA cops rarely pulled you over if you were only five miles over the limit. Ten miles, you never knew, especially in a residential neighborhood. As he had noticed earlier, Beasley had something to prove. Was this was her first bust? If Shelby would keep quiet a little longer, maybe Power would be able to extricate himself from his scrape.

"Can I see your driver's license, sir?" said Beasley.

This was going to take longer than he thought, decided Power, disheartened.

He dug his wallet out of his trouser pocket and offered it to her.

"Just the license, sir," said Beasley, looking askance at the wallet. "You know better."

"I've never been pulled over before, Officer."

"A citizen above suspicion."

Power couldn't tell if she was being sarcastic. "It's true."

Beasley's face registered nothing. "The license, please."

Power pulled his driver's license from his wallet and handed it to her. He wasn't getting on the good side of her, he realized. He wasn't worried about his license passing inspection. He had an expertly forged California driver's license. He had an expertly forged driver's license for several states. His only legitimate one was for Virginia, where he lived and commuted to Langley when he wasn't on a mission.

Beasley inspected his license, her expression all business.

She would be a good-looking woman if she wasn't so deadly serious, he decided.

"And your car registration, sir," she said.

Power hesitated.

Which didn't go unnoticed by Beasley. "This *is* your car, isn't it, sir?"

"Not exactly. It's my employer's."

"The registration," said Beasley, holding out her empty hand.

She was becoming less polite, Power realized. As long as she didn't raise her voice and disturb Shelby.

He reached for the glove compartment.

She reached for the Smith & Wesson M&P 40 holstered on her hip. Power froze, his heartbeat ratcheting upward. His hand never made it to the glove compartment.

"Slowly," said Beasley, her hand hovering over her Smith & Wesson.

"No problem."

Looking apologetic Power took his time opening the glove compartment. He flicked through the assorted maps and papers inside it, brushed aside a pair of Wayfarer shades, withdrew the car registration, and handed it to Beasley.

Beasley scrutinized it. "American Persuasions LLC. That your company?"

"I work for them. This is a company car."

"Wait a moment."

Beasley retreated to her Harley with Power's driver's license and the car registration.

She was going to run his creds through her CHP computer to see if they raised any red flags, Power knew. They shouldn't. The CIA had provided them to him, and he knew from experience their forged documents were top-notch. American Persuasions was a shell company set up and funded by the CIA. The owners' names were anonymous, since the agency had created the LLC in Delaware, a state that didn't require their names. There was no way anyone could pierce the corporate veil and trace the LLC back to the agency.

Power was grateful for one thing. Shelby hadn't started kicking the trunk where he was imprisoned. Power didn't know how long his luck was going to hold in that regard. Maybe Shelby couldn't hear their voices. But he must be wondering why Power had stopped the Audi.

Power was relieved cops liked to speak under their breath. They thought it made them sound tough like Clint Eastwood's Dirty Harry. Still, hadn't Shelby heard Beasley's siren? Power wondered. Then again, maybe the siren was the reason Shelby wasn't making any noise. He, too, had secrets to conceal from the cops. Or maybe he thought the siren was for another driver. Power knew Shelby couldn't see a thing in the rear trunk. The guy could barely move thanks to its poky confines.

What was taking Beasley so long? wondered Power, glancing in his driver's-side mirror at her. She appeared to be absorbed in running his ID through her Harley's CHP computer.

Shelby wasn't going to keep quiet forever, decided Power. Tapping a nervous tattoo on the steering wheel, he thought he heard a sound in the trunk. Not good. He stopped tapping. He didn't hear the sound anymore. He had to get out of here. He wanted to honk his horn to get Beasley to shake a leg. Wrong move. If he made any attempts to pressure her, she would react with suspicion and might even ask him to pop the trunk.

He told himself to be patient.

He had been so close to getting Shelby to the safe house on San Vicente Boulevard only a few blocks from here—and then Beasley had spoiled everything.

Agitated, he felt like firing the engine and peeling off. Another wrong move, he knew. Beasley could outmaneuver his Audi on her motorcycle—and she would also call for backup. Forget it, he told himself. He had to sit here and do nothing. He had no other options.

The CHP motorcycle's menacing blue and red lights kept flashing in Power's rearview mirror. The noise in the trunk hadn't resumed. Maybe he had imagined it, decided Power. Or maybe a passing car had made the noise.

He saw Beasley break away from her Harley and return to his Audi. He couldn't tell anything from her expression, which hid in the shadows. Her helmet and the night teamed to obscure her features.

He heard the heels of her gleaming black jackboots crunch against the sand on the tarmac.

Despite his conviction that his documents were foolproof, he felt edgy at her approach.

She handed his documents back to him, her face leaning toward him as if she was trying to smell his breath. Fine, he decided. She could smell it all she wanted. He hadn't had a drink in hours. He could use one now, he decided, his throat dry.

He accepted his documents.

"Everything's clean," she said.

"Of course."

"Let me give you a word of advice. Pay attention to your driving. Paying attention is 99 percent of safe driving. You wanna be a good driver, don't you?"

"I do."

"I'm letting you go with a warning, is all."

"Thanks, Officer," he said, wishing she would get away from his car so she couldn't hear Shelby should he decide to shift his position in the cramped trunk.

"Drive safely."

He noticed she was scoping out his car's interior. Now what? he wondered. What the hell was she looking for? An empty beer can? Drugs?

"Who does your cleaning, by the way?" she said. "I've never seen such a spotless car. It's immaculate. Most of the cars I pull over, you wouldn't believe the mess inside. Your car, it's like you just drove it out of the showroom. It's a car without an identity."

She was cutting a little too close to the bone, Power decided.

"My company keeps it clean," he said. "I don't have anything to do with it. You'd have to ask them."

"Funny," she said, raising her eyebrows but not laughing. "I've never seen a car this spick-and-span." She paused. "Almost as if it's been wiped clean of evidence. You don't even have a burger wrapper on your floor."

What was she talking about? Cops didn't bust people for having clean cars, decided Power.

"I'll pass on your compliment to my boss," he said.

"It's hard to believe someone as neat as you wouldn't pay attention to your speed."

She was convinced he was up to something, but she had no idea what.

Best to beat it, he decided. If she asked him to pop the trunk, he would be dead. Or she would be. One way or the other he couldn't let her find Shelby.

He inserted his key into the ignition.

She retreated to her Harley, still admiring the cleanliness of his car.

With a start, he heard a thump in the trunk. Thinking fast he fired the engine to drown out the noise so Beasley couldn't hear it, signaled, and pulled away from the curb.

He glanced apprehensively in the rearview mirror to see if Beasley was pursuing him. She was standing near her bike, adjusting the strap on her helmet and looking downward. A good sign, he decided.

The briny odor of a sea breeze swept into the Audi through his open window.

Power turned right onto San Vicente Boulevard.

He wondered why Shelby hadn't pounded on the trunk to get attention. Maybe the guy was asleep. Could he have died from carbon monoxide fumes in the car exhaust? Power doubted the trunk was airtight. Some fumes might get in, but there shouldn't be enough to kill Shelby. The car was moving when the engine was running and the tailpipes were spewing out the exhaust into the rushing air. Power didn't see how exhaust could poison Shelby.

Had the guy suffocated? Power wondered with apprehension. The trunk was so cramped he had had a devil of a time shoehorning Shelby into it. Luckily, the guy wasn't tall, or Power wouldn't have been able to close the trunk lid.

Power couldn't interrogate a stiff. He had to get to Shelby to make sure he was alive.

If Shelby *was* alive, why wasn't he pounding on the trunk? The guy should have pounded on it when Beasley pulled over the Audi, decided Power.

It didn't take long for Power to reach the safe house. He glanced at the rearview mirror to make sure Beasley wasn't following him. He didn't see her. He drove around the block once to see if she was tailing him. No sign of her.

He pulled into the safe house's driveway, put the car in park, got out of the car, pulled up the wooden roll-up garage door, returned to the car, shifted into drive, and parked in the garage. He killed the engine, got out of the car, closed the garage door, and popped the trunk with his key fob.

Bound and gagged with duct tape, Shelby lay motionless in a fetal position in the trunk.

"Don't die on me," said Power.

Winterboro wanted answers. It was Power's job to pump Shelby.

Power shook Shelby. "We're here."

Shelby launched a kick with his bound feet at Power. Thumped in the chest, Power staggered backward and crashed into the garage's drywall, cratering it with the back of his head.

"Crap," said Power, gathering himself against the wall.

Shelby struggled to crawl out of the trunk. With his arms and legs bound, he reminded Power of a monstrous worm trying to squirm out of the car.

Angrily, Power snagged Shelby's bound wrists, yanked him out of the trunk, and stood him unceremoniously on the cement floor.

"Try that again and I'll rearrange your face," said Power. "Let's go into the house."

Shelby struggled to speak through his gag.

Power tore the duct tape off Shelby's mouth. Shelby winced as the skin around his mouth smarted.

"My body's killing me," he said. "I got muscles aching I never knew I had."

"Get moving."

"My circulation's cut off."

Grimacing, Shelby groaned as he struggled to walk. He moved his sore neck to the right and left, stretching its burning muscles.

"Don't worry," said Power. "I'll give you a massage when we're inside."

Shelby shot a glare at him. "Bastard."

The garage was attached to a small square lemon stucco Spanish-styled house with a flat red-tiled roof. The house had room enough only for two bedrooms, a living room, a bathroom, and a kitchen.

Power thrust Shelby onto a wooden chair in the living room and drew the half-open white linen curtains shut behind the picture window.

"What the hell's going on?" demanded Shelby.

Power stood in front of him. "The inspector general wants answers."

"I don't know what you're talking about."

"Good answer, if I was a cop. But I'm not. I work for the CIA like you, Shelby. I'm a criminal investigator for the OIG. Isn't 'Shelby' the legend you're using?"

Power didn't have to explain OIG was the Office of the Inspector General of the CIA, since Shelby worked for the CIA's Operations Department, which included covert action, Shelby's expertise. Shelby knew all about how the CIA was set up.

"I don't know what you're talking about," said Shelby.

"I'm talking about the murder of Barbara Malone."

Despite Shelby's CIA training to withstand interrogations, Power noticed a flicker of recognition in Shelby's eyes.

Shelby said nothing.

"You were dating her," said Power.

"What's my personal life got to do with anything?"

"Nothing. As long as it doesn't include murder."

Shelby shook his head. "You're coming at me from outer space."

"Cut the bullshit, Shelby."

Shelby said nothing.

"Somebody murdered Malone, and we believe that person is you," said Power.

"That's ridiculous."

"You don't sound very upset she's dead."

"I'm not convinced you're on the level. Is this some kind of agency test to see how I react?"

"She's dead, all right."

"Then why hasn't it been on the news? This is the first I've heard of it."

"The inspector general ordered us to sit on it. He doesn't want cops digging into a CIA agent's life and finding out he works for the agency. They could blow your cover if they start investigating Malone's murder."

"I dated her a couple times. I didn't murder her. I didn't even know she was dead."

Power drew up a wooden chair, spun it around so its back was facing Shelby, and straddled it, crossing his arms on the back and facing Shelby.

"It was a little more than that, Shelby. You flew into a jealous rage when you found out she was seeing someone else."

"That's ridiculous."

Power knew Shelby would be a hard nut to crack, what with Shelby's CIA interrogation-resistance training. Still, Power had a job to do. He was investigating Malone's murder for the inspector general. He needed to find out if Shelby was involved. If he was, the inspector general would see to it that the cops never found out about it. The CIA's name must under no circumstances be connected to a homicide. The CIA avoided publicity like the plague. Nobody but the CIA must find out if Shelby, one of their agents, had indeed murdered Malone.

"We need to know if you did it," said Power.

"I already told you. No. Now it's my turn to ask a question. How do you guys know about Malone's murder if even the cops don't know about it?"

"I was tailing you when the murder occurred."

"Oh, yeah? And you saw me murder her?"

"No."

"Of course not. Because I didn't."

"I was watching you pay her a visit. Winterboro wanted me to inform him of the nature of your involvement with her. You know he doesn't like sexual liaisons cultivated by agents, covert or otherwise."

"It's none of his business, really."

"He believes sexual liaisons cloud the mind and interfere with your judgment as a spy."

"He believes wrong," said Shelby, his face smug.

"This isn't about him. It's about you."

"Get on with it, then."

"I knocked on Malone's door after you left, and nobody answered."

"How soon after I left?"

"Uh—I'd say twenty minutes. I wanted to make sure you were gone and wouldn't double back."

"And?"

"And I knocked again. She didn't answer. I used a lock pick gun on her door and entered her apartment. I looked around and found her lying in her negligee faceup on her bed in her bedroom, a scarf tied around her neck. She was quite dead."

Shelby stared at him. "She was quite alive when I left her."

"You didn't let me finish. There were bruises on her face, and her nose was broken. Somebody did a number on her. A couple of her teeth had been knocked out, and there were burn marks on her forearms."

"Shit. A psycho got her."

"More like a crime of passion. A beating handed out by an enraged jilted lover. Somebody who knew how to inflict pain. Like a covert CIA agent in the Department of Operations. Like you."

"She was alive when I left her. Maybe the other guy got to her, the one you say she was seeing when she was dating me."

"Who's the other guy?"

"I have no idea. You're all wrong about me."

"Lemme get this straight. She was alive and well when you left her?"

"She was."

"I didn't see anyone else enter or leave her apartment after you left."

"Maybe he was hiding in the closet and beat the crap out of her after I left."

"Then why didn't I see him there?"

"Maybe he escaped out the window."

"Why would he? He had no idea I was watching Malone's door. Why not just walk out the door—like you did?"

"Who knows? He was scared. People do weird things when they're scared."

Power stood up and walked around, mulling it over. "Which legend were you using when you dated her, or were you using your real name?"

"I never use my real name. That person doesn't exist anymore."

"You used the Max Shelby legend?"

"I did."

"You don't even use your real name when you date a woman?"

"Why should I?"

"The question is, why shouldn't you? Don't you want to be honest with her since you're dating her?"

"You don't know anything about women."

"We know you dated her several times, so this wasn't a one-night stand. This was a relationship you wanted to last."

"What makes you the great expert on what I want? And I don't appreciate being spied on."

"Your private life can't interfere with your professional life. You know better. You're not an amateur."

"Maybe *you* don't have a life. *I* do. I'm not a machine."

Power rounded on Shelby. "Tell me the truth."

"I didn't kill her."

Power strode up to Shelby, pushed the chair he had been sitting on out of the way, glared at Shelby, and planted a right hook spang on Shelby's jaw. Shelby fell off the chair from the impact of the blow, his chair toppling over with him.

"Bastard," spat Shelby, lying on his side on the hardwood floor, blood leaking out the corner of his mouth. "Hitting a guy that's tied up? That takes a pair."

Power didn't respond to Shelby's sarcasm. "All I want from you is the truth. Then we can settle this."

"I'm telling you the truth."

"You're the one that tortured her and strangled her because you found out she was seeing another guy."

"Read my lips. It wasn't me."

"She betrayed you."

"So you say."

"She did. And you knew it. You beat her face to a pulp so she was all but unrecognizable and burned her arms with cigarettes before you strangled the life out of her."

Power stepped on Shelby's left cheek and ground his face into the floor. "Want me to be nice to you?"

"Asshole."

Covert agents were the hardest to get to tell the truth, Power knew. Their whole lives were lies. They lied so much that it became second nature to them. Some of them were so well trained they didn't even know they were lying. They believed they were telling the truth. They were sociopaths. Those were the hardest to crack.

They formed compartmentalized personalities that weren't even aware of the other personalities, or legends, they manufactured. Shelby might even now be pretending to be another legend while he was talking about "Shelby"—a separate legend who didn't know Shelby had strangled Malone and therefore could state with absolute certainty he didn't kill her, having no idea the legend Shelby had done it.

It was maddening, decided Power. It was like dealing with a schizophrenic with multiple personalities, each personality as convincing as the next and unaware of what the others had done.

"Admit you killed her," said Power, grinding his shoe into Shelby's carotid artery in the neck, knowing it would cut off the blood to Shelby's brain and kill him if Power did it long enough.

"I didn't do it," Shelby gasped, barely audible.

Power didn't believe him. He had no plans to kill Shelby. Yet.

Power removed his foot from Shelby's neck.

His face red, Shelby took a deep breath.

"The IG ordered you to whack me?" Shelby managed to say.

"He ordered me to remove you if you're guilty of Malone's murder."

"'Remove,' huh? Erase me from the face of the planet like I never existed, you mean."

"We can't have the cops investigating a CIA agent. There's no telling what they'd dig up about you. And your espionage career would be ruined. It would bring shame on the entire agency. We'd never live it down in the media. They'd rake us over the coals. *CIA Agent Murders Lover in Love Nest*. No, we can't have that in the headlines. And you might spill the beans about your job in order to save your neck when they put you on trial. Nobody in the agency must talk about the CIA to anyone. You know that."

"How many times do I have to tell you? I didn't kill her."

"The problem is, you're a consummately trained liar. So I can't believe you."

Power set Shelby's chair upright then hoisted Shelby up by the shoulders to sit him in it. Shelby tried to ram Power into the wall, but his feet couldn't get any purchase because they were bound at the ankles. Shelby stumbled forward. Power caught him and thrust him into the chair. Shelby tried to bite Power's throat. Power backed away. Shelby snapped his jaws shut on empty space.

"Knock it off," said Power. "You have no chance. Just tell me the truth."

"If you didn't call the cops, what did you do with the corpse?"

"I left it where it is."

"The stench of decaying flesh will alert the neighbors. And they'll call the cops."

"That's not your problem. Your problem is telling me the truth."

"I didn't kill her," said Shelby, looking beaten.

"We're sending a cleanup crew there to dispose of the stiff and clean the apartment," said Power, though Winterboro hadn't given him any such orders as yet.

"Then nobody will ever know someone wasted her, including the cops. If they don't find a corpus delicti, they won't know a murder was committed and they won't investigate. Everybody will be happy. Why grill me?"

"Because you might murder again. You're a loose cannon. And we can't afford having loose cannons in the agency. SOP. We police our own. Nobody else must ever know what goes on in the agency."

Power walked into the kitchen, opened a cupboard, peered inside, withdrew a package of Fig Newtons, and returned to Shelby.

"These Airbnb safe houses come with provisions," said Power. "Want a Fig Newton?"

"Yeah, sure."

Power withdrew a cookie from the package, guided it toward Shelby's mouth, and pulled it away at the last moment.

"After you tell me the truth," said Power.

"I told you the truth."

Power slapped Shelby on the side of the head. "Did you murder Barbara Malone?"

"No."

Munching a Fig Newton Power searched Shelby's face. Finishing the cookie he set down the package on a sideboard, fished an encrypted burner out of his trouser pocket, and called Winterboro.

"He says he didn't do it," said Power, ambling to the other end of the living room, where he could keep an eye on Shelby as he talked on his burner.

"Do you believe him?" said Winterboro, his voice low.

"He says someone strangled her after he left. I was watching Malone's apartment for twenty minutes after he left. I didn't see anyone enter it."

"What's his explanation?"

"He says the killer was already in the apartment waiting for Shelby to leave before he strangled her."

"Did you see anyone else in the apartment when you found Malone's corpse?"

"No."

"What do you think?"

"Shelby's lying through his teeth. He used his agency legend as 'Shelby' to whack Malone and figured he could get away with it because there's no such person as Shelby. He didn't know I was tailing him."

"A failure in his tradecraft."

"Spies don't kill for personal reasons, either. Another failure in tradecraft."

"Did he identify the murderer?"

"He thinks it was the other lover in the triangle. Found out his girlfriend Barbara was cheating on him with Shelby and offed her."

"Barbara?"

"Malone. Barbara Malone."

"Opinion?"

"If the other lover was in Malone's apartment, why didn't I see him? Also, Shelby had a certain bounce to his step when he left the apartment. Like he was energized."

"Because he just took someone out?"

"The act of murder gets the adrenaline flowing. He was juiced up. Not only did he whack her, he tortured her."

"Have you informed the cops of Malone's murder?"

"Not yet. But neighbors will find her corpse soon because of the stench."

"I want Shelby removed before the cops find out about Malone."

"To an undiscovered country?"

"Posthaste. And use a cleanup crew afterward."

"What about Malone?"

"Is her apartment clean?"

"I haven't had time to check. Shelby's DNA may be there."

"I'll have someone spray the apartment with DNA remover. Even if the cops find some, it won't do them any good. Max Shelby never existed."

"I don't know if that'll be enough."

"I'm listening."

"There might be pictures of Shelby or other evidence of his existence on Malone's computer. I took her cell phone and destroyed it."

"Her computer's still in her apartment?"

"It is."

"I see." Winterboro paused. "What do you suggest?"

"We need to deep clean the apartment. It'll cover up the murder so the cops won't know it happened and won't investigate."

"Does she have a gas range or electric?"

"Gas."

"It'll develop a leak and explode. Malone will become the victim of an explosion and fire, not a murder. The fire will incinerate her stiff, eradicating any evidence of murder. No murder, no murder investigation. I'll get a crew on it right now."

"Are you dispatching another cleanup crew here?"

"They're on their way." Winterboro fetched a sigh. "I don't know what happened to Shelby. He used to be one of our best covert agents. He was at the top of his class at Camp Peary."

"He got emotionally involved."

"What happened to his training? One of the first things we train agents is never to become emotionally involved. The mission is all that matters."

"Did he pass his psychological analysis?"

"With flying colors."

"He knew what answers he was supposed to give and lied."

"Which makes for a good spy. You can't fault him on that."

Power shrugged. "I'll take care of him."

"Did you get him to confess?"

"No. He's well trained for interrogations."

"But he forgot everything he learned about avoiding emotional involvement."

"He's never gonna confess. Unless we use sodium pentothal and waterboarding. Maybe electrodes—"

"We don't have the time. He needs to be dealt with now. Every minute he stays alive he's a threat to the agency. Take care of him."

"My pleasure."

Winterboro was about to hang up then came back on the line. "Are you sure he's not confessing because he's telling the truth when he says he didn't murder Malone?"

"Positive."

Winterboro hung up.

"Emotionally involved," Power muttered.

I'm sure Shelby strangled her because I'm the one Barbara was seeing. Beautiful Barbara. Babs. Tortured to death by Shelby because he found out. But not my name. Or does he know it and isn't confessing it, certain it will be his death sentence if he tells me? Like he isn't confessing to murdering Babs.

It didn't matter, decided Power.

He fixed a suppressor to his SIG P365's muzzle. He was going to enjoy making Shelby disappear.

Emotionally involved. Power knew all about being emotionally involved, feeling vindictive rage boiling inside him.

Dead Reckoning

Power didn't know how he was going to kill LeHaigh—*if* he had to. And he figured he *would* have to.

First, he had to determine if LeHaigh was guilty. Winterboro was still giving LeHaigh the benefit of the doubt and was willing to listen to LeHaigh's explanation. Though Power doubted LeHaigh could explain his way out of this one. The only thing that could save LeHaigh now was documentary proof of his innocence, something that could explain his lavish lifestyle.

Taking out LeHaigh could present a problem, decided Power. No doubt LeHaigh had a gun on his premises. After all, he was a gunrunner.

An erstwhile Navy SEAL who had completed two tours of duty in Afghanistan and won a purple heart for a bullet wound in his leg inflicted by an AK-47–wielding member of the Taliban, he worked now as an independent contractor for the CIA, smuggling guns into Venezuela to aid Juan Guaidó in his battle to overthrow the dictator and indicted narcoterrorist Nicolás Maduro. It was a given LeHaigh would have arms on his premises.

Inspector General Winterboro of the OIG suspected LeHaigh had gone rogue and set up shop selling guns for his own profit without the agency's knowledge. If Winterboro's suspicions turned out to be on the money, Power's job was to terminate LeHaigh before any other government agency, such as the ATF or FBI, discovered what he was up to, in which case they would arrest him, try him, and blow his cover. If, indeed, LeHaigh had gone rogue and in the future ended up busted, Winterboro couldn't trust him to keep his mouth shut about working for the CIA. Hence Power's current mission.

Power was driving along the five-mile-long Rickenbacker Causeway that crossed Biscayne Bay from Miami to Virginia Key. He drove through Virginia Key, got back on the causeway that spanned Bear Cut, and made for Key Biscayne, where LeHaigh was living.

It was hot and humid, and Power had the AC in his rented BMW cranked full blast. He could stand the heat, but not the oppressive humidity. He maxed the volume on the radio the better to hear AC/DC's "Highway to Hell" over the AC's drone. Oddly, the song calmed his nerves, despite its unapologetic brashness.

Power drove onto Key Biscayne, where the houses were either white or pastel shades to reflect the sun's intense rays.

It didn't take him long to find the modern-style house where LeHaigh was living. Its front yard skirted by sea grape bushes, the two-story house was white with sliding planes with an infinity pool in the backyard facing the Atlantic Ocean, where the house had a small wharf. A thirty-foot cigarette boat moored to the wharf was bobbing on the ocean, its hull glinting like a knife in the sun.

A house like this would cost a pretty penny, Power knew, as would the go-fast boat. CIA agents didn't make that kind of money.

Power drove onto the pale coquina driveway and parked behind a late-model black Porsche 911 Carrera Cabriolet Turbo S, which could rocket from zero to sixty in a little over two seconds.

As he climbed out of his car, the humidity smacked him like a wet glove. His polo shirt was wet with sweat by the time he walked up to the house's front door and rang the doorbell. Maybe he should have worn Bermudas instead of his jeans.

A bald, swarthy middle-aged butler with a furrowed brow answered the door, wearing white gloves.

"Sean Power to see Philip LeHaigh," said Power.

"Come inside. He's expecting you. He's poolside."

Power followed the butler, who walked with a curious penguinlike gait, through the spacious, air-conditioned house out onto the terrace and then to the infinity pool.

A five-ten, square-jawed man pushing forty in navy blue bathing trunks was sitting on a lawn chair on the cement deck gazing across the pool out at the ocean. To his left a grill station constructed of cinder blocks containing a large electric barbecue stood on the deck behind the diving board.

"Have a seat," said LeHaigh on seeing Power.

Power sat on a lawn chair beside LeHaigh.

Once fit, LeHaigh had the makings of a potbelly. A three-inch-long scar slashed his right calf.

His tanned face covered with two days' growth of dark stubble, his hair bushy and black, his eyebrows caterpillar thick, LeHaigh reached for an ice-cold mojito on the glass-topped metal table beside him.

"Pour our guest a mojito, Antonio," he told the butler. "And some water."

Antonio poured iced water out of a pitcher into one glass then a mojito into another for Power. Power listened to the ice cubes chinking.

"That'll be all for now, Antonio," said LeHaigh.

Antonio departed.

His face beading with sweat, Power took a pull on the water.

"See how still the pool is," said LeHaigh. "Not even a ripple. It could be a mirror. I almost hate going into the water. It's like desecrating a work of art."

Power sipped his mojito, but he didn't come here to get high.

"Does the agency have a new mission for me?" said LeHaigh.

"No."

"Then why are you here?"

Power got down to brass tacks. "The IG suspects you've gone into business for yourself."

"Why does he think that?"

"For one thing, he doesn't think you could afford a house like this."

"It's not mine. An LLC bought it."

"Who owns the LLC?"

"I dunno. They hired me to house-sit for them. I jumped at the idea. You can see why," said LeHaigh, gesturing with his arms at the spectacular view. "I love the lifestyle of the idle rich. I take to it like a duck to water."

"You should've been born rich."

"Somebody didn't get the message. I had to work for a living."

"Like everyone else."

LeHaigh eyed him. "Some jobs are easier than others—and better paying."

"The question is, how can you afford this kind of lifestyle on what you get paid at the agency."

"I play the stock market. I'm very good at it."

"You're not running guns for yourself?"

"No."

"You're not smuggling guns to the opposition in Venezuela?"

"Not me. I only do it when the agency orders me to. Why do you think I care what happens in Venezuela?"

"You might care about the piece of change you could pick up smuggling guns there."

"I only did that when the agency hired me to. Is that why you're here? To call me back into action for the agency?"

"The IG is calling the shots on this mission. Not your employer the DDO."

LeHaigh knew he meant the deputy director of operations, decided Power.

"That's a disappointment," said LeHaigh. "I was hoping you came here with a job offer from the agency."

"You wouldn't need a job offer from them if you've gone into business for yourself."

"Who sold you that bill of goods?"

"If you're smuggling guns on your own on the black market, you're breaking the law. The feds could bust you. The agency can't allow that to happen."

"I'm curious. Exactly what job do you have at the agency?"

"I work for the Office of the Inspector General."

"You're checking up on me." LeHaigh fetched a sigh. "I was looking forward to a mission. I was getting bored with sitting around."

"Is that why you went into business for yourself?"

"That's not what I said."

"You're not smuggling guns into Venezuela?"

"Nope." LeHaigh paused. "What if I was? What's the big deal? The agency orders me to do the same thing when they hire me. You would think they'd be happy if I was doing it on my own."

"You'd think wrong. If the feds bust you, it'll turn into an international incident. The agency doesn't want that kind of publicity. We do everything under the radar, and we don't want anyone to know we're in Venezuela."

"Don't worry about it. I know what I'm doing. I keep everybody happy."

Power cocked an ear. "Are you admitting to freelancing?"

"I admit I know what I'm doing," said LeHaigh, smiling.

He tasted his mojito.

Power couldn't tell if LeHaigh was lying about going into business for himself selling guns. Not surprising, since the guy worked for the CIA, where everybody lied as a way of life. If this multimillion-dollar house belonged to LeHaigh, the guy was most certainly freelancing.

Winterboro suspected LeHaigh had gone rogue, which was why Winterboro had dispatched Power to take care of the situation and disappear LeHaigh if Power ascertained LeHaigh's guilt.

Power could blow LeHaigh away right here—if it wasn't for the butler Antonio. Antonio had seen Power and would tell the cops about it. The cops would then put out a BOLO on Power.

If Power took out LeHaigh, he would also have to take out Antonio. Power saw no way out of that inescapable consequence. Power wondered if he could make it look like Antonio had scragged LeHaigh and taken his own life after. But why would Antonio kill himself after whacking LeHaigh? Because he felt guilt for killing his master?

Power didn't think that scenario would play.

He considered another option. What if he made LeHaigh's death look like an accident that even Antonio would believe? LeHaigh could drown in his swimming pool, for instance. Would the cops investigate such an accident? Power doubted it.

First, Power had to determine LeHaigh's guilt to his satisfaction. Was the guy running guns to Venezuela on his own? Living in this pricy manse on the waterfront suggested he was.

"How'd you meet up with this LLC that hired you to house-sit?" said Power.

"Do you like your mojito?"

"It's fine."

"Antonio makes a mean mojito," said LeHaigh, and tossed his down.

He reached across the tabletop for the glass pitcher and poured himself another one.

"You didn't answer my question," said Power.

"What's with all the questions? I'm tired of questions."

"I need to do my job."

"What exactly is your job?"

"I told you, I work for the IG."

"In what capacity?"

"This isn't about me. It's about you. Winterboro wants to know what you're up to."

"You make it sound sinister. Just because I'm living in a nice house."

"You also have a Porsche 911 Carrera Turbo S parked in your driveway. A car that costs north of two hundred grand."

"Is that all that's bugging you?"

"Well?"

"It came with the house."

"The LLC with anonymous directors owns the car, too?"

"It does."

"What's this LLC's name?"

"XYZ LLC."

"You have no idea who owns it?"

"None. How can I? It was formed in Delaware, where the owners don't have to list their names."

"Who did you cut this deal with?"

"I'm tired of all your questions," said LeHaigh, getting up and walking around, mojito in hand.

"You had to cut a deal with someone from XYZ to get this house."

"I didn't 'get' this house. I'm house-sitting."

"Somebody had to give you the keys. Who was it?"

"He said his name was John."

"John what?"

LeHaigh thought about it. "I had to sign an NDA that I wouldn't disclose his identity to anyone."

"You can tell me. I work for the agency, like you."

"No, I can't. The guy would sue my ass off."

"Could I see a copy of the NDA?"

"I can't show it to you. That would violate the NDA."

"Don't you realize how suspicious this looks—your living in a multimillion-dollar mansion on Key Biscayne?"

"I can't help it if people envy me. Including you."

Power ignored the dig. "You can see why they would, though."

"Looks can be deceiving," said LeHaigh, standing facing Power.

"How so?"

"I'm sure I seem like a nice guy to you. The truth is, I killed a lot of guys to get where I am today. You don't get anywhere in this world by being a sheep."

"I know you're an ex-SEAL. Is that what you're referring to?"

"The agency didn't hire me to be a priest. They know I have talents they want. I'm not afraid to kill to get the job done."

Was LeHaigh's mask slipping? wondered Power. But as yet, LeHaigh had not admitted committing a crime on his own.

"Why'd you leave the SEALs?" said Power.

"They had a motto at the SEALs: 'No Easy Day.' I never liked that motto. What's wrong with an easy day? I'm loving it," said LeHaigh, turning his face to the sun and soaking up rays.

"Let's cut the crap. Are you saying this will-o'-the-wisp XYZ LLC hired you to do a job for them and paid you off with this house?" said Power.

"I'm not saying that. Listen. I don't own the house. I'm house-sitting."

Power shook his head in confusion. "Then why did you bring up these killings you've committed?"

"To show you you're not dealing with a babe in the woods."

"I already know that."

"Then let's stop with all these questions," said LeHaigh, wiping sweat off his forehead with the back of his hand.

"Just one more. How were you so fortunate as to meet up with this LLC?"

"I was looking on the Internet for a place to live, and I saw XYZ's ad for a house sitter," said LeHaigh, pouring himself another mojito. "I was in the right place at the right time."

"And?"

"And I called the number in the ad."

"And?"

"I met a man who gave me the key to the house."

"And to the Porsche and the cigarette boat?"

"Those, too."

"No questions asked?"

"He asked me my name and phone number."

"A trusting sort of guy, huh?"

LeHaigh gave Power a look. "Are you suggesting I'm not trustworthy?"

"I'm trying to understand why he's giving a complete stranger all of his expensive toys to play with. He *is* a stranger, right? Or do you know him?"

"Never met him before."

"Then I can't get my head around it. He's handing you well over a million dollars."

"He's leaving the country, and he needs a house sitter. Simple. It was first come, first served. He didn't have time to be picky, he said. He had to leave pronto."

"What's this guy's name?"

"I can't tell you. Remember the NDA."

"Let me get this straight. He handed millions of dollars' worth of valuables over to you and he didn't give you his name?"

"He gave me his name. I can't tell it to you, is all." LeHaigh bridled. "And what's with the third degree? I resent your tone."

Not to be deterred, Power pursued his line of questioning. "He's not in the least afraid you'll steal his luxury car and boat?"

"Why should he be?"

"I'm not in the habit of handing over my car keys to a complete stranger. I don't even like giving them to a valet. And I don't own a car that costs over two hundred grand."

"These rich guys. They're a different breed of cat from you and me."

"He sounds like a gibbering idiot."

LeHaigh laughed. "Some rich guys are. Any idiot can win the lottery. What makes you think it takes brains to accumulate money? In my experience, luck is the deciding factor. Lucky to be born with it, most of 'em."

"And they have a willingness to break the law. Behind every great fortune is a crime."

"I didn't say that."

"No. Balzac did."

"If you're so smart, why do you take home such a mediocre paycheck? Think about it."

"Knowing the right people doesn't hurt when it comes to making money," said Power. "Unless you win the lottery. Did this John guy win the lottery?"

"I have no idea how he got his money. He didn't tell me."

"How do you know he isn't a narcoterrorist?"

"I don't. And I didn't ask him. I don't stick my nose where it doesn't belong, like you do. He wouldn't've sealed the deal if I was too nosy. Where is this leading? You're wearing out your welcome."

Power wasn't done yet. He didn't find LeHaigh's answers satisfactory.

"I want to check this guy out. What's John's last name?" said Power.

"My lips are sealed."

"Didn't you check him out before you cut a deal with him?"

"Why should I? He gave me a good deal. What's to check out?"

"Did you tell John you killed people to get where you are today?"

"Why would I do that?"

"Why'd you tell me?"

"Because . . ."

"Because why?"

"Because we both work for the agency."

"Is there any way I can talk to John?"

"So you can take my place as his house sitter?" LeHaigh laughed. "You think I'm a fool? I'm not giving away a cushy job like this."

"I want to know more."

"Because you're jealous. You know a good thing when you see it."

"I wanna talk to someone who can verify your story. I'm having a hard time believing it. It sounds too good to be true."

LeHaigh advanced on Power. "Are you calling me a liar?"

"I'm doing my job. Winterboro has his suspicions of you."

"Tough."

"He'll interpret your refusal to cooperate as corroboration of your guilt."

"Guilt of what?"

"Of smuggling guns to enrich yourself."

"What evidence does he have?"

"This house, the Porsche, and the cigarette boat."

"Which aren't mine. As I already explained."

"Without any verification."

"I don't have to verify anything for you. I don't have to explain myself to you. You don't have the authority to arrest me."

"I'm not arresting anyone."

"Then what are you doing here? I thought you came to offer me a business deal. Instead, you're taking advantage of my hospitality and making unfounded accusations. Maybe you better take a hike before I tell Antonio to give you the bum's rush."

"I haven't completed my job yet."

"Listen. You don't make the kind of money I'm making by teaching Sunday school. There are skeletons in my closet. Skeletons that would make your blood run cold."

"A confession?"

"I killed for my country. And not just once. Many times."

"But how are you making all this money you're talking about? That's the question. And Winterboro thinks he has the answer. You've gone into business for yourself smuggling guns."

"It's time to tell Antonio to get you off my property."

LeHaigh reached for his cell phone that lay on the coffee table.

"I thought you said it wasn't your property," said Power. "It belongs to some guy named John." Power made air quotes around the name "John."

LeHaigh leveled a glare at Power then took a pull on his mojito. "You're trying to confuse me."

"You're trapping yourself in your own web of lies."

LeHaigh gazed at his cell phone with annoyance. "It's dead."

He snagged an orange extension cord that was plugged into an outlet near the barbecue, took it to the coffee table, plugged a recharging wire that lay on the tabletop into his cell phone and into the extension cord, and began charging his cell phone, which he set on the table.

"The battery dies a lot when I'm outside," he said, "and I'm outside a lot doing business on the phone. Can you blame me with this weather and this view?" LeHaigh motioned to the polished blue sky and the aquamarine ocean. "That's why I have the recharging wire out here. Success is all about being prepared. And taking risks." He paused a beat. "And being willing to kill to get an edge."

"You're revealing your true colors."

"You already revealed *your* true colors," said LeHaigh. "You're an unwelcome guest."

"I'm bending over backwards giving you the benefit of the doubt. Did you sign a document with John proving you're house-sitting for him?"

"I never sign anything. I work for the agency. You know their rules as well as I do."

"You said you signed John's NDA."

"That's different. I had no choice."

"Did John write you out a check for your house-sitting services?"

"He paid me in cash. Can you imagine? Not only do I get to live here, I get paid to live here."

"You're making your story harder and harder to believe."

"You know what they say. Truth is stranger than fiction."

"You're not making a strong case for your innocence."

"This isn't a court of law," said LeHaigh with an edge to his voice.

"I don't think you understand the gravity of your situation."

"*Your* situation is far worse than mine. What if I told you that right now there is a Barrett M95 sniper rifle with a Schmidt & Bender PM II High Power scope mounted on it aimed at your tiny head?"

Power scrutinized the mansion for signs of a rifle barrel sticking out of a window.

"Winterboro would never let you get away with it," said Power, wondering if LeHaigh was lying to him, seeing no sign of anyone in the mansion's windows.

Power wouldn't be surprised if LeHaigh, indeed, owned a Barrett M95 since the guy trafficked in guns. But to risk blowing away a fellow CIA operative would be going beyond the pale. LeHaigh had to know there would be payback for such a crime. He would become a pariah and a hunted man without a country. No place would be safe for him. Or was the guy so scared now he would do anything to save his neck?

The thing was, LeHaigh didn't look scared, decided Power. Did LeHaigh really think he could get away with icing him?

"Winterboro discovered you have an offshore bank account in Turks and Caicos," said Power. "Is that true?"

"What if it is?"

"There are millions of dollars in that particular account."

"Where do you get the authority to investigate personal bank accounts?"

"If dirty money is being funneled into those accounts, the IG has the authority to investigate them."

"Who said anything about dirty money?"

"We're trying to find out. That's why I'm asking you."

"I'm not disclosing my personal finances to anyone. That's an offshore account. The American government has no right to investigate it."

"Who's gonna stop them?"

"You've overstayed your welcome."

"It looks like Winterboro was right to suspect you. I'm sorry to say, everything adds up to your guilt."

"I'm going for a swim," said LeHaigh. "By the time I get out of the pool, you'll either be gone, if you know what's good for you, or you'll be quite dead with a .50 caliber bullet buried in your brain."

"You got a pair, I'll say that for you. Either that or you got a death wish. Do you really wanna risk messing with Winterboro?"

"I've heard rumors about the guy. Nothing else. What is he? Like the CIA's version of the Gestapo?"

"The less you know about the inspector general and the OIG, the better for you."

"Is that a threat?"

Power sipped his mojito. "At this point, we're beyond threats."

LeHaigh took two steps toward the infinity pool. "Then this is where you say good-bye."

"Not before I get proof you're house-sitting. Or your stay here is coming to an end."

LeHaigh contemplated the unruffled stillness of the pool's water. "Such a shame to crack the mirror."

He dove into the pool.

Power walked over to LeHaigh's cell phone, fished out a pocketknife with a rubber handle from his trouser pocket, flicked out a blade, nicked the orange plastic sheath of the extension cord till the blade hit the wire, folded the blade, pocketed his knife, turned, and watched LeHaigh surface in the pool.

"You still here?" said LeHaigh, blowing out his cheeks and shaking water from his face as he dogpaddled in the middle of the pool. "You don't like living?"

Power called LeHaigh's bluff.

"It's for you," said Power, picking up LeHaigh's cell phone from the coffee table and tossing it toward LeHaigh.

The cell phone fell short of LeHaigh and dropped into the water, sinking, pulling the frayed extension cord after it. His muscles tensed and his eyes bulged out of his head as the electric current coursed through his body and triggered cardiac arrest.

"I don't envy you now," said Power.

No bullet from a Barrett M95 tore through Power's brain.

To Power's relief.

Too Many Bodies

Power was driving a rented Audi sedan on the Overseas Highway that spanned the Florida Straits on his way back to Miami after getting in some marlin fishing and doing a job in Key Largo when he got the call from Winterboro.

Winterboro's cleanup crew had found two corpses on the kill site at the Paradise Inn in Key Largo where there was only supposed to be one—left by Power.

"Explanation?" said Winterboro over the phone.

On speaker his husky voice rumbled through the air-conditioned Audi's interior.

"Somebody piggybacked," said Power.

"What's the point?"

"The job called for one removal. I removed one. I left behind only one stiff. I'm as much in the dark as you are."

"You need to get back to the cleanup site and find out what's going on."

"Is that wise?"

"We don't have much choice."

"What about the cleanup crew?"

"I told them not to touch anything."

"We don't have a lot of time. The longer the bodies go without being removed, the more chance there is somebody'll discover them."

"I know that. Which is why you need to return there this minute."

"On my way."

Power made a U-turn on the Overseas Highway and headed back to Key Largo, the turquoise and mint green straits fanning out on either side of him.

This smelled like a frame, he decided. Was somebody trying to set him up for two murders? If so, the culprit might have notified the authorities by now. He had left nothing behind at the crime scene that would implicate him. How could they convict him for two killings when they couldn't even convict him for one?

It took him over an hour to get back to the Paradise Inn, where he had whacked the double-dealing CIA agent Raymundo Neves. Winterboro had discovered that Raymundo had been secretly working for the Cuban Intelligence Directorate in Havana while feigning to be a CIA operative. He had everyone in the CIA duped for over five years.

Not only was Raymundo working for the CIA and the Cuban DI, he was also lining his pockets with narco money from the Jalisco New Generation cartel in Guadalajara. He had all three organizations convinced he was working for them. Power didn't know how Raymundo had pulled it off for so long without being discovered.

The fact that Raymundo was working for the CIA and dealing drugs for CJNG put him at the top of Winterboro's most wanted list. Winterboro had ordered Power to disappear Raymundo. Power had shot Raymundo dead in Raymundo's Paradise Inn motel room after arranging a meet to buy flake.

Power parked his rental on the inn's half-empty coquina parking lot and got out. The sky was becoming overcast, and the wind was picking up. The warm air was thick with humidity. They could be in for a storm. He hoped it wasn't a hurricane headed this way. He wasn't a Florida native and wasn't familiar with the hurricane season.

He cut across the parking lot, entered the pink and aquamarine one-story inn that needed a new paint job, and made for Raymundo's room.

He rapped gently on the door.

Winterboro's cleanup crew should be inside, he decided.

They didn't answer.

Maybe they were playing it safe, decided Power.

He tried the doorknob. Surprised it gave, he circumspectly pushed open the door. He slipped inside and eased the door shut behind him.

He spotted Raymundo's corpse lying on its back on the rug. Warily, he wondered where the cleanup crew was. Bending down he withdrew his SIG P365 from his ankle holster, expecting trouble. As he was straightening up, he heard movement in the bathroom. He tensed.

Two guys appeared out of the bathroom. Both about the same height, one was wiry, the other burly. Bart the former and Matt the latter, the cleanup crew. They were wearing surgical gloves and booties along with their Bermudas and aloha shirts.

Power put away his SIG.

"We weren't sure it was you," said Bart.

"Why didn't you lock the door, Bart?" said Power.

"Winterboro told us not to touch anything. To leave everything the way it was until you showed up. The door wasn't locked when we arrived."

"I knew you didn't have a key, so I left it unlocked. Risky, but I knew you would be arriving shortly."

"You could have waited for us to arrive."

Power shook his head no. "I had to get back to Miami." He looked around the room. "Where's the second stiff Winterboro was talking about?"

Bart led Power past the corpse and around the bed. On the other side of the bed was another stiff. Lying on his back was a five-eight Hispanic male with long thick black hair dressed in jeans and a black T with the name Lamborghini printed on its chest in white cursive letters.

"Which one is the target?" said Matt, who had followed Power around the bed to the second corpse.

"The other one," said Power. "I didn't do this guy. Did you check his ID?"

"We didn't touch anything. Winterboro's orders. When we saw two stiffs instead of one, we called it in."

Power rubbed his chin. "Somebody must know I offed Raymundo. Or why deposit another body here?"

Power inspected the cadaver. A trickle of drying blood from its temple left a squiggly trail down the side of its livid face. A bullet had drilled a hole in the temple.

"Do you know this guy?" said Bart.

"I never saw him before. Maybe he was working with Raymundo."

"If you didn't ice him, who did?" said Bart, pointing his forefinger like a handgun at the unsub.

"We're not gonna have time to figure it out. You need to dispose of the two bodies."

"Our assignment was for only one."

"Change in plans. This room was rented in Raymundo's name. If the cops find a corpse here with a bullet in its brain, they're gonna be all over this place. And then they'll start digging into Raymundo's life. We can't have that because Raymundo was spying not only for the Cuban DI but for the CIA, and Winterboro doesn't want the cops to open *that* can of worms."

"Deep clean?"

"Right. Scrub the place down and get rid of all traces of blood. Use anti-DNA spray to get rid of all DNA traces."

"The other killer will go unpunished if we get rid of his corpus delicti."

"That's the chance we have to take. We can't have the cops investigating Raymundo. He was supposed to be working for the CIA, though he was really a mole. It would cause all sorts of problems if the cops found out he was aligned with the CIA."

"Was this other stiff working for the agency?"

"Maybe his ID will give us a clue."

Power knelt down beside the corpse, lifted it, reached under it, and retrieved the wallet in its rear trouser pocket. The wallet had been picked clean.

"The guy could've been a victim of a robbery," he said. "Or it was made to look that way. I figure the latter. I can't figure out why a robber would put his victim with another murder victim. What would be the point?"

"It's above my pay grade," said Bart. "I'm in the disposal unit. We aren't told the whys or wherefores in our line."

Power noticed it was a Gucci leather billfold in his hand. "Expensive wallet. The unsub wasn't some bum."

Power withdrew his burner from his trouser pocket and took several pictures of the corpse. He noticed the corpse's wrists had rope burns on them.

"Do we get on with our job?" said Bart. "Winterboro told us to wait for you."

"I'll call him," said Power.

Burner in hand, Power wandered over to the window, which gave onto a view of a canal with a mangrove with a tangle of grey gnarly roots growing in the water. A saltwater crocodile was scuttling along the cement parapet of the canal with a Chihuahua-sized mutt in his mouth. Somebody's dog hadn't been on a leash.

As long as the creature wasn't heading this way, Power wasn't concerned, though he wasn't in the habit of looking out his window and seeing a crocodile. He felt an impulse to try and save the dog, but the dog wasn't moving. If it was still alive, it wouldn't be shortly. He had a job to do, and it was time sensitive.

"I'm here at the disposal scene," Power said into his burner.

"Who's the second victim?" said Winterboro.

"I don't recognize him. He was stripped of ID."

"You had nothing to do with his death?"

"Nothing."

"How did he die?"

"Violently."

"If it was a heart attack, I could see where the sight of the murder victim might've triggered it."

"It was a bullet to the temple."

"I see." Winterboro paused. "Any chance of suicide?"

"Why would he commit suicide in a room with a corpse? He also has rope burns on his wrists. He was held hostage before he was shot."

"I need to know what happened. I don't like puzzles at the scene of one of our disposals."

Power cast around the room. "You can rule out suicide. There's no sign of a gun anywhere."

"Somebody could have removed it."

"The killer."

"Any idea who the stiff is?"

"None. He has a fancy wallet, but no money in it."

"The perp didn't want him ID'ed."

"He didn't want to leave behind any money either."

"So robbery's on the table?"

"I doubt it. Why dump a robbery victim in a room with a corpse?"

"Then what are we dealing with?"

"That's what's bugging me. Some kind of setup?"

"You had nothing to do with this guy's death?"

"I took out Raymundo. Not this guy."

Winterboro fetched a deep sigh. "What's your explanation?"

"Somebody blew away this guy here after I took out Raymundo."

"Then we got a problem."

"Meaning?"

"Whoever took out this unsub might have seen you waste Raymundo. In which case, he could ID you to the cops. Was anyone else in the room when you did Raymundo?"

Power had thought he was alone with Raymundo when he had screwed his suppressor onto his SIG P365 and put a bullet in Raymundo's brain.

"I didn't see anyone," said Power.

"Then somebody you didn't see could've been in the room with you when you took out Raymundo?"

"Anything's possible." Power considered it. "If others *were* in the room, they were hiding."

"Was somebody in the closet? Do you think that's possible?"

"Unlikely. Why would somebody be hiding in the closet? It makes no sense."

"If somebody witnessed your taking out Raymundo, you need to take care of it."

"There were rope burns on the stiff's wrists."

"I heard you the first time. The killer led the unsub—"

"Let's call him Gucci."

"Gucci?"

"He had an empty Gucci wallet in his pocket."

"The killer led his captive Gucci to your crime scene and wasted him." Winterboro paused. "If he's setting you up to take the fall for the two murders, you better get out of there posthaste."

"Or . . ."

"Or what?"

"Or the killer wants our cleanup crew to dispose of both of the stiffs."

"That would mean the killer knows about our cleanup crew. Something only a handful of people know."

"Which means this second hit could've been sanctioned at a very high level."

"In the agency?"

"Or maybe an opposition foreign intelligence agency."

"Are you suggesting the Cuban Intelligence Directorate had something to do with this?"

"We can't rule it out."

Winterboro fetched another sigh. It sounded like a wheeze. "Piggybacking on our cleanup crew, huh? I know they're a cheap outfit, but that's a bit much."

"I took photos of Gucci. I'll e-mail them to you."

"This doesn't make a whole lot of sense."

From Winterboro's tone Power got the impression Winterboro was having trouble believing him. Did Winterboro actually think he, Power, clipped Gucci and Raymundo? If Winterboro thought Power was lying to him, he might send someone to take out Power. Power hoped he was misreading Winterboro.

The problem was, this job was all about paranoia, decided Power. It was impossible to look at anything from an objective point of view. The paranoid aspect of the job kept creeping into and swaying decision-making, Power's as well as Winterboro's.

"All right," said Winterboro. "We'll figure this out later. Right now you get yourself out of there and tell the cleanup crew to shake a leg."

Power couldn't tell if Winterboro believed him about his claim of innocence in blowing away Gucci. It would help if he could see Winterboro's face, decided Power. Not that it would help that much, since Winterboro's aging visage gave away little.

Power watched Bart and Matt unroll a green plastic tarpaulin on the living room floor, lift Raymundo's corpse, and place it on the tarp.

"We only came prepared for one stiff," said Bart.

Matt scoped out the tarp. "I think we can cut the tarp in half and use the other half on Gucci."

"Or we could roll them both inside this tarp."

"It would be too heavy for us to carry. It's gonna weigh well over three hundred pounds."

Bart nodded in agreement. "Let's make two packages."

He retrieved a pair of scissors from the suitcase he had brought with him and proceeded to cut the tarp in half.

He and Matt retrieved Gucci's body from the other side of the bed. Matt grasped Gucci's arms while Bart grasped Gucci's ankles, as they hauled the corpse over to the tarp next to Raymundo.

"Why are you limping?" said Matt.

"I think I have an ingrown nail in my big toe," said Bart, wincing.

"Get a toenail clipper," said Matt with disgust.

"I have one. The clipper doesn't get the nail out."

"Go to a pedicurist."

"What's that?"

"It's a manicurist for feet. Don't you know anything?"

"That's girly stuff. Men don't go to manicurists."

"You'd rather hobble around like a gimp," said Matt, shaking his head.

They deposited Gucci's corpse on the tarp and wrapped the tarp around it. They were about to wrap the other tarp around Raymundo when they heard a cell phone chime. They halted.

"I thought you checked his pockets," said Bart.

"I thought *you* did," said Matt.

Power pocketed his burner and retrieved the chiming cell phone from Raymundo's corpse.

He accepted the call from a private caller. The voice was on speaker.

"*Hola, Jorge. El patrón quiere saber donde está el yeyo.*"

Power didn't answer. He thought whoever was calling would know it wasn't Jorge if he spoke.

"*Jorge? Jorge? Quién es? Chingado.*"

The caller terminated the call.

"What did he say?" said Matt.

"He said the boss wants to know where the blow is," said Power.

"Why'd he call Raymundo Jorge?"

"Because this isn't Raymundo's phone. I removed all of his ID and his cell phone after I took him out. The other killer must've planted this phone on Raymundo. I'm willing to bet it's Gucci's."

"Why would he do that?"

"As part of a frame."

"What's the point?"

"It sounds like Jorge/Gucci here was dealing drugs. One way or another it got him whacked. And the killer wants to involve Raymundo in the drug dealing by planting Gucci's phone on him."

"I still don't get it."

"The killer obviously didn't know Winterboro sent a cleanup crew here to dispose of Raymundo's corpse. Which defeats the frame."

Power's cell phone vibrated in his trouser pocket. He took the call.

"I received your e-mailed photo of the second victim," said Winterboro. "He's a wanted member of the Jalisco New Generation cartel by the name of Jorge Batista."

"That gibes with what we found here."

"Namely?"

"Jorge's cell phone was planted on Raymundo's corpse, and we just got a call from someone who wanted to know where the blow is."

"A drug deal gone south?"

"The killer may have the blow and is setting up Jorge to take the fall. With Jorge dead, who's to say otherwise?"

"The cops'll think Jorge and Raymundo are both narcos. Hmm. Maybe that's a good thing. It gets the agency out of the picture, which is the reason I had you blow away Raymundo. So he wouldn't spill the beans about the agency."

"Does he still want us to dispose of these bodies?" Matt asked Power, finishing helping Bart wrap Raymundo's corpse in the tarp.

Power relayed Matt's question to Winterboro.

"Good question," said Winterboro. "Is there any way these murders can be traced to us?"

"We'd be better off if the cleanup crew completed their mission. My DNA might be in here somewhere—and the cleanup crew's. A deep cleaning would keep us out of this. Otherwise, I can't guarantee it. My returning here might've contaminated the crime scene."

"I've been thinking. Could Cuban intelligence have had anything to do with Jorge Batista's murder?"

Power heard sirens in the distance. "We need to make a decision fast. I hear squad cars. We have to figure they're heading here."

"Wait a second. We may be able to spin this to our advantage."

"How?" said Power, feeling his heartbeat accelerate as adrenaline kicked into his system at the sound of the sirens.

"We at the agency let it be known to the Cuban DI that Raymundo was moonlighting as a coke dealer. It should please them by drawing attention away from the fact that he was working for Cuban intelligence."

"How does that help us, though?"

"The Cubans would suspect a narco, namely Jorge Batista, knocked off Raymundo thanks to a botched drug deal. That would let you—and, by extension, the agency—off the hook for his murder."

The sirens were getting louder.

"What are we supposed to do?" Matt asked Power, becoming edgy thanks to the sirens.

Power held up his hand, gesturing to Matt to hold on.

"I heard that," said Winterboro. "Who was it?"

"Matt," said Power.

"What's the problem?"

At that moment an unwelcome stranger paid a visit to the motel room. He scampered into the room, scooped up Jorge's head in his jaws, clamped down on the skull covered with the tarp, and hauled the body out of the room into the hall.

"What the hell?" said Matt, his eyes bulging. "A friggin' croc."

"Is that supposed to happen?" said Bart, trying to come to grips with what he just saw.

"I guess he was hungry."

"We got a problem," Power told Winterboro.

"Give it to me," said Winterboro.

"You're not gonna believe it."

"Just tell me."

"A crocodile took Jorge's body."

"What?"

"He came into the room and took it out of here."

"That's not funny."

"It's not funny, but it's true. What do you want us to do?"

"Can you get the body back?"

"I'm not playing tug of war with a crocodile."

"Shoot the goddamn thing."

"It's illegal to shoot them here. They're endangered species. It'll bring the cops down on us."

"All right. Let me think."

"The sirens are getting nearer."

"Hold on."

"What do we do with Raymundo? Do we take him out of here?"

There was a pause on the line.

Power heard his heartbeat increase in volume with every tick of the clock, as the sirens neared.

"Leave him," said Winterboro. "And make sure you leave Jorge's cell phone on him, making it look like narcos had something to do with his death. That'll divert any attention from the agency."

"We already wrapped Raymundo in a tarp. It'll take too long to unwrap him."

"What about Jorge's cell phone?"

"It's next to Raymundo's stiff."

"Is the cleanup crew wearing gloves?"

Power scoped out Matt's and Bart's clothing. "Surgical gloves and booties."

"What about you?"

"Driving gloves and shoes that are two sizes too big for me."

"Shoes that don't fit?"

"To throw off investigators. I always wear them on a hit."

"Spray everything with anti-DNA spray and get out of there. Leave the tarp. The cops can't tie it to the agency. It'll give them something to think about."

Bart packed up his suitcase, while Matt sprayed the area with anti-DNA spray. Bart then sprayed the same area with alternate DNA spray.

Erase and replace, decided Power, watching them. Whatever trace amount of DNA remained after erasing was replaced with the foreign DNA.

"Beat it," said Power when the cleanup crew had finished. "But don't run. You don't want attention."

"We know our job," said Matt.

Bart snagged his suitcase and followed Matt into the hall.

Power inspected the room one last time and turned to leave. Jorge's phone chimed. Power halted midstride. For some reason he couldn't explain he turned around, picked up the phone that lay next to Raymundo's tarp-wrapped corpse, and answered.

"*Jorge, dónde estás, querido?*" said a female voice.

Jorge, where are you, dear?

Power swallowed. He dropped the phone and ducked out of the room, feeling bad about Jorge's girlfriend. He didn't even hear the sirens arriving, as he exited through the motel's back door.

ABOUT THE AUTHOR

Bryan Cassiday writes thrillers and horror fiction. His latest Scott Brody crime thriller is *Murder LLC*, which followed *Bolt*. He wrote *Zombie Apocalypse: The Chad Halverson Series*. His short stories have appeared in numerous anthologies, such as *Shadows and Teeth Volume Two*, which won the International Book Award for best adult horror fiction anthology series 2017. He lives in Southern California.

www.ingramcontent.com/pod-product-compliance
Lightning Source LLC
LaVergne TN
LVHW091135080826
845145LV00008B/2167

* 9 7 8 1 7 3 2 9 7 6 3 9 9 *